MW00856163

The traveler can only observe.

By Philip Fracassi

NOVELS

Sarafina

Boys in the Valley

Gothic

A Child Alone with Strangers

Don't Let Them Get You Down

STORY COLLECTIONS

No One Is Safe!

Behold the Void

Beneath a Pale Sky

NOVELLAS

Commodore

Shiloh

Sacculina

THE THIRD RULE OF TIME TRAVEL

PHILIP FRACASSI

orbit

orbitbooks.net

This book is a work of fiction. Names, characters, places, and incidents
are the product of the author's imagination or are used fictitiously.
Any resemblance to actual events, locales, or persons, living or dead, is
coincidental.

Copyright © 2025 by Philip Fracassi

Cover design and art by Stephanie A. Hess
Cover copyright © 2025 by Hachette Book Group, Inc.
Author photograph by Stephanie Simard

Hachette Book Group supports the right to free expression and the value of
copyright. The purpose of copyright is to encourage writers and artists to
produce the creative works that enrich our culture.

The scanning, uploading, and distribution of this book without permission
is a theft of the author's intellectual property. If you would like permission to
use material from the book (other than for review purposes), please contact
permissions@hbgusa.com. Thank you for your support of the author's rights.

Orbit
Hachette Book Group
1290 Avenue of the Americas
New York, NY 10104
orbitbooks.net

First Edition: March 2025
Simultaneously published in Great Britain by Orbit

Orbit is an imprint of Hachette Book Group.
The Orbit name and logo are registered trademarks of Little, Brown Book
Group Limited.

The publisher is not responsible for websites (or their content) that are not
owned by the publisher.

The Hachette Speakers Bureau provides a wide range of authors for speaking
events. To find out more, go to hachettespeakersbureau.com or email
HachetteSpeakers@hbgusa.com.

Orbit books may be purchased in bulk for business, educational, or
promotional use. For information, please contact your local bookseller
or the Hachette Book Group Special Markets Department at
special.markets@hbgusa.com.

Print book interior designed by Bart Dawson

Library of Congress Cataloging-in-Publication Data
Names: Fracassi, Philip, 1970– author.
Title: The third rule of time travel / Philip Fracassi.
Description: First edition. | New York, NY : Orbit, 2025.
Identifiers: LCCN 2024017290 | ISBN 9780316572514 (trade paperback) |
    ISBN 9780316572521 (ebook)
Subjects: LCSH: Time travel—Fiction. | LCGFT: Novels.
Classification: LCC PS3556.R24 T55 2025 | DDC 813.6—dc23/eng/
    20240415
LC record available at https://lccn.loc.gov/2024017290

ISBNs: 9780316572514 (trade paperback), 9780316572521 (ebook)

Printed in the United States of America

LSC-C

Printing 1, 2024

For Stephanie. Again, and always.

Of course, there are rules...

I'm in an airplane.

A small propeller plane. I look to my left and see my sister, Mary, seated next to me. A large headset covers her ears, but I make out her profile easily. Her mouth, her cheekbones, her eyes. Chestnut-brown hair falls to her shoulders. She wears jeans and a black down jacket.

My vision turns toward the front of the plane.

I have no choice but to follow.

A windshield filled with blue sky. A man seated to the left. I can only see the back of his head, but I know it's my father. Seated on the right is my mother. Between them, the plane's console is a smattering of buttons, levers, and lights.

Even through my noise-dampening headset, I can hear the whine of the propellers. The sound is like a swarm of hornets.

I continue looking forward.

My feet, flat against the metal floor of the narrow cabin, vibrate unpleasantly.

As a young girl, I'd flown in this little plane dozens of times. Dad's Cessna. The last time any of us flew in the Cessna I was twelve years old. My sister, Mary, was fifteen. I think...

No... it can't be.

I feel a concussion to my right—as if someone punched a hole in the sky—and my vision jumps toward the sound. Out the window, a thick stream of black smoke flows past. I lean forward and glance far below, where an earthen carpet of dense, endless forest rolls past. The plane shakes with a sudden violence. It dips and sways, battered by currents of air.

My father's voice erupts in the headset.

"Hold on!"

The windshield tilts sickeningly and Mary's hand clutches my arm. My head turns toward her and I see my own terror reflected in her wide eyes and oh God, no . . . please, no . . .

No!

Why have you brought me here?

RULE NUMBER ONE:

*Travel can occur only at destination points
during the previous lifetime of the traveler.
These destination points are random.*

The plane shakes with such violence that I'm forced to clench my jaw to keep my teeth from rattling. My vision is vibrating, turning everything around me into a blur of trembling colors. I can barely understand what I'm seeing. Everything is distorted. Focus is impossible.

I turn to look at Mary, and then the plane drops. The engine shrieks like a demon and my stomach leaps into my throat. My hips and chest strain painfully against the locked seat harness, fighting gravity. I watch in shock and wonder as Mary's hair *rises* into the air, naked fear on her bloodless face.

My dad is screaming into the headset, but all I can make out amid the savage fury engulfing our plane are the words "Hold on!" and "I'm sorry, I'm so sorry!"

Mom is yelling into a hand mic attached to the plane's radio. I don't know what she's saying—I can't hear her—but I assume it's a distress call.

Her lips form the words: *Mayday! Mayday!*

I think I'm screaming but can't be sure. It's too chaotic. There's too much stimulation.

The windshield is no longer blue; it's green.

We're plummeting; we're going to crash.

Again.

RULE NUMBER TWO:

*The traveler has only enough energy
to maintain contact with the arrival world
for approximately ninety seconds.*

The ground rushes toward us as smoke and fire billow past the plane's windows. A piece of the engine snaps free, slams against the door next to me. The window splinters, and if I wasn't already screaming, I'm screaming now.

My sister claws at my arm; her fingers and nails dig painfully into my flesh, but I don't bother turning toward her. My eyes are fixed ahead. Even in the maelstrom of the plane's descent I can make out individual trees growing closer as my dad yanks helplessly on the controls, desperate to somehow slow our downward plunge.

We hit the top of the first tree just as my mom whips her head around, twisting back for one final look at her children. In that split second her face wears a mask of unimaginable sorrow I'll never forget. Then the windshield implodes and thick branches rip into their bodies, shredding them like tissue, and I'm sprayed with a burst of glass and blood; the plane lurches sideways as it's torn apart.

Something sharp and hard smacks into my face, shatters my arm.

I no longer feel Mary's grip. It's vanished.

The cabin rolls as we slash and tear through endless branches. I'm turned upside down as dark earth flies toward us through the ragged hole that was, only seconds ago, a cockpit. My parents.

My legs drop upward and I'm suddenly hovering in midair like an astronaut in zero g, and then we crash into the ground like the blow of a hammer.

RULE NUMBER THREE:

*The traveler has no ability to interact with
the world they have traveled to…*

What's left of the plane settles to a stop.

I'm hanging. My arms and legs dangle, lifeless.

My vision blurs everything a swampy gray.

I turn to my left to find my sister. I see nothing but torn metal and ruptured dirt.

Her empty headset.

I try to twist my head to look behind me, to find her, but the harness strap is cutting into my neck and my chest blossoms with a pain so deep it steals my breath.

In the end I suffered broken ribs, a broken arm. A concussion. Internal bleeding.

I steel myself against the pain, force my head to turn toward what remains of the rear cabin. Spattered against metal walls I see broad sprays of dark blood and parts of my sister's body. I'm not sure which parts they are.

I vomit into the dirt a few feet below, my body limp, suspended in the wretched belly of the shattered Cessna like a broken marionette.

When this happened—the first time—I remember what I was thinking:

I'm in a tomb.

I'm alive, somehow alive.

I'm alone.

...the traveler can only observe.

ONE

Beth wakes to her tablet's alarm. A chorus of birds.

Five AM.

Time to run.

She groans, taps the screen to still the alarm, and throws her legs out from beneath the covers. The early morning air is brittle cold, chilling her skin, causing her bare arms to break out in goose bumps. Gray light seeps in through the window. The room hums with the shimmering sound of rainfall.

"Perfect," she says with a tired sigh, not thrilled to be starting her day with ten miles in the rain, but she pushes herself off the bed and heads for the bathroom to brush her teeth.

Minutes later she's sitting on a bench in the mudroom, her breathing measured and steady through her nose as she prepares her body, her mind. Wearing a rainproof windbreaker and workout leggings, she slips on her well-worn Asics, ties them tight.

Breathe in. Hold it. Breathe out.

She taps the face of her watch and a steady beat of music plays through her earbuds. She opens the front door of their home (the spacious, classic Craftsman being their lone big splurge when moving to the Pacific Northwest), steps onto the porch, and stretches her hamstrings, her calves. A few yards away, rain shatters the quiet street, slicks the crooked pavement of the sidewalk that waits down the steps and past a small wooden gate, aged white, like the rest of the picket fence lining her modest yard.

She lifts a wrist toward her mouth. "Start morning run," she says. A timer lights up on the watch face. She nods, jogs quickly down the steps, through the gate. She makes a right on the sidewalk, not wanting to brave the street in the early dark, nor the streams of ankle-deep water already flowing down its sides. The heavy rain drenches her almost immediately.

Beth focuses on her breathing as the Asics slap the wet pavement. After a few moments, she picks up speed.

While she runs, her focus is on her breath, the steady beating of her heart, the pulse of the music pumping into her ears. She pushes away any thoughts of being cold, of being wet or tired. She does everything in her power not to think about the day ahead, or that brief visit to her past the day before, when she was forced to relive the most horrible ninety seconds of her life.

ᔆᕆᔆ

When she returns to the house, the rain has lightened to a drizzle; the emerging sun has brightened the dark gray sky to a less oppressive shade of pewter. She taps the face of her watch, pleased she managed to clock her run in at a reasonable time, despite the slick surfaces.

Marie Elena waits on the porch, standing beside the door, wearing a blue raincoat. A waterproof babushka, patterned with pink flowers, is pulled tight over her head. She clutches an oversize bag in her hands, smiles warmly at Beth as she climbs, sweating and winded, up the steps.

"You're early," Beth says, smiling through panted breaths.

"Robert had to be downtown this morning, so I dropped him off and came straight here. Besides, I knew you'd be up," she says with a wink.

Beth nods and opens the door. "Yeah, you know...Well, come in out of the cold."

Marie Elena—a spunky woman in her early seventies with three grown children of her own—has been their nanny, for all practical purposes, since the day of Isabella's birth. Beth doubts she could have ever made it this far without the woman's help, her strength. She was a stable force in Beth's tumultuous life, had been so even prior to Colson's death, when the pair of them worked insanely long hours at the lab, making full-time parenting an impossibility.

And then, when Beth found herself shockingly, tragically widowed a year ago, she knew there would be no way she could continue working at the pace she needed—the pace she *required* of herself—while also being a responsible, dependable parent, especially given the grief and depression that engulfed her world like an unforeseen eclipse in the months following her husband's fatal accident.

"She's still asleep," Beth says, kicking off her shoes, "and I obviously need to shower, but there's fresh coffee in the kitchen, and I picked up some muffins from Lenzi's yesterday. Help yourself."

Marie Elena nods and shoos Beth toward the bedroom. "Yes, Beth. I'm okay. You go. Go get ready for work."

ᶜᴼꓸ

When Beth reenters the kitchen twenty minutes later, refreshed after the hot shower and the change into dry clothes, she feels a pang of disappointment at seeing her daughter already seated at the kitchen table, eagerly eating a bowl of oatmeal. Waking her daughter is one of her favorite parts of the day, and now it's just another moment she's missed, another memory snatched away by time, never to be returned.

Marie Elena, setting a glass of juice in front of the little girl, seems to read Beth's mind. She shrugs. "Yes, look who's up. She must have heard us talking. Came out of her room saying she was hungry." Marie Elena smiles and strokes the girl's hair.

Isabella, still in pink pajamas, her hair wild from sleep, twists around and sees her mother hovering at the kitchen entryway. "Mommy!" she yells brightly, holding out one hand, flapping her fingers open and shut in a *come! come!* gesture.

Beth dismisses her ill thoughts and goes to her daughter, takes her hand in both of her own, kisses each tiny finger. Her heart swells with a surge of love so strong she doesn't know how she can possibly contain it. Releasing her daughter's warm hand, she settles herself at the table to watch the little girl eat breakfast.

She ponders how Isabella is nestled in that wonderful age between four and five years, the time in a life when the soft baby parts are being stretched and honed—her cherubic face taking on more defined angles at the cheeks and chin, her limbs lengthening as she begins the unstoppable metamorphosis that will transform her from a lovely child into the beautiful young woman she would become.

Marie Elena sets a cup of coffee in front of Beth and joins them at the table, her own cup steaming. "You should eat as well," she says earnestly. "Stay for a minute."

Beth nods and sips her coffee before completing the rote back-and-forth the two women seem to have multiple times a week, if not daily. "I don't have time. I'll get something at work."

Marie Elena tuts, shakes her head. "There's always time, Beth," she says. "It's what you do with it that matters."

Beth starts to reply when her daughter interrupts.

"Mom! We're making butterflies at school today," Isabella announces, her mussed, silky black hair cresting with a casual elegance down the side of her face, brushing her narrow shoulder, enhancing her wide, bright brown eyes. "I'll bring one home for you."

Beth stands, kisses her daughter on the head. "Please do, baby. Now, be good for Marie Elena. I'll be home tonight for dinner and bath, okay?"

Isabella puts down her spoon. She slides her arms around her mother's neck, kisses her loudly on the cheek, then whispers into her ear. Like a secret.

"I love you, Mommy."

TWO

To the average passerby, the headquarters of Langan Corporation appears more like a Cold War–era military complex than a cutting-edge tech company with a market value over fifty billion dollars.

Atop a broad hill, reached only by helicopter or via a single winding road, nestled within a high-fenced perimeter monitored 24/7 by a military-grade security team (the parent company of which regularly competes for wartime mercenary duties), Langan Corp. is a single-story Brutalist-style concrete and glass structure. A square city block of impenetrable intelligence and hidden secrets.

Only those permitted inside—a group that includes some of the greatest scientific minds on the planet—realize that the building is not the single-story structure it appears to be, but a massive sunken compound traveling five stories down, each sublevel entrenched deeper and deeper into the earth.

As Beth guides her car to the top of the hill, she sighs heavily at the grim sight of her place of employment these last four years, the slate-gray sky a sodden backdrop to the dark concrete fortress, a utilitarian monument to knowledge that is brazenly ominous, colorless, cheerless.

And yet.

Inside that building, nearly a hundred feet belowground,

resides her greatest achievement. Hers and Colson's. And not just theirs alone...

What sits far beneath the surface has the potential to be one of the greatest achievements in human history.

A machine that could change everything.

And so, despite the drizzly day, the heavy gray atmosphere, and the grim setting, she never fails to feel a tingle of excitement as she drives nearer the security checkpoint and pulls her badge from her pocket, already thinking about the day to come: The data she'll check and recheck after yesterday's travel, the scrutinous unraveling of mysteries that lie within the complex configuration of algorithms, electricity, and steel. The quest to control a power not meant for human control—a power that lies beyond the science, beyond the machine and the screens of scrolling equations.

Something undefinable.

But she *will* define it. She *will* harness it. And then...

And then she'll change the world.

ᘓ⊕ᘔ

Stepping through the glass front doors and into the dim lobby— diamond-polished concrete walls, floor, and sunken lighting giving it the feel of a white-collar prison—Beth shows her ID once again, this time to the burly no-nonsense guard positioned next to a full-body scanner, noting for the thousandth time the bulk of the sidearm the security personnel keep clipped to their waists beneath ubiquitous black sport coats.

Just past the security station is a thick smoked-glass wall with three entry points, and when the guard nods and buzzes her through, Beth walks to the entry at the far right, toward a door-size tinted panel that slides open to reveal a long hallway. Passing through the opening, Beth feels as if she's entering a different building altogether. The walls are deep cherrywood from floor to ceiling, the carpeting plush, the color of dark chocolate. Ornately framed mid-twentieth-century paintings—primarily abstracts in hues of mustard yellow, crimson, burnt orange, and sea blues—hang along the walls, giving the place a vintage feel, a callback to a world she's never known. Beth once heard the offices described as an old-school law firm by some of her older peers, but she doesn't have a clue what that means. Regardless, she has no problem understanding the underlying ideology being presented:

Stodgy. Plain. Archaic.

Langan Corp., she knows, is anything but.

It's still early, quiet. The doors lining the hallway are closed as she passes them by, making her way toward the lone elevator waiting at the far end of the corridor, an elevator that can be reached only from the ground floor, is wholly exclusive to her lab, and only goes down.

"Don't fucking touch me!"

Beth spins, breath catching in her throat. Behind her a door bursts open and a man—a man she knows well—is pushed roughly from the office's interior and into the hallway. Papers flutter from his hands, spill onto the floor. He wields a briefcase as if it were a weapon. A pair of armed security guards—their uniform black suits straining against the muscular, predatory frames all the guards here seem to have—follow him out, their faces stone, their eyes steel.

One of the guards casually pushes aside the hem of his sport coat, rests his hand on the butt of a deadly-looking firearm.

Beth takes a step toward the commotion, moving closer to the hostile trio of men less than ten feet away. "Jerry?"

The older man spins to look at her, his face ghastly pale, his white hair mussed, his suit frumpy and wrinkled. He stares at her with wild eyes. "Beth," he says, his tone unreadable. "Can you believe this shit? They're getting rid of me."

Beth shakes her head, begins to take another step closer but stops when one of the guards—the one with the hand settled conspicuously upon his sidearm—gives her a warning glare. She halts mid-step. "I don't understand. Jerry, what's going on?"

The other guard, a tall older man who looks almost bored with the encounter, clamps a hand onto Jerry's shoulder. Jerry jerks away, backs toward the lobby as the guards watch passively. "I said don't fucking touch me!" Jerry snarls. Then his eyes look past the guards.

At Beth.

"This is because of you," he says, pointing at her with a long, crooked finger. "Your ridiculous machine is sucking the rest of us dry. But don't worry, Beth, you'll be next! Just wait and see..."

Beth starts to reply when Jerry turns on his heel and walks briskly toward the lobby, briefcase clutched to his chest, loose papers floating to the carpet—almost comically—in his wake. The two guards follow closely, neither sparing a glance back.

She watches until the three men exit through the sliding glass door and disappear into the lobby. Jerry's office stands open, pale light bleeding into the warm tones of the hallway, illuminating the forgotten scatter of papers left on the floor like dead leaves. She eyes the doorway for a moment, wondering how many others have lost their jobs, were told to not bother coming into work that morning.

Shaken, Beth turns and walks to the elevator.

When the elevator arrives, the doors slide silently open and she steps inside, glances toward the camera—a penny-size eye to the left of the doors—then waves her ID card in front of a black sensor. There's a soft *beep* as a glaring red light next to the sensor turns green. The doors slide shut.

There are buttons for five floors on the elevator's panel, all of them set vertically below the sensor and the ever-watching eye of the camera.

She presses the one at the very bottom, and the car descends.

∽⊕∾

Moments later the doors open into a cavernous space two stories in height. Every architectural surface—walls, floors, ceiling—is formed from glass, concrete, or steel. In the middle of the room, set into a recess and surrounded by a series of computer consoles, is a machine.

Made primarily of polished steel components, the machine appears, in many ways, similar to an ultramodernized hospital X-ray machine. At the center of the machine is a flat metal surface, or bed. Hovering above the bed is a bubble shape with a red-eyed proboscis—the laser—that points downward, aiming directly toward the head of the bed. A clear flow tube, banded along its length with steel rings, extends from the bubble-headed laser to a massive power generator the size of a small bus. Two steel half spheres, each three feet in diameter and set vertically, sit on either side of the steel bed, the protuberant sides facing the same area as the pointed laser, presumably where a person's head might rest.

Across the room from the machine are a series of glass-walled rooms, two of which are offices, currently dark. The third is a break room, which contains a full kitchen, sofa, and dining table. Above the offices, running the entire length of one wall, is an observation balcony. Massive viewing screens, nearly invisible unless activated, hover from the ceiling on extended arms between the balcony and the main laboratory.

Seated at one of the consoles that surround the machine, wearing a pristine white lab coat over black slacks, button-down shirt, and tie, is a young man, eyes intent on the screen before him. As Beth approaches, he glances up, simultaneously concerned and mildly frustrated. "I thought you were taking the day off."

"Good morning, Tariq. No. I have the debrief."

Beth stops at one of the consoles, types in a command. Tariq stands, folds his arms. "There's still time. You could do it tomorrow."

Beth raises her eyebrows, but her eyes stay on the screen in front of her as her fingers fly across the keys. "And come into work on a Saturday?"

Tariq scoffs. "Right, because that would be shocking. If memory serves, you and Colson were never great adherents to days of the week when it came to work."

Beth ignores the reference to her late husband, studies the screen before her intently. "I see you're already running diagnostics," she says, moving on. "Anything abnormal?"

Tariq shakes his head and sits back down, knowing rebuke is a lost cause. "No. Nothing so far. Whatever you experienced yesterday was within the parameters of what we've seen before." He pauses a moment, as if debating, then says, "There was one thing."

Beth feels an acute thrill climb up her spine, the rush of adrenaline that comes when one scientist tells another, after years of experimentation: *There is* one *thing that seemed different this time.*

She lives for it.

"Go on."

"You'll see it yourself when you look at the data. It's hard to miss. But there were a couple of seconds, right before the machine kicked in, where you had a significant spike."

"Spike? Like adrenaline...?"

Tariq shakes his head, taps his temple. "No... this was cognitive. Your amygdala threw a little shit fit right before takeoff. I've seen similar stuff when doing dream research as an undergrad. The type of brain wave activity we'd see when someone was having, for example, a particularly bad nightmare."

Beth thinks about it but doesn't recall thinking *anything* particularly impactful prior to her travel the day before. In fact, she remembers being even more relaxed than usual. "Nothing comes to mind that could have caused it," she says. "So if it happened, it certainly wasn't conscious."

Tariq shrugs, his slim shoulders barely lifting the stiff fabric of his pristine lab coat. "Still, it seems strange, doesn't it?"

Beth starts toward the small kitchen. "I don't think so. Why do you?"

Tariq stands once more, follows her toward the break room, where Beth opens the cabinet above the sink, grabs her favorite mug—the one screaming ALOHA! across the ceramic surface in bold, happy letters, a faded rainbow riding beneath it, the colors aged from use. The mug was her lone souvenir from a trip to Hawaii when she was a young girl. The last vacation she'd ever have with her family.

Tariq leans against the doorway. "You know what I mean, Beth. Where it dropped you. The arrival point. Come on, that had to be..." He shakes his head, searching for the right word. "Traumatic."

Beth fills her mug with coffee, notes the digital clock on the microwave. "I'm fine. It was just bad luck. We both know that." She sighs, dumps a spoonful of sweetener into the mug. "Look, I don't need you to worry about me. I need you to focus on the data and the travel diagnostics. We need to find what drives these targeted arrival points, Tariq. It's vital—"

Tariq holds up his hands. "I know, I know. I work here, too, remember?"

Beth nods. "Well, that's what I need from you. I already have a shrink. Speaking of which, I gotta get settled. My debrief is at nine sharp. Will you have a report before I'm back?"

"Should be done soon, yeah. I'll send the whole file over to you once I've added my notes." Tariq takes a step closer, so they're both enclosed within the walls of the break room. He lowers his voice. "Did you hear about Neural Prosthetics?"

Beth takes a sip of the hot coffee, relishes the rush of caffeine to her weary body, then shakes her head. "No, I hadn't. But I just saw Jerry Wilson escorted out of the building by security. I figured it couldn't be good. What'd he do? A little corporate espionage?"

"No, Beth. It's not just Jerry is what I'm saying. It's the whole damn division. They dissolved it."

Beth lowers her cup, stunned. "What? The entire group? That's, like...sixty people. They're a huge part of Langan's med line."

Tariq shrugs, a sardonic smirk on his lips. "Gone, baby."

"Why? That makes no sense."

"Above my pay grade. That's a Jim question. Still, makes one wonder—"

"Don't worry, they're not cutting our funding. Look, I gotta get going..." Beth turns back toward the counter to add more coffee to her mug, inadvertently hits the edge. The mug is knocked from her fingers and falls to the concrete floor, smashing into ceramic pieces, the spill of coffee a dark snowflake.

"Shit!"

Tariq drops to his knees, begins gathering pieces. "Hey, I got this. You go do what you need to do."

Beth puts her hands over her face, tries to stem a sudden rush of emotion, her eyes burning—shockingly—with tears.

Get a grip, Beth.

"Goddamn it. I loved that stupid mug."

Tariq looks up, worried. "Hey, you okay?"

Beth is momentarily confused by the concern in his eyes, then feels the wetness on her cheeks and realizes, despite her best efforts, that she *is* crying. She swipes angrily at her face. "I'm fine. Fuck."

She storms out of the room, leaving her bemused assistant staring after her.

Beth enters her office; the cube lighting, triggered by her motion, brightens the space from within, revealing the only warm area of the entire lab. Oriental-style rugs cover the concrete floor. The oversize desk is dark oak, an antique. Standing floor lamps, shaded with beige fabrics, replace the cold white lighting that permeates the rest of the laboratory. She settles down into her leather desk chair, puts her face in her hands.

"Stupid stupid stupid," she murmurs, knowing that any signs of emotion in front of her assistant will only deepen the ever-widening cracks in her authority.

Crying over a fucking coffee mug? That's gonna go over just great, Beth. Would Colson have ever cried at work? Over a cup? It's just one more reason for Tariq to doubt you.

For all of them to doubt you.

THREE

Beth gets out of the elevator on the second floor. Like the rest of Langan Corp., the floor is seemingly vacant, the hallway eerily devoid of activity.

The few well-spaced doors along each side, she knows, are entryways to labs as big as her own, if not bigger. Neural Prosthetics took up half of the entire ground floor on their wing, a space filled with equipment and testing areas, offices and independent data centers. But to a visitor it might have appeared to be nothing more than a broom closet.

When Beth and Colson first sold their technology to Jim Langan, agreeing to come on board as project managers (in perpetuity), they were happy to have the security of benefits and high salaries, and *thrilled* to have the funding to continue the development of the machine, but they'd both noticed right away how strange the atmosphere was at the immense tech company.

"So much happens behind closed doors, it's impossible to know how it truly functions," Colson said after their first week of employment, both of them still riding a wave of joy and enthusiasm after being given their incredible laboratory space. "I feel like we're moving into the Pentagon."

On their first day of orientation, Jim Langan himself gave them a tour of the entire facility, and Beth quickly lost count of how many times she and Colson exchanged glances behind the old man's back while he continually gestured toward closed doors or sealed-off areas, saying only the name of the department, a rote one-liner about their general function or project, then followed it up with some variation of "Of course, that's off-limits."

Still, Beth couldn't complain. The last thing she or her husband wanted was a bunch of other scientists and tech geniuses coming down the elevator to their lab, sipping coffees and making idle chat while their eyes inspected the machine, the occasional open file, or a random data dump on a console monitor.

But that didn't make it less eerie moving through the seemingly empty hallways. The outburst with Jerry that morning was one of the few times she could remember seeing another employee someplace other than the semiannual corporate debriefs, which were typically held in a rotunda that could comfortably seat hundreds, or the corporate cafeteria (a space that was hardly used, since most employees took their meals in their respective workspaces).

Truth be told, Beth didn't know just how large Langan Corporation was, either in number of employees or in physical dimensions. The main lobby split three ways, and she had clearance to access only two of those routes: one that went to the wood-paneled hallways of her own section, which she only later discovered was referred to as the "developmental tech" wing, and the other to a central division that strangely had only three levels (seemingly); the cafeteria and auditorium were on the first, or ground, floor, while CEO Jim Langan's office, along with the other corporate officers', was on the second. She'd never been to the third.

The other branch of the subterranean structure—like many things that happened at Langan Corp.—was a mystery. Beth had heard rumors it was pharmaceutical, but Colson had always insisted (only partially joking) that it was alien spaceships, a theory expressed with such earnestness and excitement that it had always brought a smile to Beth's face.

One more memory for her broken heart to hold on to.

Beth reaches the end of the hallway, stopping beside a set of double doors on her right. A subtle copper placard above the polished wooden doors reads simply: FORUM.

She takes a moment to close her eyes, take a deep breath, and let it out.

Then she pushes through the doors.

Inside, the circular room is dimly lit by sconces placed along glossy wood-paneled walls. The thick, dark carpet acts as a silencer for any sound of movement or life. Beth knows the room is completely soundproofed, something she's reminded of every time the door suctions closed behind her after she enters.

At the near end of the room is a podium centered beneath a hazy spotlight. Behind the podium is a sectioned-off area of empty leather chairs that Beth always thinks of as a jury box. At the far end of the room is a dais, on which sit three people, their lower halves hidden behind a low wall like a judge's bench, already awaiting her arrival. As always. She moves to stand behind the podium, grips the edges. A small black mic extends toward her from the top of the podium. She adjusts it slightly and waits.

"Good morning, Beth," the man to the far right says.

"Good morning," she replies. She takes a moment to steady her breath, force herself to relax. The man who spoke, a youngish, roguishly handsome psychologist named Jonathan Greer, is the only one of the three she knows well, but she's had direct experience with each of them over the years, to varying degrees.

Jonathan is a clinical psychologist (a fancy way of saying therapist), one she's forced to speak with weekly, at a prescribed time and for a predetermined duration. At first, both she and Colson found the arrangement disarming, uncomfortable. For Beth, it was almost... confrontational. After all, Greer has all the power. If he decides to indicate that the mental health of a Langan employee is not, as he likes to put it, "fit for service," then said employee is immediately suspended until further notice. Likewise, Terry Adams, an ancient-looking man sitting in the middle of the three, is Langan Corp.'s private in-house MD. Health checkups for all employees are monthly (instead of weekly, thank God), and over time Beth has found it harder to be annoyed by them, especially during her pregnancy, when she almost welcomed the reassurance of a second opinion that her baby was doing fine. Besides, it's free medical care, and if she were to ever show signs of a long-term sickness or disease, one of the monthly checkups would catch it early on.

Of course, Adams also has the power to shut down a project, or an employee, if he determines they aren't physically fit or able to perform. Still, she likes the old man. He's never been anything but kind in the years since she arrived.

The woman to the far left is Abigail Lee, the program director. Lee is technically—at least according to some corporate flowchart somewhere—Beth's direct supervisor. Of course, Abigail has only been in the lab itself a handful of times and, as far as Beth knows, has absolutely no idea how the technology (or *any* technology, for that matter) works. She's certainly never shown an interest in their work, at least not to Beth, or to Colson when he was alive. Beth thinks they are fairly close in age but cannot imagine two more disparate personalities. Still, Lee is always there for an annual review, and her signature miraculously appears on all finance requests for the day-to-day operational needs of the lab. Beth sees her more as a babysitter than a boss, one who doesn't say a peep unless called upon, for which Beth is grateful.

It's Abigail who leans forward, cautiously addressing the microphone before her, as if it were a cup of tea she was worried might be too hot. When she speaks, however, her normally reedy voice is loud and clear. Perfect for recording. "Dr. Darlow, are you ready to begin the redundant question session, matching to date of travel March 17, 2044?"

Beth nods. "I am."

There's a beat of silence, then the program director taps a few keys on a console hidden from Beth's view. The room fills with the soft sound of static—the chamber's surrounding speakers, hidden in the dark-paneled walls, coming alive. A man's sonorous voice fills the room, as if coming from everywhere and nowhere.

Please state your name and today's date.

Beth clears her throat, makes a point to enunciate clearly. "Beth Darlow. March 18, 2044."

Who is the president of the United States?

"James Whitmore."

Describe your marital status.

Beth's words hitch in her throat for a fraction of a second, then she sighs softly and answers. She does not lower her eyes. "Widowed."

In one word, describe your childhood.

For Beth, this question has been—from the first time she heard it—a complicated one. Going through this process early on, she made the mistake of overthinking the questions, as if it were an exam, or a study of her life, rather than scientific variables. She could literally give any answer she wanted, as long as those answers were consistent. During the questions, consistency is everything.

Still, easier to stick with the truth.

"Happy."

Name two members of your immediate family.

Another puzzler. She's never fully understood why they created a question that offered so many variables, and it was Colson who came up with the idea that, in addition to consistency for comparison's sake, they must also be using the answers, in some respects, as evaluators of some kind. A psychological test weaved in with scientific variables. Beth had asked Jonathan about it in one of their sessions and he'd refused to answer. Which was an answer in itself, she supposed.

In the beginning, Beth had answered the question using her husband's name, and then her uncle, Brett, since both of her parents and her only sibling were long dead. Further, when she first traveled, Isabella hadn't even been born.

And now, death had changed things once more.

"My uncle, Brett Hawkins. My daughter, Isabella Darlow."

If you could change one moment in your life, what would it be?

This is the question that always hurts the most, no matter how many times she's heard it. Still, it's an easy one. There is only one moment in her timeline, were fate allowing do-overs, she'd want to change. That she'd have the *power* to change.

"I would stop my husband from leaving on the day he was killed."

The speakers continue their live-wire humming, the hair-raising sound of electricity filling the air. But the questions, she knows, are over.

There are only six. And they never change.

The program director clears her throat, tilts her head toward the mic. "End of questions recorded for transmission." Everyone remains silent until a soft, low-pitched tone emanates from the speakers, followed by a *click* as the speakers turn off. The room is plunged into a deep, heavy silence. "Thank you, Beth. Do you need a moment before playback?"

Beth shakes her head. "I'm fine."

"Very well," Abigail says, leaning once more toward the mic. "Begin playback of original travel questions, dated March 17, 2044, Dr. Beth Darlow."

Again the speakers click on, and the same emotionless, mechanical voice fills the room.

This time, Beth doesn't speak, but only listens to the questions, along with her prerecorded answers, the ones she gave yesterday morning prior to traveling.

Please state your name and today's date.

Beth Darlow. March 17, 2044.

Who is the president of the United States?

James Whitmore.

Describe your marital status.

Widowed.

In one word, describe your childhood.

Happy.

Name two members of your immediate family.

My uncle, Brett Hawkins. My daughter, Isabella Darlow.

If you could change one moment in your life, what would it be?

I would stop my husband from leaving on the day he was killed.

No one speaks until the recording terminates, the invisible speakers once more going silent with a *click*.

After a moment, the program director looks to the other two members of the panel, who both nod in confirmation. She leans in, voice softer now that she's only addressing Beth, versus posterity. "Let the record show there are no discrepancies. We will now continue with the debrief." She turns toward Jonathan. "Mr. Greer, do you want to begin?"

Jonathan nods. "Director, could we put video for the travel session of Beth Darlow, dated March 17, 2044, on the screen, please? Hold playback."

The program director nods, types another command into her keypad. A large, clear-tech screen lowers to Beth's right. A still-frame image appears on the screen, bathing Beth in a dull white glow.

She turns her head to stare at a lightly distorted full-color image of the Cessna interior. The view is from her perspective, the image slightly skewed by mild tunnel vision. Seen clearly, however, is the swath of blue sky through the windshield, and her soon-to-be-dead parents sitting side by side in the tight cockpit.

Beth unconsciously rests the fingers of her right hand across her left forearm. The same place Mary's fingers nervously clutched her before their plane went down and her sister's teenage body was torn to pieces.

Seeing it like this, shown as a video broadcast instead of her private memory, does nothing to lessen the sense of association her feelings have toward the event. Rather, the image throws open a locked door inside her head, and she steels herself against the fresh flood of pain that comes surging through at the sight of this moment of time snatched from her life.

The arrival point of her travel.

FOUR

Can you describe this for us, Beth?"

Beth stares at the frozen image, willing it not to play.

She can't relive it again. Not here. Not with them judging her every intake of breath, every nervous twitch of her lips. Her own memory—her *present* memory—overlaps uncomfortably with the ninety seconds her consciousness spent on that plane yesterday, as if her brain can't separate the decades-old trauma with yesterday's experience. Beth knows it's the psychological equivalent of tearing open an old scar, never fully healed, to let it bleed out all over again.

She wills her emotions to flatline, her mind to focus. She forces herself to stare at the image with the detachment of a scientist, of an impartial observer.

Part of Beth wishes she had been in the mind, the body, of her sister instead. The clinical part of her very much wants to see the expression on young Beth's face, to observe her reactions.

Specifically, her eyes.

Beth knows that if she could somehow go back to that moment, choose a different perspective, and look into her twelve-year-old eyes, they'd be *flickering*, like the rapid clicking of a camera shutter, between her natural eye color—an aquamarine blue—and pure white. That flickering is the only way to know if someone is traveling inside a past version of themselves.

Watching. Recording. Reliving.

She'd seen it herself once. Just once.

In the eyes of her husband.

The two of them had been sharing an anniversary meal over plates of steak and glasses of Cabernet at their favorite restaurant, their go-to for celebration meals since the prices were insane but the food totally worth every gratuitous penny. Across the table, halfway through a conversation about what to name their unborn baby—Isabella for a girl, Brett for a boy—his eyes had begun to . . . *shutter*.

It was so subtle that she first thought it was nothing but a trick of the light, the flicker of the tabletop candle reflecting in his irises. It wasn't until two years later, after he had documented travel to that exact moment, that she realized what she'd been seeing:

His future consciousness had been inside his mind, watching her.

A spy sent from the future to observe.

When she first told him about the strange tell, he refused to believe it. But future traveling revealed it to be true.

They never came up with a sound reason for the bizarre physical effect. The soundest theory was that it was the body's response to the stress of an invading consciousness—aggressively dilating the pupil, which in turn would (theoretically) spread the pigment of the iris to such an extent that it created a strange flickering in the eyes.

The other theory—one that Beth kept to herself—was that the two consciousnesses were sharing the same brain, causing the eyes to bounce between one and the other with such speed that it created a physical response in the iris muscle.

Regardless, it wasn't a huge priority for them to understand, just another lingering mystery, something to shelve for future analysis when their funding was ramped up and more investigative help could be brought in.

But after they'd discussed it, and Beth realized what she'd seen at that long-ago anniversary dinner, she'd found herself watching her husband's eyes more closely. Nearly every moment they were together, she'd be looking for that strange flutter, an indicator that a second consciousness—a future *him*—was observing her.

The memory of that dinner—of those eyes—still gave her chills.

Shaking free of the past, Beth turns her gaze away from the frozen image on the screen and focuses instead on the three faces watching her, half-hidden in shadow, from across the room. Since it was Jonathan who'd asked the question, she addresses him directly.

"Not sure what there is to describe, as I think it's fairly obvious. It's the day my family was killed," she says, focusing all her energy on keeping her voice level, her emotions stilled. "My father was a pilot, although both my parents were licensed to fly, and often did. My parents were scientists, albeit in two unrelated fields, my father an epidemiologist, my mother an ethnobotanist. Given the nature of their research, it was important for them to have a plane at their disposal, and the ability to fly it anywhere in the world on a moment's notice. This particular trip was a rarity, since the destination was of interest to both of them, their respective fields intersecting. They were eager to study a certain flora said to be used within a small aboriginal community. The Inuit who have settled in the boreal forest region were rumored to be using the flora extract as a medicine for a particular strain of flu virus. The plan had been to land just past the border and refuel, restock. My sister and I, not in school at the time, were just along for the ride."

Beth shrugs, smiles crookedly. "A scientist's version of a

family vacation, I guess. Anyway, as you saw in the video, we lost an engine..."

Beth pauses, swallows, and once more forces her mind to separate from the memory, as if she were a surgeon performing heart surgery on a loved one. "We crashed in Jasper National Park, near Chungo Creek. About twenty minutes from Edmonton's airport." Beth intertwines her fingers on the podium. "I was the only survivor."

Dr. Adams, his face a mask of empathy, leans forward. "My God, Beth. How old were you?"

Beth shifts her eyes to the physician. "I was twelve at the time. My sister was fifteen."

Now Jonathan also leans forward intently, as does the program director, who is growing noticeably uncomfortable.

Poor Abigail, Beth thinks, although not unkindly. *Forced into empathy.*

"Well..." the program director says meekly, the strength of her voice during the question session now diminished. "Why don't we...?" She looks to Jonathan, who nods and takes over.

"Beth, reliving this trauma must have been gut-wrenching. Horrible..." He shakes his head sadly. "Hell, I don't even know what the right word is. But being forced to relive, reexperience, what I imagine is the worst moment of your life, an impossible tragedy... How in the world are you dealing with it?"

Beth feels her lower lip quiver and, below the edge of the podium, tightens her intertwined fingers until the knuckles turn white. "I'm fine."

Jonathan mumbles something to the old physician, who turns and mumbles something to the program director. Finally, Jonathan returns to the microphone, the sidebar apparently over. "I'm requesting a full psychological examination before you're allowed to travel again."

Beth's worming feelings of sorrow evaporate in a rush of hot anger. Her jaw drops, then she clamps it shut, twisting her lips into a mocking smile, her tired eyes suddenly blazing. "I'm sorry, *allowed*? That's not your decision."

"I'd also like a full exam," the physician chimes in, as if Beth hasn't spoken. "If Dr. Darlow shows any signs of physical trauma, it will be noteworthy as to how straining the consciousness can impact the body."

"Director, this is ridiculous. May I speak?"

Abigail holds up a finger, then covers her microphone.

Beth's anger, and impatience, grows.

"Excuse me…"

Beth glares at Jonathan as the other two whisper between themselves. She does her best to stare daggers, but his eyes don't flinch away. If anything, they study her more closely.

"Excuse me, Abigail…Dr. Adams…"

The program director and the doctor continue to ignore Beth, who raises her eyebrows at Jonathan, looking for help, but he only reclines in his chair, hands folded below his chin, as if he were almost enjoying himself.

Righteous prick.

"Hey!" Beth yells, enjoying the sight of Jonathan's eyes widening in surprise. The two others stop their rushed conversation and turn to focus on Beth. The program director scoots back into her spot, leans into the mic.

"No need to shout, Beth."

Beth scoffs. "Look, I appreciate your concern. The bottom line is that the travel was successful. Data is being compiled now that will give us more information on the arrival point and how that point was determined by the machine." She points to the screen, to the endless blue sky outside a doomed cockpit. "This is *research*. My husband had similar experiences when traveling, and

I don't recall a rush for brain scans or demands for colonoscopies being thrown around." She looks at each of them in turn, eyes wide with indignation, fingers no longer intertwined but clenched into tight fists. "So allow me to repeat: I'm *fine*."

For a long moment, no one speaks, the soundproofed room deadly silent.

Not waiting for permission, Beth turns and walks out.

FIVE

Beth! Wait a second..."

But Beth doesn't wait. She's already halfway down the long hallway, heading toward the elevator that will take her to her lab, where she can, ironically, stop feeling like a test subject, a guinea pig, and start feeling like the scientist she is.

Jonathan followed her from the Forum at a near jog after she stormed out at the end of the queries. She knows that being overly emotional or reactionary—or God forbid, *angry*—isn't helping her case as a competent leader, but sometimes she just can't help it.

The decision to keep her from traveling until she's been cleared both mentally and physically after the incident with the airplane is infuriating. Not because she wants to travel again anytime soon (she doesn't) but because they are taking the choice out of her hands. They are *controlling* her, and she doesn't like that. She doesn't like being handled.

Of course, if the machine had just sent her *anywhere* else—a birthday party might have been nice—she wouldn't be in this mess.

Just bad luck, she thinks, fuming. *Stupid random luck that it would send me to that exact moment...*

She and Colson had often discussed what triggered the machine's process for choosing an arrival point. It was always a little embarrassing to reveal to others that they didn't really understand that (rather important) component of the travel sessions. But they figured it was just another variable to work out, a problem to analyze, a puzzle to solve. Unfortunately, it had been more difficult than either one of them anticipated.

The mind was the most complex machine in the known universe, and when it came to making choices, the mind had plenty to say. A volcanic stew of emotions and memories and patterns with an almost bottomless depth of data. For better or worse, it was also a key part of the functionality of the machine. What made the machine *go*. And yes, it made sense that moments of strong emotional import might act as beacons of sorts, showing the machine a hot landing pad for the traveler, but it hadn't been *proven*.

Was it emotion that drove the arrival point, or something else?

Beth hadn't been thinking about that crash on the morning she traveled. It wasn't the "spike" that Tariq referred to. She hadn't thought about that fateful day in years...

So, then, what was it? What was the machine using?

"Beth, please... damn it, will you stop?"

Beth spins on her heel so suddenly the psychologist—a head taller and a solid fifty pounds heavier—takes a cautious step back, hands up, as if she were turning around with a cocked right hook. She locks her jaw to hide the small tinge of pleasure at seeing his fear.

"What?"

"Hey, whoa, okay? I just want to talk. Look, I think you're misreading what happened in there."

Beth laughs, crosses her arms tightly over her chest. "Oh, really? Because it sure sounded like you three were debating pulling me off my own goddamn project."

Jonathan shakes his head. "That's... No, Beth. No. Not at all. Come on, we're talking about making sure you are *safe*. To make sure going through a traumatic experience like that isn't having repercussions, damage we can't see unless we analyze you."

"So then why was Colson never analyzed after a trip? Huh? He traveled, what…seven times? I don't recall him getting the kid-glove treatment."

Jonathan sighs. "First of all, this has nothing to do with the fact that you're a woman. Psychological trauma affects men and women the same. If anything, men are more susceptible to long-term—"

"Yeah, Jon, I know." Beth takes a deep breath, lets it out. "Look, I'll do the tests, okay? But believe me when I tell you that *I'm fine*. The second I landed I knew where I was, what was happening. Yes, it was scary. Yes, it was very sad to go through that again. But keep in mind that I survived, Jonathan. A twelve-year-old girl *survived*. Not just physically, but psychologically as well. I'm still here. So if it didn't knock me down then, it sure as hell isn't going to knock me down now."

Jonathan nods. "I hear you. And I appreciate your agreeing to the examinations. But please understand, if I or Dr. Adams find something we don't like, we will recommend you halt traveling until further notice."

"Jesus Christ, you don't stop."

"Damn it, Beth, I'll halt testing altogether if I think there's a danger here—"

"Well, good luck with that, Jonathan. Really. Good luck. I'm sure Jim will be happy to put his top asset on the shelf until the frail little scientist gets her shit together. I mean, we're only talking about throwing away billions, right?"

Jonathan looks her in the eye, neither one of them backing down. "Either that or someone else will have to travel."

Beth shakes her head. She can feel the blood rushing to her face, fingernails digging into her palms as she clenches her fists.

Maybe I will *hit the son of a bitch.*

Instead, she takes a step back and lowers her voice, wanting to be sure what she says next is taken for what it is. A threat.

"Over my dead body. I'll tear the fucking thing down before that happens without my consent."

"You're overreacting. You need perspective."

"You know Colson would have *never* allowed that," she says. "And neither will I."

"So you're trying to impress a dead man."

Beth's eyes widen with a sudden, burning fury.

Jonathan takes a step back, hands rising defensively once more. "I'm sorry, that was uncalled-for."

Beth glares at him another moment, hating him for what he said, what he *thinks* of her.

Hating that he's right.

Hating him for that most of all.

"Fuck you, Jon."

Beth turns her back to him and walks briskly to the elevator, eager to get back to work, to get away from these dark halls and prying minds.

As she punches the call button and waits, she feels his stare on her back; she's grateful when the soft *ding* finally comes and the doors slide open. She steps in, taps the button for the lab, and forces herself to stare back at him, refusing to be cowed, to show weakness.

It's only when the elevator doors close on the exasperated face of the psychologist that she allows herself to relax. As the car descends, part of her wishes desperately that Colson *were* here, so they could rant and scream together, stand shoulder to shoulder—as a team—against the waves of politics and money that crashed against them, that now crash mercilessly against *her.*

But he isn't here.

She is alone.

And now the machine is hers and no one else's, no matter what the spreadsheets say.

I'll never let them take it from me. Never.

She thinks about what she said to Jonathan, how she felt when saying it.

Over my dead body.

She meant every word.

SIX

When the elevator slows to a stop, Beth checks her watch.

Damn, almost ten AM.

Hating to have wasted so much of her morning with the worthless Q and A session, she feels a rush of eagerness to bury herself in work, in doing what she loves. Solving the final threads of mystery in her grand design.

The doors slide open and she steps out quickly, already thinking of the checklist she wants to address with Tariq...

She takes three steps, then stops.

The elevator doors swish closed behind her.

A guilty-looking Tariq sits meekly at one of the consoles, his face an apology.

You have got to be kidding me.

Leaning on the desk next to Tariq is an old man in a finely tailored dark blue suit; bushy white hair sits disheveled atop his head, pale blue eyes sparkling like Santa Claus's. The old man's lips are curled into a familiar smirk Beth despises, a seemingly perpetual leer, an unchanging visage of disdain worn like a mask, regardless of which of his many moods (mostly aggravated) he happens to be in. When he notices Beth's entrance, he stands up straight, folds his hands neatly in front of him, and smiles at her as if she were a long-lost friend he was getting a chance to see one last time, face-to-face.

Beth's eyes dart from the man in the blue suit to Tariq, who suddenly busies himself with whatever happens to be on his monitor. She cocks her head, makes a show of her confusion.

"Jim? What the hell are you doing down here?"

Jim Langan holds his hands up expansively, seemingly unbothered by Beth's rude greeting. "Just taking in the sights, my dear." He smiles wider, showing his very white teeth, a feature of his she knows he takes a ridiculous amount of pride in. "You look tired, Beth."

"Uh-huh," Beth says under her breath, approaching the two men and giving Tariq a death stare when he turns to face her. "Well, I just had the debrief from yesterday's travel."

"And it didn't go to your satisfaction, I take it."

Beth keeps her eyes on him steadily, as if he were something dangerous, a tiger in the brush. "I wouldn't call it hilarious."

Jim laughs. "Oh, I agree. The whole thing is very stodgy, what with all the dim lighting and posturing, the inane questions and answers. So personal, yet so clinical, am I right? Anyway, no need to rehash it on my account," he says, blue eyes twinkling mischievously. "I know all about it. Those doctors do like to worry, don't they?"

"You were listening?"

"Of course I was! I hear everything, my dear. I see everything. In this building, I'm omniscient, didn't you know?" Jim steps closer, rests his large hands on Beth's shoulders, as if imparting some ancient wisdom. She makes an effort not to pull away in disgust. "Seriously, I am worried about you, though."

Beth scoffs. "I think my quota of overprotective men has been filled for the day, but thanks." Now she does pull away, relieved to have those gnarled knuckles and long fingers off her arms. "What do you want, Jim? I have a lot to do, as you know."

Jim's grin disappears, and Beth hears Colson's voice inside her head.

Take it easy, Beth, he whispers. *This man could make things very uncomfortable for you. So try to play nice, okay?*

Beth sighs, knowing Colson always was the more diplomatic one, especially when it came to Jim. "Look," she says, attempting a more convivial tone. "Why don't we go in my office? I could use a cup of coffee."

Jim's smile returns, as do those twinkling Santa Claus eyes, cold as chipped ice.

"Perfect. I was about to suggest that very same thing."

ᘓꙬᘔ

"Okay, so what's with the visit? Don't tell me you've missed my sparkling personality."

Jim sits heavily on the small leather couch. He glances through the blackened glass wall to his left, a barrier between Beth's office and an unlit room filled with deep shadows. "Must be hard, sitting next to the dark."

Beth's eyes cut to the darkened wall, the other side of which contains Colson's office, a room she hasn't stepped foot in since the week after his death. She knows it's cleaned every week by the rarely glimpsed janitorial crew. Cleaned, but unused.

She pulls her glare away from the shadows, brings it back to the man on the couch:

Jim Langan, the founder, CEO, and all-around head honcho of Langan Corporation. One who rarely deigned to visit her lab.

Just the way she liked it.

"Why are you down here, Jim?"

"Always to the point with you, Beth," he says, blue eyes momentarily darkening. Or, at the least, certainly no longer twinkling.

She can almost hear Colson's voice, seeping from that darkened room, whispering into her ear. *Take it easy, Beth. We need him.*

"Sorry," she says. "I just—"

"No, no...Say no more. You're busy. I get it. So, enough chitchat." Jim folds his hands in his lap, looks down at them a moment. "Would you believe me if I said I just wanted to check on your well-being? That was some tough sledding yesterday."

Beth watches him cautiously. "Uh-huh. And?"

Jim looks up at her. Perhaps he's startled at how easy he is to read, perhaps giddy to get to the real reason he's here. Regardless, he's giving her his world-famous smirk once more. A twisted smile that doesn't come anywhere near his eyes. "*And*...in addition to inquiring about your welfare, I wanted to give you a heads-up. On Monday morning, at nine AM sharp, you'll be doing a one-on-one interview. Here, in the laboratory."

Beth sits up in shock, leans forward on her desk. "I'm sorry? An interview? Here? Jim, this is highly classified—"

"I'm aware of that, Beth," Jim says, overriding her. "Believe me, if anyone is aware, it's me. Don't forget, it's your talent, but it's *my* money. The last thing I'd ever do is jeopardize the return on this particular investment."

Beth sits back slowly, cautiously mollified. "Okay, so what gives?"

"This reporter, and her magazine, and, well, the conglomerate that owns the magazine, have signed enough NDAs to wallpaper this office three times over. The reporter has been handpicked, Beth. She's a...What's the word?" Jim's eyes light up, and his smile turns somewhat malicious, like a shark who's just spotted a swimmer's kicking legs. "A ringer."

"A ringer for what?" Beth's eyes widen as a cold hand of panic grips her heart. "Jim, are you selling?"

Jim looks at her steadily for a beat, his mischievous smile wavering only slightly. "No..." he says. "But I suppose you could say that a capital infusion would be beneficial. To everyone."

Beth's mind races. This time, Colson isn't just whispering in her ear; he's sitting right next to her, arms folded, foot bouncing like a rabbit—a tic of his when angry.

Cripes, Beth. The old fucker's out of money.

She glances sidelong toward Colson's darkened office, an abyss of loss and sorrow that she finds somewhat comforting, as if visualizing the pain keeps it tactile, manageable. Beatable. She pushes away the image of him sitting over there, in the dark, watching her. Waiting to see what she'll do next.

"Okay, Jim, okay..." she says, stalling for time while she figures out just how bad things have gotten. "I don't know what the magazine could possibly print that wouldn't be covered by that NDA wallpaper you mentioned, but I won't fight you on the dog and pony show. What's the publication?"

"Business Weekly."

Beth can't help it. She laughs out loud. "Jesus, the first interview I ever do for the machine...and it's a *business* article? I've created the most ambitious science project of the last hundred years, and I'm telling Wall Street?"

Jim spreads his hands wide, eyes all innocence. "Who the fuck else would you tell?"

Beth scoffs but bites her tongue.

"Look," he says, placating now. "You'll get your science pieces, Beth. But those space nerds will want details I'm not willing to give them, at least not yet. This is more...Oh hell, it's a fluff piece, Beth. Something to get the board to loosen their wallets a little. Maybe bring in some outside interest. If it all goes to plan, we'll be expanding the board and bringing in fresh capital. Good for me, good for you. Good for the machine."

Beth nods. "I get it. Play dumb on the tech, go big on the vision."

"Don't worry about playing dumb. By the time the piece goes to print, it'll be so whittled down by their editors—and my lawyers—the only thing that will translate to the general public are two beautiful words."

Beth sighs heavily. "Time travel."

Now the smile does meet his eyes, and Beth doesn't know which version she finds more unsettling. "You've read my mind."

"It's not hard," Beth says sharply. "I just think about making money and I've got a crystal ball straight to your brain."

"I take that as a compliment," he says, bowing his head in mock salute. He takes a sip of the coffee, winces, sets it down on the small table in front of him. "You drink that shit?"

Beth shrugs, still thinking. Worrying.

Money… it's always the damn money.

Jim stands, brushes his pants, buttons his tailored suit coat. "Like I said, let me worry about what the rag prints or doesn't print. I want you to give them full access. Nothing is out of bounds. Answer every question the best you're able. I'll handle the rest."

Beth stands as well, hands firmly on the desk, as if the solidity of it will somehow keep this billion-dollar ship from rocking. "I'll play nice."

"See that you do. Have a lovely weekend. Kiss that little girl for me."

Beth follows Jim out of her office and to the elevator, watches until the doors settle closed before turning to Tariq. "What the hell, Tariq? Meeting with Jim behind my back?"

Tariq scoffs and shakes his head, but his eyes don't leave his monitor. "You're being paranoid, Beth. He came down here looking for you."

"Oh yeah? It's interesting he thought he'd find me here while I was scheduled for a debrief."

This time Tariq doesn't respond. Instead, he taps the keypad with the relentlessness of someone with something to hide, his face a mask of indifference.

Beth sighs heavily, rubs at one temple, annoyed to be getting a stress headache after being at work for only an hour. "Whatever," she says. "Playtime's over. Where's my report?"

"Just uploaded it to the server. But I didn't find—"

But Beth is already striding away. "I'll read it for myself, thanks. Please run the mechanical diagnostic," she says over her shoulder. "If you're done kissing ass, that is."

Tariq sighs, turns back to his monitor. "Uncalled-for," he yells after her, already typing in the commands.

SEVEN

I brought you a butterfly, Mommy."

Beth arrived home later than she wanted (again) after spending the afternoon and early evening running new scenarios through the data Tariq had acquired, seeing if the "pre-spike" was indeed something to focus on or just a visceral response caused by anxiety; undue stress born from having a powerful laser beam pointed at one's face, for example.

When she stepped through the door of her home, yelling out a greeting and kicking off her work shoes, she immediately caught the scent of Marie Elena's famous baked chicken coming from the kitchen, and her mouth flushed with saliva. She'd skipped lunch (again) and had forgotten to eat much for breakfast after the surprise meeting with Jim and the childish fight with Tariq. Smelling the spicy chicken (and whatever else the amazing woman had concocted) made her realize that she wasn't just hungry; she was *starving*.

Now she makes her way quickly to the kitchen, noticing with a pang of guilt that Isabella is already seated at the table, stuffing her mouth with small cuts of chicken. Marie Elena is bent over the stove, spooning sauce over a plate filled with chicken breast and green beans with the care and precision of a gourmet chef.

"Just in time," she says, smiling as she walks the plate to the table.

Beth kisses Isabella on the head, all but runs to the bathroom to wash up, then hurries back to find her lovely daughter smiling up at her and a plate of food waiting on the table, a full glass of red wine standing sentinel beside it.

"Marie Elena, you're too good to me," she says, sitting down and making a funny face at her daughter. "Where did you get this wine?"

"At the farmers' market this afternoon, along with the beans," she says, sitting down with her own plate and her own glass of red wine. "But I figured you could use some color in your cheeks, Beth. You're too pale, dear. Just don't tell Robert," she adds slyly, winking at Isabella, who giggles.

While Beth fought back against being emotionally "handled" by the men at work, she is more than happy to be mothered. In fact, she welcomes it. "My lips are sealed," she says, taking a long sip before digging into the hot meal.

They are partway through their supper when Isabella gasps theatrically, leaps from her chair, and runs from the room. When she returns she's holding a purple-and-blue butterfly cut from construction paper, decorated with glued beads, glitter, and pipe cleaner antennae.

"I brought you a butterfly, Mommy."

After dinner, when the dishes are cleaned up and Marie Elena has left for the night, Isabella takes her mother's hand and leads her down the narrow hallway that stretches from the front of the house. "We need to hang the butterfly I made you," she says.

"I can't wait," Beth replies; the weight and stress of her workday—already sweetly muted by the wine—is now massaged completely away by her daughter's touch. Stopping in the hallway at the part they affectionately refer to as the Gallery, Beth flips a switch on the wall, filling the corridor with the milky-white glow of the overhead light. Together, mother and daughter stand, holding hands, side by side, studying the montage of colorful creations Isabella has made over the last couple of years: drawings of flowers and insects, clowns, and animals; a particularly colorful portrait of Beth, the word *MOM* scrawled daintily beneath in green crayon, the *O* in the shape of a heart; several decorated paper plates; a 2-D representation of their house assembled with pink Popsicle sticks; a family portrait Isabella made when she was only three years old, drawn just a few weeks before Colson's death, their small family represented by colorful stick figures with bizarre hair, big eyes, and bigger smiles, holding hands, a yellow sun nestled in the picture's top corner, green grass beneath their feet.

That one is Beth's favorite.

"Where should we hang my butterfly?" Beth asks.

"There, Mommy," Isabella says, pointing to a small clearing of space high up on the wall, a clean spot on the wallpaper of drawings filling the space above the cream wainscotting.

Together, they carefully tape the butterfly to the wall.

At Isabella's request, Beth agrees to leave its bright blue wings free so that it can flutter at will through the innocent images of her baby girl's imagination.

ꙮ

Later, Beth and Isabella lie in her large bed, Isabella in her brown onesie pajamas (the ones Beth thinks match her eyes), her long black hair still damp from the bath. Tucked under one of Isabella's arms is her favorite doll, Singing Sally, slightly larger than a normal figurine doll (just over a foot in height when stood straight) with posable arms and legs, interchangeable outfits to match her programmable singing style (rock, country, or pop), and a largish head with transparent eyes that glow while she sings, pulsing to the tempo of a small variety of recorded songs. Isabella's favorite was the country tune, the one that made Sally's eyes glow yellow, her bright plastic smile unmoving while an internal speaker played out tinny guitar and a woman's (somewhat yodeling, Beth thought) voice:

I hope to see you soon,
In the country,
In the country.
Just follow my sweet croon,
To the country,
To the country . . .

Thankfully, Singing Sally is currently taking a stage break while Isabella is occupied flipping the pages of a classic children's book—*Where the Wild Things Are*—her dark brown eyes flared wide at the sight of the massive troll-like creatures and the young boy in a crown dancing under the moonlight. Beth, having made the transition to sweats, warm socks, and an oversize T-shirt, lies contentedly beside her, staring at her tablet, reviewing portions of Tariq's analysis she hadn't been able to get to while at the lab.

Isabella closes the book and yawns, rolls over, and clings to her mother, staring tiredly at the pages of scrolling text and numbers, wondering what it all means.

"Mom, show me the pictures," she says, tapping the tablet with a small finger.

Beth looks over, offering her best mock outrage. "The pictures? Again?"

Isabella giggles, nodding excitedly. "Yeah. And do the video. My first day at preschool."

Beth's heart simultaneously sinks and swells at the request. It's a difficult memory for her. A glimpse of a better time, a happy time, snatched away by a greedy, malicious fate.

"Oh, I love that one," she says, and closes her work file.

She taps another icon, scrolls through to find the file she knows by heart, the one Isabella can't seem to get enough of, and taps it.

The tablet goes momentarily dark before the image of a low brick building pops into view, filling the screen.

A sunny day. A wide sidewalk leads to a large wooden door painted sky blue. A wall of bursting jasmine hedges the sidewalk to one side, the flowers so full Beth can almost smell their fragrance all over again. The bubbling sound of children comes from nearby like the chatter of hidden fairies in a meadow.

The sound is overrun by a man's voice, hidden behind the camera. He speaks to Beth from the tablet speakers and she feels a clutch in her throat, a soft pain in her heart. Her fingers tighten their hold on the tablet as he speaks, his voice a river of memory flooding through her.

How are we doing?

In the video, Beth turns to face the camera, smiling and radiant. She holds the hand of a younger, tinier version of Isabella, only two years old at the time. Beth is wearing jeans and a white blouse, Isabella a bright yellow sundress, fine dark hair falling past her shoulders, the ends lifting slightly with the push of a soft breeze.

As they near the sky-blue door, it opens from the other side. An older woman in white sneakers, blue jeans, and a polo shirt the same color as the door steps out to greet them. Her eyes glance briefly at Beth, then the camera, then focus on Isabella.

"You must be our newest friend," she says gleefully.

The soft chimes of Isabella's laughter trickle through the speakers.

The Isabella lying in the bed with Beth clutches her arm more tightly, giddy at the thrill of seeing her past self. "Mrs. Thomas," she whispers into Beth's ear, quietly, as if not wanting to break the spell of reliving the moment.

"That's right," Beth says.

In the video, Beth shakes the teacher's hand, says something the video recording fails to pick up. Then she turns to face the camera, one hand extended toward the lens.

Let's get you in here! Come on, Colson, hand it over.

The image jostles for a moment, then Colson's face fills the frame, eyes wet with unfallen tears, his expression one of pure joy.

You got it?

I got it.

Isabella points a finger at the screen. "Daddy!" she yells happily, just like she always does at this point in the video. And every time—every time—it's a knife in Beth's heart.

"That's right," she says. "Your daddy and I were so happy that day. We were both..."

"Nervous," Isabella offers, pulling words from their prior conversations in this exact bed, watching this exact video, as if it were something they'd experienced over and over in a continual loop of time. A glimpse of eternal heaven.

"Nervous, yeah. A little bit. But we were also excited. One day you were just a baby, and then...then you were this amazing little girl."

"And now I'm all grown up," Isabella says matter-of-factly.

Beth starts to reply but realizes she has no idea what to say.

In the video, Past Beth follows Colson and Isabella through the blue door...and disappears.

EIGHT

After Isabella is tucked into bed, Beth pours what's left of Marie Elena's wine into a tumbler and settles onto the couch, eager to continue studying the analysis from her last travel, consumed with the idea of making the ultimate discovery:

How does the machine choose the arrival point?

She thinks about Jerry Wilson being hauled away by security, his papers left strewn on the carpeted hallway floor like forgotten memories. She recalls his words, and the disgust on his face when he spoke them:

Don't worry, Beth, you'll be next!

She takes a sip of wine, shakes the cobwebs of doubt from her mind, and focuses on her tablet. She's about to close the folder containing the old video files when she spots an icon near the bottom. It's labeled: FIRST TRIP.

Her finger hovers over the icon for a beat, then she taps it.

The screen becomes a still shot of her lab at Langan Corp., but instead of a wide-open empty space filled with no one but her and Tariq, there are multiple techs standing around in lab coats, a fist-pumping Colson in the middle of them.

God, did we really have so many staff?

Budget attrition has taken most of them over the last year or so, and she finds herself struggling to remember what it was like in the early days. She stares with a sense of wonder at the smiling, excited faces of the other scientists, most of them graduate students, and can't bring herself to think of them as real people. Instead, it's as if she's looking at ghosts, or something drawn from her imagination. A pretend version of the "better days" that may or may not have truly existed.

That's... Suzanne, Beth thinks, staring hard at the faces, trying to recall details about each of them, and surprised at how difficult it is. *And that boy in the back, he was so funny... Ron. And the pretty girl, she had a crush on Colson, but she was also a brilliant physicist. Ellen... or, no, Ellie. I used to tease him about it but secretly worried about an affair.*

"As if we had time..." Beth mutters, dazed by the cheerful faces she wishes she'd gotten to know better.

When Colson died, a few of the remaining staff left of their own volition, ready to move on to other projects, other dreams, not believing Beth could finish what she and Colson had started.

Her request to replace them had been denied.

Over the ensuing months, the rest were laid off as a result of more extreme budget cuts.

All but one.

Beth feels a surge of guilt at how she treated Tariq today. Accusing him of something based on nothing other than her own insecurities. He was the only one who chose to stay, who gave Beth a vote of confidence that he believed in her, in the project. She made a vow to make it up to him, to be less bitchy, less internalizing... She'd need him in the months ahead. And besides, the idea of losing another person in her life, creating another ghost were there was once flesh and blood and *belief*... it would be too much.

Grimacing, Beth taps the screen, and the video plays.

Hoots of congratulations and excitement leap from the tablet speaker as the techs and engineers and scientists slap one another on the back, slap Colson on the back. She smiles at his smile, his *joy.* After a moment, her own voice overrides the audio, because of course she's the one holding the tablet, hidden behind the lens filming it all, the woman behind the man, despite their equality of workload.

What would they all have thought if we'd told them the truth? she thinks. *That the machine was initially* my *project. My idea. That it was my formulas and theories that created time travel.*

"Okay, mister," Beth's recorded voice says, interrupting her present-day thoughts. "You've just become the first successful time traveler in history. How do you feel? And please, be very specific!"

Past Beth laughs, as do Colson and a few of the staff. But they quickly grow quiet as Colson ponders the words he'll say for posterity.

"I felt like God," he says quietly, eyes focused on a distant spot, on the memory of what he'd just been through. Then he smiles shyly, as if self-conscious about how egotistical he must sound. He clears his throat, starting over. "What I mean to say," he says carefully, "is that, for me, it was a glimpse of what it might mean to be omniscient." He pauses, looks at the faces around him, each of them beaming and eager. "I mean, to leap into a mind, to relive a moment and watch it play out...to *observe* the past from the perspective of another consciousness, from *inside* a past version of yourself." He shakes his head in obvious wonderment. "There are no words."

Beth's voice breaks in once more, shattering the spell of reverence. "I hate to be a downer," Past Beth says, "but it was all pretty boring from our end." There are a few laughs at this, and even Colson nods along. "You just sort of...lay there."

Hearing herself now, she wonders if she did it purposely, maliciously. She tries to recall if she was bothered at the time, annoyed at those admiring faces, the naked *want* of their expressions, by his talk of omniscience. Jealous at the attention he was receiving.

In the past, Colson looks directly at the camera, and even now, sitting on the couch, holding a tablet portraying a digital image, Beth shivers at the focus in his eyes. It's the same look she remembered seeing over the many years of their partnership, their marriage. That burning *drive* of his that kept them both going, both reaching for the impossible.

Then his face relaxes and he looks away from the lens, back toward his acolytes. He begins speaking animatedly, gesturing with his hands for emphasis, and she knows he's thinking of the future, of the generations that would watch this moment over and over.

He's gone into Teacher Mode.

That's what she called it whenever Colson would spontaneously begin lecturing, going over and over the science to anyone who would listen, as if he were constantly politicking, driving home the bullet points of his dreams until they were cemented in the minds of others.

"Unlike the movies," he begins, "there is no grand flash, no tunnel of light to travel through. As Beth so aptly remarked, my body didn't glow like an overcharged light bulb and then wink out of existence."

"Not a bad idea," Past Beth says. "Maybe we should incorporate some strobe effects. The board would shit themselves."

Colson laughs. "Wouldn't hurt. But look, science aside, what this project reveals...what it revealed to me, only moments ago...is that humans are made up of memories. It's the constitution of who we are. Our minds hold the reflections of a billion lives, infinite parallel worlds...but only fate can decide which of those we are allowed to see and touch."

He looks past Beth and points. "That machine isn't God; it's just a tool. Hardware. Energy. Algorithms."

"It's a lot more than that," Past Beth says. "I think you're giving fate too much credit." A few of the faces in the lab turn toward the camera, smiles fading uncertainly at Beth's tone. "It's the machine that decides where we travel; we just don't know what that decision process is yet. But I guarantee you it's a scientific answer. There's a rational formula."

Colson steps closer to the camera, his upper body filling the screen, bright eyes boring holes into the future. "Let me ask you something, Beth. What if it's *we* who decide? What if it's us, you and I, who harness the power to choose from infinite possibilities? Forge our own path to the moments of our past selves, our other lives?"

There's a beat. Sitting here on the couch, years later, Beth swallows the lump in her throat, remembering her answer.

"Then I suppose you'd be right," she says. "We'd be gods."

Colson nods, an almost sad smile on his face...when the screen freezes. A window pops open over the video as a *blurb blurb blurb* sound emanates from the tablet. Beth, more deeply engrossed in the video than she realized, jolts in surprise, nearly spilling her wine.

"Damn it."

The pop-up graphic announces INCOMING CALL, showing the face of her best friend, Lucy. Beth sets the wine on the table, closes the video file, taps the answer icon.

"Hey, you," Beth says, her tablet screen now filled with the upper half of a young woman wearing flannel pajamas, her head nestled into a stack of pillows. "In bed, I see."

"Hey yourself. Yeah, I just got the little monster to sleep and I'm wiped. Before I conked out, I wanted to make sure we were on for tomorrow."

Beth nods. "Of course. Thorne Park, nine AM sharp."

"Correct. We'll take turns hitting the coffee shop across the street while the kids go *Lord of the Flies* in the playground."

"Hey, it's important to cull the weak," Beth says, laughing.

"Oh God, I hope not. So tell me, how's life... Oh wait, that's right. You have no life."

"Ouch?"

"Let's try this: How's work... Oh wait, that's right. We can't talk about your work."

Beth's smile fades a little. "We can talk about you. I'm happy to live vicariously."

"Great, tomorrow I'll fill you in on the joys of dating men when you have a preschooler at home. The reactions are *hilarious*. Real top-drawer humor."

"I bet."

Lucy kisses the screen. "I'm off to dreamland. See you in the morning."

"See you."

The screen goes dark and Beth finds herself staring at it a moment, unsure what to do next. Part of her wants to continue down the rabbit hole of the past, watch more videos of her lost husband, her idyllic history. Another part of her knows there's work to do. Data to analyze.

Instead, she sets the tablet down on the table, picks up her glass, and finishes off the wine in one swallow. "No more memories," she says, staring into the empty glass, almost wishing it were true, not realizing the impact, and irony, of having such a wish.

Because Lucy was right. Sometimes, it does seem like her life is empty.

That memories are all she has.

NINE

Thorne Park is filled with parents and children. A popular Saturday morning destination for kids under twelve, the park features toddler-safe equipment and is one of the few parks near Beth's neighborhood that is completely fenced in. One gate in and out keeps the smaller kids from wandering where they shouldn't, and any strange characters from doing the same. There's ample parking, and across the two-lane street is a large neighborhood coffee shop that caters to park patrons—one more reason for parents to love it as a destination. It's a warmer day than Beth expected, and she finds herself holding Isabella's jacket, folded over her arm along with her own, while sitting on the bench with Lucy.

The two women watch Isabella and Lucy's little boy, Timothy, run through, under, and over the pirate ship–themed equipment. Seeing their carefree play, Beth has a familiar thought: how nice it must be to laugh openly, to have fun without worry, to love life without the psychological or emotional boundaries that rise—unbidden, unwanted—as a person grows into adulthood.

"So what, the old guy's out of money?" Lucy asks, picking up the thread of their conversation, her eyes never leaving the children.

"Guys like Jim Langan don't run out of money," Beth replies. "They don't have dwindling bank accounts, or needless debt, or hand-wringing accountants. What they do have are thresholds of pain."

"And he's reached that threshold with your...you know... machine."

Beth smirks. For years she's had to keep her closest friend, her college roommate, her maid of honor, in the dark about what—what *exactly*—the machine does. Sure, the information would most likely be safe...but what if?

What if Lucy got a little tipsy one night and let it slip to a work colleague that her friend Beth dabbled in time travel? What if she thought it would be okay to tell her mother or her father? And what if Mom or Dad happened to have a friend whose kid works for a news source?

Then the NDAs would come crashing down, and Beth's dreams right along with them.

"Sorry, I know it's annoying," Beth says, like she always does.

Lucy waves a hand. "It's okay. I like to imagine you're out there saving the world, finding a sustainable vaccine for the T-1 virus, or curing baldness. You know, hero stuff."

"Listen, it's my turn to get coffee," Beth says, anxious to change the subject. "You wanna keep an eye out here while I make a run across the street?"

Lucy nods. "Yeah, sure. Oh! Get me a blueberry scone, will ya?"

"Done. Do we need waters for the kids? It's hot today."

"Might as well."

Beth looks around until she finds Isabella across the enclosure, sitting on the soft foam flooring of the play area with Timothy, happily distracted. Feeling better having put eyes on her daughter, she heads toward the gate. "Be right back."

∽⊕∾

On the sidewalk just outside the park's exit is a crosswalk leading to a row of shops across the street, including the coffee shop. A few people stand with her, waiting for the light to change. On a whim, Beth turns her head to the left, noting the fence extending to the end of the block, comforted by the four-foot barrier that separates the kids from the bustly sidewalk and the busy street beyond. Absently, she scans the faces of the people hanging out along the park's perimeter.

That's when she sees Colson standing near the end of the fence line, no more than twenty yards away. He's wearing dark pants and a worn blue work shirt—exactly the kind of outfit he'd wear on the weekends around the house.

Or to the park.

Beth's mind freezes and her mouth drops open as if, fueled by pure instinct, she is preparing to call out for him.

To call out her dead husband's name.

Instead, she mumbles it under her breath, her thinking slow and fragmented, her thoughts foggy and distant, as if her brain has been reset and is now slowly booting back up.

"Colson..."

He's staring into the park. Beth turns her head to see what he's looking at...

And of course, it's Isabella. He's watching his daughter play. He's—

"Colson?" This time her voice is louder. Loud enough that she senses the people around her take notice. One woman, holding the hand of twin little girls, glares at Beth with worried eyes, perhaps sensing the strain, the *fear*, in her voice.

Beth takes a step toward her husband—*her dead husband, the one she saw in the morgue, his face torn in half, brain fluid leaking from a crack in his skull, limbs shattered, his chest concaved with enough force to have smashed his ribs like toothpicks, pulp his beating heart into jelly*—yes, *that* husband, who is now casually leaning against the low chain-link fence as if he doesn't have a care in the world.

As if he's not real at all.

As if he's a ghost.

"Colson!"

This time Beth knows people can hear her, because she's yelling like a madwoman in the middle of a crowded throng of parents and children. Her hands are shaking, her skin prickling with shock.

The man—*just a man who looks like Colson but can't possibly be*—at the end of the fence straightens; his head begins to turn toward her...

And then someone is grabbing her arm, tugging hard. Beth spins around, frantic, and finds herself staring into Lucy's worried face.

"Beth? What the hell?"

Then Beth looks back, pointing, straining to see—to *show* Lucy—her husband, who's standing on the sidewalk, watching the children play in the park. Watching his daughter...

But the man is gone.

"He's...I saw..."

Beth realizes that more than a few people are watching now, clutching their children tight, wary of this woman yelling and trembling on the sidewalk outside a children's playground. Her mouth opens and closes wordlessly as she searches for answers.

"Mommy?"

Beth's head jerks toward the sound, toward her daughter. Isabella's standing at the fence, watching her, brow furrowed, eyes worried.

"It's okay, love. One second..."

Beth turns and grabs Lucy's hand, points with her other hand toward the end of the fence.

"Did you see him?"

Lucy shakes her head. "Who?"

Beth stares at her friend, meets her eyes. She lowers her voice, as if anyone around them would have a clue who she was talking about. "*Colson*. Lucy, I saw Colson…"

She points again, thrusting her finger toward the area where he was standing, no more than a stone's throw away. "He was right there, Lucy. He was alive, and he was *right there*."

"Beth," Lucy says slowly, the way someone speaks to a child. Or a crazy person. "What are you talking about?"

Beth looks left and right, squeezes Lucy's hand harder. "I saw my husband. Just now. He was standing right over there."

Lucy doesn't look down the sidewalk. She doesn't show alarm or surprise.

Instead, her face shows confusion. Concern.

"Honey, Colson is dead. I mean, okay, maybe you saw someone who looked like him…and it triggered something. Like a mind trick. But, Beth…come on…"

Beth grunts, lets go of Lucy's hand, and takes two determined steps toward the fence. She drops to her knees in the grass in front of her daughter, the metal mesh separating them. Isabella looks scared, confused. Beth tries to smile, to defuse her daughter's fear, but her body is trembling like a live wire, as if her nerves are raw and exposed, the slightest breeze painful as fire when it brushes her skin…because she *knows* what she saw.

If I could just stop shaking…

"Baby, sweetheart, it's okay," Beth says, and puts her hand to the fence, coils her fingers around the cool metal. "Did you…did you see your daddy?"

"Beth!"

The word hits her like a slap, and Beth jerks away from the fence as if shocked by an electric current. She twists her head to see Lucy staring down at her, no longer worried or confused but bordering on something else. Anger.

"Beth, that's enough."

Beth stares down the length of sidewalk once more, straining her eyes for the blue work shirt, the back of her husband's head, his eyes meeting hers through the churn of people walking, obscuring his existence like a flickering candle...

Then she lowers her head, exhales. "Okay, you're right. I'm sorry. I'm okay."

Lucy steps closer to the fence, where Timothy and Isabella (along with a few other curious children and their bored, nosy parents) are now carefully watching Beth. Lucy claps her hands to get their attention, to break the spell of their innocent fear.

"Hey, who wants to get pancakes?"

Beth doesn't hear the children's answer. She doesn't know if they say yes or no or beg to stay or cheer for the idea of fucking pancakes. She only hears the blood pounding in her ears, and when she closes her eyes tight she sees him again, standing straight, turning to look at her... and for a split second, their eyes meet...

And then...

And then they lock you up because you're fucking nuts.

Beth sighs and wipes her hands over her face, tries to scrub away the image of her husband, as if it were a dream she wanted to forget. A nightmare.

"I'm not crazy..." she says under her breath, but takes no solace from the words, because she doesn't know if they're true.

Then she stands, brushes clippings of grass from her knees, and follows Lucy back toward the park entrance to find her daughter.

TEN

Beth sits in a leather club chair, twitchy and tired.

She didn't sleep well over the weekend.

After the park on Saturday morning (and subsequent awkward pancake breakfast with Lucy and the kids), she felt as if she'd only gone through the motions over the ensuing forty-eight hours with Isabella. No matter how hard she tried, or internally scolded herself, Beth couldn't focus on her little girl or enjoy their time together because her mind kept plaguing her with that image, over and over again...

For a split second, their eyes meet...

Jonathan hands her a mug of coffee and sits across from her, crossing his legs casually. "I have a theory."

Beth nods, sips the coffee, absently realizing it's a thousand times better than the stuff they cook up in the lab. She emailed Jonathan Sunday night, asked if he could meet her early for an impromptu session. She wanted to talk with him about what had happened—clear her mind a bit, if possible—before meeting whatever old-school business reporter dragged their spectacles and suspenders down to her office at nine AM.

She isn't crazy about Jonathan, and she doesn't always trust him, but they've known each other for many years and she likes to think there is a grudging respect between them. He is the only one who knows all her secret worries, how deep the trauma of losing Colson is, the conflicts and hardships of being a world-class scientist on the brink of one of humankind's greatest discoveries, and a single mother. She's never had reason to regret opening up to him in the past and hopes she has no reason for doing so now. After Colson's death, he was instrumental in steering her emotions in a constructive way that allowed her to keep working, gave her the tools to fight off the near-debilitating moments of grief and depression.

Which was why, after a weekend of headache-inducing confusion, she decided to talk with him about what happened at the park. A big part of her hated (and feared) the idea of sharing what she'd seen (or what she thought she'd seen), because if he concluded that she was mentally or emotionally unable to perform her work duties, it could mean trouble for her with Jim. But given what they'd already been through, specifically about Colson and the ensuing hellish aftermath, she thought he'd be somewhat open-minded about the fact that she'd seen her dead husband hovering at a playground on a bright Saturday morning. He might even be helpful.

Or so she hoped.

Regardless, she was willing to risk it. Because if she didn't talk to *someone* about it, she really would go crazy. "Please," she says. "I'm all ears."

"You're gonna be shocked to hear this, but I don't think what you saw is, quite frankly, all that strange. It certainly doesn't surprise me and, further, doesn't worry me. I'm telling you because I know my response to all this is on your mind, so you needn't worry on that front. As a doctor, and as a friend, I appreciate your trust, Beth. I'll never misplace it. That's a promise."

Beth nods. "I know. Thank you. But what do you mean about it not being strange? Because I gotta be honest, it felt *really* fucking strange, Jonathan."

He laughs, sits up, and settles his elbows on his knees, hands intertwined. Eyes focused on Beth's. "I know, and I'm sorry. Aside from being confusing, I'm sure it was traumatic."

Beth lets out a held breath, grateful to be taken seriously. She doesn't know if she'll ever forgive Lucy for the way she reacted, looking at her like she was mad. Like she was somehow *dangerous.* "Okay, so what's this theory?"

Jonathan sits back, his entire posture that of a man relaxed and in control. A man confident in his answers. Despite herself, Beth finds herself clinging to that feeling, that strength. God knows she needs it.

"Let's start with facts. One, you and Isabella had been watching old videos of Colson the night before the park, right?"

Beth nods. "Yeah, I thought about that, too."

"Good. Another fact. We are a few days away from the anniversary of Colson's death, which also happens to be your birthday. It's the twenty-seventh, right?"

"Yeah, that's right. It'll be a year."

"Both of these are what I call stress events. The fact that they happen on the same day makes it doubly so. But let's continue with a few more facts." Jonathan lifts a well-manicured hand, begins counting off fingers. "One, we both know you're under a tremendous amount of strain. Two, your staff has been reduced to practically nothing and you're essentially doing the work of half a dozen people. Three, you've lost not only your husband but your partner in one of the most important scientific endeavors in human history. Four, you're raising a beautiful little girl who, let's not forget, is also dealing with the grief of losing a parent, albeit in her own way. Fifth, and last, you're literally experimenting on yourself with this machine, and just a few days ago you blasted your mind back in time to reexperience the most tragic moment of your life."

He drops his hands, leans forward again. "Beth, when you add all this up . . . it's no wonder your mind is showing you phantom images of your deceased husband. Your subconscious is being battered by wave after wave of trauma. It's grasping at straws. For help. For support."

Jonathan extends one hand across the narrow coffee table separating them, rests a warm palm on Beth's knee. His intense gaze locks onto her eyes. "I want you to know I'm here for you, Beth. That I believe in you and in what you're doing. And besides all that, I consider you a friend. I'm on your side, and I'll help you through this."

Beth's eyes flick to his hand, but she forces herself not to shift away. She offers a weak smile and nods. "I know."

Jonathan removes his hand, reclines once more. "Let's do this. Let's keep talking. Maybe, for the next month or so, we increase our sessions to twice a week, just to keep things open and conversant. I don't want you feeling stuck with any of this pressure. In the meantime, don't sweat this Colson vision. It's simply your internal self's way of telling the outside you, the focused-on-work you, that it's hurting. Let yourself mourn. Hell, let yourself feel a little crazy, all right? I mean, sometimes repressing these natural emotions in stressful times can do more harm than good. Let yourself be sad, cry into a pillow at night, spend time with Isabella looking at old pictures from happier times. And be cognizant to let *her* mourn as well. And look, I'm confident you're going to get through this with flying colors, but for the next week or two these feelings are going to be fresh. The wounds aren't healed, Beth; they're just bandaged up with work and parenting, or whatever busywork you come up with, which is why those bandages slip a little during quieter moments—when you're relaxed, when your mind is free to wander. It's in those moments that your mind is free to let you know it wants to grieve, to not ignore the pain of loss. And believe me, it'll do what it has to do to get your attention."

"Like showing me my dead husband."

He smiles slightly, nodding, fingers dancing on the arms of his chair. "That's right. And besides, you won't be traveling again for a while, right? So we have time to get things settled, get through this rough patch. And in the meantime, if you need me to prescribe something mild, something to take the edge off, that's okay, too."

Beth thinks about this. "I don't know. It's hard enough getting people to see me the way they saw Colson. You know, genius man scientist versus genius female sidekick. If people knew I was medicated…"

Jonathan sits up. "Beth, this is all between us. Completely confidential."

Beth stares at him a moment, wondering how far she can trust him. Wondering if she's already made a huge mistake by confiding in him. "Plus, like you said, we're friends, right? You'd never, you know, fuck me over."

Jonathan laughs. "Never. Doctor-patient et cetera."

"Fine," she says, exhaling a held breath. "Then yes, on the meds. I think it might be a good idea."

Because if I see my dead husband again, those bandages you talked about might be yanked clean away, exposing the wound beneath.

And that can't happen.

Jonathan stands and walks to his desk, scribbles a prescription on a pink pad. He rips it off, hands it to her. "Not a big deal, just something to keep the anxiety in check, help you sleep at night. Take it with food or before bed."

Beth takes the slip, tucks it into her pocket. "Thanks. And thanks for letting me vent all my crazy."

"Of course," he says, smiling warmly. "That's what friends are for."

⌒⊕⌒

When the elevator doors open, Beth is surprised to see a pretty young woman she doesn't recognize stepping inside to stand next to her, apparently heading down. Before Beth has a chance, the young woman swipes a guest badge at the sensor, turning the light to green. She taps the *B* button on the console.

She's going to the lab.

As the doors close Beth turns toward her, about to say something, when the woman's eyes light up. "Oh my God, you're Beth Darlow!"

Beth is confused, her thoughts still jumbled from her session with Jonathan. The only response she can come up with is to nod mutely. The younger woman, wearing jeans, pristine white sneakers, and a black blouse, and carrying nothing but a tablet, sticks out her hand, smiling brightly.

"I'm Chiyo Nakada."

Beth shakes the extended hand as the elevator drops them lower, her brow furrowed in puzzlement. But the woman only smiles all the wider, dark eyes sparkling, showing perfect white teeth.

"I'm your nine o'clock."

ELEVEN

You'll have to forgive me. You're not at all what I was expecting."

Beth sits behind her desk, the reporter seated across from her in what she and Colson used to jokingly refer to as the Most Uncomfortable Chair in the World. Beth likes having the awkward seat for visitors to use in her office, hoping they'd spit out whatever they wanted and leave as soon as possible.

She doesn't think she'll get so lucky with the seemingly undaunted reporter, whose small frame and elegant posture look impossibly relaxed as she studies Beth from across the jumble of books and reports, discarded pens and other bric-a-brac that covers the desk's surface.

"No problem. I get that a lot. Although rarely from young successful women such as yourself," she says chidingly, but in such a way (throwing in *young* certainly doesn't hurt) that Beth takes no offense. In fact, she knows she deserves the rebuke and is pleased the journalist is open enough to offer it, even if it's with a wink.

"I just meant…Well, no, you're right," Beth says, stumbling through an apology. "I guess when I heard 'business reporter,' my mind went straight to a middle-aged white guy with a potbelly and a comb-over."

Chiyo laughs. "Please don't worry about it. I'd hate for our relationship to start with a mea culpa."

Beth raises an eyebrow. "Relationship? Are we moving in together?"

"Well, I mean, you will be seeing a lot of me, right?"

Beth shakes her head. "I don't understand."

For the first time since their meeting in the elevator, the reporter's smile falters. Then, as if a slipped mask is put back into place, the dazzling smile returns. "I'm sorry, bad choice of words. Look, I know you're busy, so why don't we start the interview? If that's okay?"

"Sure, sure." Beth leans forward. "Where should we start? My childhood? My academic background? Favorite flavor of ice cream, that sort of thing?"

Chiyo laughs, nonchalantly places her tablet on the desk, and taps an icon on the screen.

The tablet is recording. The interview has begun.

"Yes, yes, and yes. I want to get into all of that. How you went from concept to funding, what the future looks like for Beth Darlow once the public is introduced to your technology...but to be completely honest, what I really want"—Chiyo leans in, her face glowing softly in the warm light of the desk lamp—"is to hear about the time machine."

"I think that's a great place to start," Beth says, crossing her arms on the desk, looking the reporter in the eye. "How's this?"

Chiyo's smile twitches. "I'm not following."

"You wanted to see the time machine, right? Well, Ms. Nakada," Beth says, warming up to the idea of (*finally*) talking about her invention. "You're looking at it."

The reporter laughs. "Okay, you've hooked me. Please explain."

"The machine? The feat of engineering and energy sitting out there in the lab? That's the gatekeeper. The doorway, if you will. But what travels, what actually moves through time?" Beth taps her temple with the tip of a chewed pen. "Right here."

Chiyo shakes her head. "Man, I have some catching up to do. Okay, I'm getting the sense we're not talking H. G. Wells here. There's no DeLorean. So, what are we talking about? Please, talk to me like I'm a newborn babe."

"Will do." Beth stands, excited despite herself. She can't deny that it's a thrill to talk to someone—someone who doesn't work in this lab, this *building*—about what she's built.

About the miracle she and Colson have created.

"Let's go meet my machine."

TO: Jim Langan <jim.langan@langancorp.net>

FROM: c.nakada@busweekly.com

SUBJECT: Excerpt for Approval

Good morning, Mr. Langan.

Please see the following excerpt from my upcoming article, "Making the Impossible Possible: The Invention of Time Travel," which is set for publication on April 4, 2044.

Once you (and your legal team) have approved Dr. Darlow's interview as written below, I will then commence writing the remainder of the piece, which I will of course submit for further, and final, approval.

As I am on deadline, I respectfully ask you respond with any requested changes, if deemed necessary, by end of week.

Sincerely,
Chiyo Nakada

The laboratory is spacious and—much like Dr. Darlow herself—intimidating.

The lab is two stories high (but secured well below-ground, like a high-tech bunker) and features the kind of equipment most major universities could only dream of. The machine itself, along with the computers that control it, are located on the ground level. A set of stairs leads to a balcony, which overlooks the lab's primary working space. The balcony harbors what Darlow refers to (with an apparent tinge of disdain) as an observation deck, complete with cushioned theater chairs, hidden speakers, and large, clear-tech monitors. Sort of a VIP section or, perhaps more befittingly, the viewing area of an operating theater, the kind you'd see in a medical college two hundred years ago, where men in dark wool suits would watch doctors perform lobotomies.

Beth Darlow herself—the one responsible for all this—looks younger than anticipated. Tall and classically beautiful, with a lean, athletic build, Darlow overflows with a manic energy, a constantly brewing hyperintelligence that often feels a gentle nudge away from physical violence—a combination of physique and intelligence that can be, as stated above, intimidating. Spending time with Dr. Darlow is akin to being trapped inside an iron-barred cage with a hungry, pacing tiger (albeit one with an IQ off the charts and a doctorate in quantum mechanics).

Were I conducting this interview a year ago, I would be talking with two Dr. Darlows: Beth and her husband, Colson. Partners in life and business, the two scientists began developing the concept of time travel through their combined research at California Institute of Technology. They devoted themselves to the project for nearly a decade, with Beth Darlow focused primarily on the theoretical physics and algorithms that would drive the programming, while Colson Darlow dedicated himself to the engineering challenges of the machine itself.

According to Beth Darlow, the key component of the machine, being the use of negative energy (see interview that follows), was something they solved as a team.

Tragedy struck when Colson was killed on March 27, 2043 (which also happens to be Beth's birthday). While he was driving through a particularly heavy rainstorm to get supplies for his wife's special occasion, his car hydroplaned through a stop sign and into an intersection, where it was struck by a delivery truck at high speed, killing him upon impact.

Now the machine is Beth Darlow's project alone. It's been her burden to continue to do the work—to cross the proverbial finish line of creating something that will change the world—for both herself and her deceased partner. It will be Beth who must somehow take up the slack of a lost, brilliant mind and find the drive to complete what began as scribbled pages of formulas and designs in the couple's shared Pasadena, California, apartment.

If the weight of the world is on her shoulders, she carries it well.

The machine, or what I'm allowed to tell you of it, is a marvel of both engineering and programming. Not much can wiggle through the hefty NDA this article is working under, but what I *can* tell you is that the machine is simpler in design than I would have imagined. Made up primarily of polished steel and high-grade plastic, it's bigger than a car but smaller than a house. There is a massive laser that looks like something you'd see in a science fiction movie, and a bed nestled deep within the machine's operating framework for a human being. In Beth Darlow's own words, it's the human component that actually drives the machine, something we dive deeper into during our discussion.

The rest of the mechanics is something you'll have to imagine for yourself, at least until Darlow's incredible technology is made public by its corporate owner, tech giant Langan Corporation.

Following are select excerpts from my initial interview with Beth Darlow, before finally being able to watch her "travel" a couple of days later.

The results of which were, it's safe to say…alarming.

BW: Let's start with the basics. At the risk of oversimplifying, how does the machine work?

DARLOW: I'll answer, but first I want to ask you something. When I'm done with this interview, I want your honest answer.

BW: Shoot.

DARLOW: Do you believe in God? Not the Christian
God, necessarily, but, you know, a higher intelligence
ruling the universe sort of thing.

BW: Okay, wow, dramatic opening. I like it. And I will
think about how to answer that.

DARLOW: Fair enough.

BW: Now, what's this impressive contraption hovering
behind you? How does the big fella work?

DARLOW: Let's start with energy. The main driver is
this scary thing above our heads.

Darlow indicates a laser—imagine a craned arm, approximately twenty feet of enclosed plastic, mysterious cables running throughout, terminating with a bulbous head, like an egg, from the end of which stems a mean-looking proboscis.

DARLOW: My husband and I were the first physicists
to harness negative energy, the most fickle and hard
to find of all forms of energy, theoretically caused
by gravity or close proximity to a black hole. This
Casimir laser is the result of our discovery and, when
at full power, is able to produce enough negative
energy to open a quantum wormhole between two
points for just over a minute. These receivers contain,
or hold open, each mouth of the wormhole.

Imagine two massive polished half spheres, one meter apart, with a steel bed between them.

BW: I'm sorry. But traveling between two spheres, only a
couple feet apart... Wouldn't one of these spheres—
from my layman's understanding of general

physics—need to be out in space somewhere? To create the time disparity?

DARLOW: No, and we'll get to why that is, and remember that wormholes don't apply to time in the way you traditionally think of it. However, since you bring up time disparity, what you're describing is one function of our experiments. Part of the post-travel debrief that we do here is a safety check, I guess you'd say, for any disparities in the space-time continuum. To make sure that when we travel, we're not disrupting the timeline in any way.

BW: Ah, you're talking about the idea of going back in time and killing your grandfather, which would mean you never existed...

DARLOW: The matricide paradox. But that's impossible with the kind of traveling I've created. Getting back to that time disparity, we have a fail-safe of sorts that allows us, in a very rudimentary way, to make sure I haven't pushed myself into an alternate timeline.

BW: Oh, my editor mentioned this. You're talking about the questions...

DARLOW: Correct. Before I travel, usually a day prior, I answer six questions. That audio file is then transmitted to a satellite that is not in Earth's orbit but traveling away from our planet toward an infinite point in space. The recording is beamed directly from this facility to that distant satellite, where it is stored on that satellite's memory chip for approximately twenty-four hours, then beamed back to Earth, thereby landing the answers approximately thirty-six hours in the past as we now know it.

BW: Sorry, I'm not following. The recording lands in the past?

DARLOW: No, it lands in the present. The data, however, is still locked into the past. See, while it was stored on that distant satellite, it was moving slower than time moves here on Earth. The longer it sits on the satellite before being beamed back, at just under the speed of light, the farther it's stuck in the past. The answers in the recording, therefore, won't be affected by the accidental creation of a new timeline, because the data hasn't caught up with our new present yet. If that makes sense.

BW: I think it does. Just to be clear, you're saying that the old answers are stuck in the past for a couple of days. But eventually they catch up to whatever new reality you've, theoretically, inadvertently created, am I right?

DARLOW: Right. When the recorded file catches up to our timeline, those answers will change to match whatever new reality I've landed in. Once that happens, the recording itself will then be forever altered.

BW: And what happens if the answers don't match up? Does the much-lauded butterfly effect take place? Does the world end?

DARLOW: It's just a variable check. With the type of time travel we're talking about, it's impossible to affect the past. I can't kill my grandfather. I can only look at him. I can only observe. (*Darlow shrugs.*) None of this is new from a scientific standpoint. It's just physics. The questions are a helpful tool we use to catch variables.

BW: Variables where, though? Only on Earth? Why isn't the timeline alteration universal? Why aren't the little green men on Mars affected by your machine?

DARLOW: Did you take physics in college? Ever heard of the inverse square law?

BW: Um…

DARLOW: (*laughs*) Sorry. Inverse square law states, essentially, that the greater the distance that energy—such as light, radiation, or, in this case, negative energy—has to travel, the less intensity that energy has. The pulse we generate here at the lab, for example, expands outward into three-dimensional space, rapidly diluting as it travels. The effects of what we do here on Earth won't carry any farther than, say, the moon.

BW: So the little green Martians aren't affected.

DARLOW: That's right. Just us earthlings.

BW: Okay, but back to actual time travel. You told me earlier that *you* were the time machine. But I'm looking at something huge and metal that begs to differ.

DARLOW: It's impressive, right? Like something out of an old pulp magazine. Okay, let's talk about the tech. As I mentioned, it all starts with the harnessing of negative energy. A feat that, quite honestly, is almost as big a breakthrough as time travel itself.

BW: Not as sexy, though.

DARLOW: Tell that to a physicist and they may disagree. Okay, here's how it works: The wormhole is created by a burst of negative energy. The amount of energy needed to maintain the wormhole, however, is massive. So, as of today, the longest we can keep the wormhole stable is about ninety seconds. After that, mounting electromagnetic vacuum fluctuations build up, and

build up, until (*Darlow smacks her hands together.*)
singularity. The pathway slams shut. Radiation and light
escape, are absorbed harmlessly. The traveler needs to
be brought back before this happens.

BW: Okay, so now we get to the good stuff. What travels
through that wormhole? You?

DARLOW: I doubt it will ever be possible to send
matter, or anything that contains mass, through a
wormhole. There's just not enough energy to sustain
that kind of pathway. Even something as small
as an atom would be crushed or blasted apart by
radiation... Impossible.

BW: But earlier, you said *you* were the time machine.
That *you* traveled.

DARLOW: That's right. But not my physical body. Just
my mind. Let me show you something.

*Darlow walks us into the center of the machine, and it rat-
tles my nerves being at the nexus of this incredible feat of
technology. She sits on the steel bed, legs dangling, and for a
moment I can see the young woman she once was, a maelstrom of intelligence and drive, a doctor three times over,
but yes, still a young woman. Now a mother. A widow.*

*She pulls a black cloth band from a small shelf, points
to a chrome square at its center.*

DARLOW: This is the microprocessor that changes
me into data. Using this tiny chip, my entire
consciousness is turned into an encoded digital
packet. All my thoughts, memories—all my data,
in other words—are packed into a tidy file by the
quantum computers you see surrounding us. That file

is then zapped away, riding a modulated pulse of the same negative energy used to maintain the wormhole, through the gateway to destinations unknown.

BW: That's a pretty big email attachment.

DARLOW: I know you're joking, but yeah, it is kind of like that. The same way we send data using unique wavelengths of light is duplicated by the machine, except the data is encoded within that pulse of negative energy instead.

BW: But humans aren't data. The brain is physical matter, explosions of electricity, blood, and oxygen. What you're describing sounds like a weak, diluted copy of an actual mind.

DARLOW: Not at all. Look... consciousness, memories, thoughts, emotions. What are they? What are they really? Electromagnetic vibrations. Your favorite moments in life are just pieces of data stored away in the hippocampus. This machine, this giant beast of metal and science, is a virtual hippocampus. A very, very powerful extension of the brain. It allows the traveler to visit any moment in their lifetime, between the moment of their birth and the moment of travel... and reexperience it, as if they were living it all over again.

BW: I'm sorry, I'm no physicist and I mean no offense, but that doesn't sound very impressive. I can close my eyes and remember my first kiss. Does that make me a time traveler? Will someone give me a billion-dollar patent?

DARLOW: But it's not a memory. It's *real*. You're there. Physically there in every way possible. Smell. Touch. You are a traveler inside your own mind.

And yes, while it may not seem practical, especially to a business magazine like yours, its potential is, well, limitless. We're doing this now, in 2044, with tech that didn't exist ten years ago. Ten years from now there will be more power, faster computing, advanced materials. This is me telling you we've created a solution for time travel. The applications will come once the world catches up.

BW: Okay, now you're giving me goose bumps. Consider me on board.

DARLOW: (*laughs*) Great.

BW: Not that you haven't thought of this, and I'm sure you have backup power somewhere in the structure, but as a hypothetical, what would happen if the power went down while your consciousness was, you know, traveling? If that wormhole door slams shut, as you said, are you trapped somewhere other than here? Would your body essentially become a vegetable?

DARLOW: You're right, that won't happen. But to consider your hypothetical, my honest answer is that I don't really know. Frankly, I'm less interested in what would become of my body, and more curious about what would become of my consciousness.

BW: The true definition of a free spirit.

DARLOW: My husband would have loved that idea.

Darlow slides off the steel bed and we step carefully outside the machine's reach, back to the main section of the lab. Part of me feels a wave of relief, and it helps me understand the stress it must cause someone who travels. There's something awe-inspiring about being able to stand beneath this metal monster that is waiting to turn my brain, my humanity, into bits and bytes, then suck the whole thing away, beam it to another time, another place.

Being so close to something that powerful is, to be frank...scary.

BW: Okay, so assuming the lights stay on, I think I understand the general idea of the mechanics here, but the software is still a mystery. And really, that's what drives this machine of yours, right?

DARLOW: I suppose.

BW: So, if you'll allow my layman's science, I want to ask if part of the secret sauce has to do with quantum entanglement. I've heard we're years away from that science having practical, real-world applications, but now I'm curious if you know something the rest of us don't.

DARLOW: (*after a brief hesitation*) I'll have to take the Fifth on that one.

BW: Fair enough. I only have one more question about the act of traveling itself. How do you tell the machine where to take your mind, or consciousness? How do you choose the destination?

DARLOW: Great question. Sadly, I don't have a great answer. What you're describing is what we call the arrival point. And the short answer is we don't get to choose. Not yet. That's one of the primary things we are heavily focused on as we move forward. After each travel, we spend months crunching data and running analysis on every second the consciousness was part of the past, try to figure out why the machine picks the arrival points it does.

BW: Months?

DARLOW: Oh yeah. Believe me, that ninety seconds creates a tremendous amount of data to sort through. Especially now that we're, well, a little shorthanded. Besides, the traveler—whether it was Colson or myself—needs that time to sort of, I don't know, regroup. Traveling can be incredibly taxing, psychologically and physically. Regardless, discovering how the arrival point is chosen is of utmost importance to the future practical viability of the machine. Sadly, it's one of the mysteries we haven't solved. But we're working on it.

BW: So what, it's just...chance?

DARLOW: My husband would have said "fate," but either answer applies depending on, you know, your beliefs.

BW: Interesting. Fate and science as lab partners. Who'd have thought. So this is the Wild West of time travel, so to speak. A bit of danger. A bit of anything goes, am I right?

DARLOW: Well, I don't know about that. There are controllers...and rules. In fact, for my machine, there are three unbreakable rules for traveling.

BW: Great. Hit me.

DARLOW: First rule. Travel can occur only at destination points during the previous lifetime of the traveler.

BW: And why's that? You can't go into the future? Can't go back and check out the dinosaurs?

DARLOW: Remember, *I'm* the time machine. That thing (*Darlow points to the actual machine*) is a conduit. A doorway. An expansion of the hippocampus. So no, I can't travel outside my own memories, my own timeline. It's just not possible, theoretically or otherwise. Since it's my consciousness going through the wormhole, I can only land where I've existed. Period. That wormhole leads to another part of *me*.

BW: I'm not sure I'm fully understanding the science, but I get the spirit of it.

DARLOW: Close enough. Second rule. The traveler has only enough energy to maintain contact with the arrival world for ninety seconds.

BW: Right. You need more power to keep the wormhole intact.

DARLOW: Very good. A-plus. Third, the traveler does not have the ability to interact with the arrival world. The traveler can only observe.

Darlow smiles, but she appears tired. I can't help but wonder if explaining all this to me has somehow emptied her out. Taken away something that was once hers—hers and her deceased husband's—exclusively. There's a silence, as if we're both taking a moment to mourn the end of this incredible tour.

Then I remember her first question.

BW: Thank you, Beth, for doing this with me. Before we wrap up for today, let's circle back to that opening question. Why did you ask me if I believed in a god?

DARLOW: Because to know what this is, what I've created, only makes sense if you understand my husband as well. And I guess I wanted him to be here for this interview. This first reveal of what we created together.

Darlow smiles, nostalgic. I notice her lone assistant, who's been keeping his distance at a remote workstation, lift his head to watch us. As if, after explaining the creation of time travel, she's finally said something interesting.

DARLOW: Colson liked to think it was the soul that travels through the wormhole, not a bunch of recorded electromagnetic waves. He often said that we were screwing with the natural order of things, that we were pissing off God.

BW: Very philosophic, but strange thinking for a scientist.

DARLOW: (*nods in agreement*) He was always the more... spiritual of us. Don't worry, I won't ask you to answer the question, because it's none of my goddamn business. But I will ask you to think about what my husband said when writing your article or when thinking about what we're doing here. Messing with nature. Angering the universe. Fucking with fate.

BW: I have to say, I think your husband makes some interesting points. What do you think?

Darlow looks at me, and for the first time since we've met, I see something dark in her eyes. An underlying anger, or hate. Maybe even a sort of brilliant, terrifying madness.

DARLOW: I think that my husband is dead. And no machine is going to change that.

TWELVE

Beth walks the reporter back to the main lobby, where they shake hands.

She feels dazed, emptied.

Sharing the intimate details of the machine with a stranger—the intricacies of the research, the backbreaking, mind-bending science that has consumed her adult life, her *marriage*—was simultaneously thrilling and terrifying beyond reason. Speaking, out loud, the details of what her machine can do, is capable of—things she hasn't shared with her family, her best friend—has left her feeling raw and strangely vulnerable.

With a pang of desperate longing, she wishes Colson had been there for it. She imagines him holding her hand as he giddily discussed the feat of engineering, the harnessing of an energy as elusive as dark matter. *Controlling* it. Pointing it like a gun, ordering it to tear into the fabric of space-time itself. To create a gateway the likes of which the world had never seen.

But Colson isn't there, and so it's Beth who must carry the burden of elation, the quickly dimming shimmer of *finally* revealing all they created together; she alone left standing on the stage while the curtains are pulled back, pinned by a spotlight, revealing the impossible.

"I can't thank you enough," Chiyo is saying. "That was... beyond incredible."

Beth takes back her hand, stuffs it into the pocket of her lab coat. "I'm glad. I know it's a lot to take in."

"Oh my God, that's an understatement," the young woman says, laughing.

As they walk toward the glass-walled exit, passing closed door after closed door, Chiyo touches Beth's arm, halting her. "Can I ask you something? Off the record?"

"Sure."

"Well, as cool as it is to be here, the infamous Langan Corporation, right? No reporter's ever had this kind of access before... so I'm flattered. But frankly, it's not what I expected."

Beth finds herself glancing toward the exit, as if wanting to be sure no one is standing there. Listening. "How do you mean?" she says, keeping her voice low in the noiseless, padded hallway.

"I mean it's like a fricking ghost town," Chiyo says, also lowering her voice, following Beth's lead. "I expected... I don't know, the Pentagon, I guess. And while the security is appropriately..."

"Threatening?"

Chiyo gives a half smile. "Right. It's like all of the security, none of the people. The parking lot is half-full at best, and aside from the gorillas with guns at the entrance, I haven't seen a soul except you and Tariq."

Beth shrugs, feeling it's not the time, and certainly not the place. "The groups are separated for a reason. Everything that happens here is very proprietary, and all of it top secret. It's a big building, bigger than it appears since most of it's underground, and they like to keep us spread out."

"Sure, that makes sense," Chiyo replies. "Still, if we're being honest, Langan hasn't had a hit in a while, a decade at least, and the massive failure of his light-propulsion tech hit the company hard. Which explains his eagerness to see you succeed. I mean, come on, what could possibly grab bigger headlines than time travel?"

Beth doesn't know how to respond, so she turns and keeps walking, wanting to be rid of the reporter, the feelings she's stirred up inside her mind, her heart, and get back to work.

"Anyway, I can't wait to see it in action," Chiyo says as she falls into step with Beth.

Spider legs of anxiety tickle up the nape of Beth's neck.

"Well," she says, keeping her tone light, jocular. Uncaring. "That will be a while. Years, I'd guess, before there's a public experiment."

The reporter stops walking, and Beth turns back to face her. "What?"

"Oh, Beth. I'm sorry. But I think there's some confusion here."

Beth shakes her head. "How so?"

Chiyo looks away as if embarrassed, awkwardly trapped with delivering bad news. "Look, I think you better talk to Langan. He obviously didn't fill you in, and I don't want to speak out of turn."

Beth takes a step closer, lowers her voice. "Tell me."

Chiyo sighs. "I'm coming back here tomorrow."

"For what? A photo op? You can't photograph the lab—"

"No, Beth. I'm coming back to watch the machine in action," she says. "I'm coming back to watch you travel."

⊂⊖⊃

Beth marches into Jim's office, leaves the door sagging open behind her like a fresh wound. "You unbelievable bastard."

Martha, Jim's septuagenarian (and noticeably distraught) secretary, looks in, her face an amalgam of alarm and embarrassment. "Should I call security, Mr. Langan?"

Jim continues to sit calmly behind his desk, shuffling through a stack of papers. "No, no, Mrs. Gimley. It's fine. And not, uh"— he glances up at Beth quickly—"wholly unexpected."

After Martha exits (glaring daggers at Beth as she goes) and closes the door gently behind her, Jim finally sets down the papers, giving Beth his full attention from across the lake of plush navy-blue carpeting.

The CEO's office is obscenely large. There are no windows—the space lit only by hidden bulbs recessed into the ceiling—but the room is stately in its decor, littered with antique furniture and cocooned by dark oak walls that were rumored to have been transported from the captain's room of an ancient cruise ship, the *Olympic*. One of the two sister ships of the *Titanic*.

"I think you pissed off Martha," Jim says, and Beth feels a wash of shame. She actually likes the older woman, with whom she'd had lunch dozens of times over the years, and who took every opportunity to tell Beth some anecdote concerning one of her many grandchildren.

But then she recalls the conversation with the reporter, and the flare of anger returns fully formed, burning the shame to cinders.

"What the fuck, Jim?"

Langan stands, pushes down the rolled-up sleeves of his dress shirt as he steps out from behind his desk. "Take it easy, Beth. Let's talk. Sit down, please. You want a drink?" Jim says, chuckling wearily, pointing toward the well-stocked wet bar stationed along the wall.

Beth sits on a frail-looking Victorian-era couch, complete with carved mahogany legs and refurbished crimson fabric. "It's ten thirty in the morning."

Jim continues around the desk, glides past the bar, and sits down across from Beth in a rosewood chair—more utilitarian than ornate—that is apparently a companion piece to the couch she tries to get comfortable on, the stiff wood backing and dainty red upholstery reminding her of swollen gums. A round coffee table completes the makeshift seating area set away from the CEO's primary workspace.

As if triggered by his movement, the sunken ceiling lights shift from milky white to sky blue, drenching the room in the color of a shallow sea. "Of course, of course," he says, feigning embarrassment. "One loses a sense of time without the daylight."

"Buy a watch," Beth snaps.

Jim chuckles again, waves his hand at her as if they were simply bullshitting about old times. "Okay, okay. No small talk. I got it. So, what's wrong? Why the drama?"

Beth leans forward, elbows on knees, fingers intertwined. "Your ringer of a reporter just informed me she was popping by again tomorrow to see the machine in action. To see me travel."

Jim's smile softens into well-lined cheeks, but his eyes stay focused on Beth. He gives a small nod. "Yes, that's correct."

"Jim, that's ridiculous," she says, doing her best to keep her voice level, her shaking hands tightly clenched. "You know this, Jim. I literally just traveled. My God, even *you* were saying I needed time to recover. We've barely started the analysis..."

"I know that, Beth. I work here, too."

"Then what the hell? How am I—"

"I never said it was you who'd be traveling, did I?" he says, eyebrows raised. "I told Ms. Nakada that she could watch one of our tests, and that was all."

"Tomorrow."

"Correct."

"Well, I don't mean to sound like a broken record here, Jim, but I guess I need to say it again. No one goes through that wormhole but me."

Jim exhales loudly, lowers his eyes to his hands, which he inspects closely, as if looking for dirt. Or blood. When he speaks, his tone is even, controlled.

Threatening.

"I'm sorry, Beth. But *someone* is going through that wormhole on Tuesday morning at ten AM. It's all set up. Most of the board will be attending as well."

Beth falls backward into the couch, the hard decorative wood digging into her upper back. "Oh, that's just great. Anyone else? Maybe Martha wants to invite her goddamn grandkids? I'm sure they'd get a kick out of it. We could sell tickets—"

"Enough!"

Jim's cheeks quake with rage; his blue eyes blaze.

Beth smiles, unfazed at the old man's threatening demeanor. A lot of things intimidate her, but male bluster isn't one of them. She leans forward, meeting his glare. "You don't want to piss me off, Jim. I might suddenly get very, very stupid."

He points a meaty finger at her. "Don't threaten me, Beth."

"And don't *fuck* with me, Jim."

They lock eyes for a moment before, finally, Jim stands, huffing in annoyance. He stuffs his hands into his pockets, paces for a few moments. When he stops, he lowers his head, keeping his back to her.

"I need this, Beth," he says, looking away, as if focused on a distant spot of the office, away from her furious glare. The room's lights shift from blue to white as he turns halfway back toward her, still not meeting her eyes. "And I'm sorry to say...*you* need this, too." He sighs heavily, shrugs the shoulders of his expensive suit. "If we don't get more funding, you'll be done before the end of the year."

Beth stands, hands curling into fists. "Bullshit," she says, a choked whisper.

Jim lifts his gaze to her, features soft once more, the fire tempered, a frown on his lips. "No, Beth. Not bullshit. Reality. Colson's death set us back months—"

Beth scoffs. "I'm sorry it inconvenienced you."

Jim doesn't waver. "Not me. *Us.* You've been doing the work of two project leaders, and it's admirable as hell. But we need to accelerate things or we die, Beth. Now, the article will go a long way. It'll get the financiers riding the fence to cave. Hell, they'll be fighting over shares. And look, I respect you. I think you know that, deep down. So, I'm telling you now that the machine will be sending someone through tomorrow, with live monitoring."

Jim steps closer as Beth's mind races, her feelings fragmented into shards of anger, fear, doubt. Anxiety bubbles in her chest, halting her breath.

"I'm giving you all the power, Beth. It's your call, and yours alone, as to who travels tomorrow morning." He spreads his palms like a magician who just performed his last trick. "That's it," he says. "That's all."

Beth's eyes go wide with shock, with fear. Her knees tremble.

Jim nods and turns his back to her once more, strides casually back to his desk.

When Beth finally speaks, it's little more than a whisper. "I'm not ready," she says, the words nearly catching in her throat.

Jim sits at his desk, picks up the sheaf of papers he was studying when she barged in, and begins turning them over, one by one, as if the last three minutes never occurred. A glitch in the timeline.

"Then *get* ready," he says gruffly. Dismissively.

Beth leaves the office, closes the door quietly behind her. She passes the secretary without a word, hands clenched at her sides, stomach in knots. She fights off the dark tendrils of terror creeping into her mind, the swirling torrent of emotions eclipsing her heart.

No one goes but me.

She repeats it in her mind, over and over, like a mantra, as she returns to her lab.

No one goes but me.

THIRTEEN

Beth checks her watch. No matter what happens next, she's not going to make it home for dinner, and she feels terrible that Marie Elena will have to stay late again. Beth knows she's been abusing the nanny's kindness these last few months, and she hates herself for it. Weeks ago she'd vowed to be home by six PM every night, regardless of what was happening at the lab. But after her confrontation with Jim, something unforeseen had come up—something that might be worth putting her amazing nanny in a bad spot, one more time.

Toward the end of the day, Beth had been buried in her office, analyzing data from her last travel, hoping—by some miracle—to find a clue to how the machine was targeting the arrival point. If she was being forced to go through again in less than twenty-four hours, she wanted to have as much control as possible.

Just as her eyes were beginning to blur and her head to ache from staring at a screenful of scrolling formulas, a phone call came through on her personal cell. A proposed meeting. One that trumped her desire to continue working.

Not wanting to explain her early departure, she gave Tariq a terse goodbye (*let him think I'm throwing a brat fit, I couldn't give a shit*), and now she's hustling toward a midtown café to meet the caller, hoping the meeting might shed some light on what she heard from Jim earlier in the day.

She pulls into a gravel parking lot, the café's front window facing her. A weathered wooden sign hung just above, tenuous as an old shingle, reads: MARIO'S.

The small restaurant is nestled between a ubiquitous auto repair shop and a private office building, complete with white-painted bars on the tinted windows. Beth hadn't heard of the café when he mentioned it on the phone, and now she understands why.

"What a dump," she says, powering down the car, wondering if the place's nondescript drabness is part of why he chose it. She has to give the guy credit; it's definitely not a meeting spot where they have to worry about prying ears.

Moments later, Beth enters the shadow-drenched café, winces at the jingle of a rusted bell above the door. She scans the small room—an order counter with a chef's window behind, scattered four-top tables with mismatched tablecloths, olive-green walls broken up by the occasional framed posters depicting lily pad–filled ponds and crop-bursting acres of farmland.

Beth sees the man she's here to meet, his back to the wall, watching her uncomfortably as he ignores the oversize cup of coffee on the table in front of him.

She walks over and sits down.

"Hi, Jerry."

"Hello, Beth. Do you want a coffee, or...?"

"I'm good. I need to get home soon; my daughter is with the nanny."

"Of course, of course... First, I want to say that I'm sorry about what I said in the hallway. It was a... stressful moment. You caught me at my worst."

Beth holds up a hand, shakes her head. "Forgiven. I'd be blowtorching the place if they did me like that."

Jerry nods, sips his coffee, and Beth takes a moment to study the man who, for all intents and purposes, was living right next door to her all these years, like a neighbor you don't make the effort to meet until it's too late, then one day there are moving trucks.

Or, in this case, armed guards.

"Why did you want to talk, Jerry?" Beth asks. "Not that I mind. But... I assume there's something you want to say to me?"

Jerry nods, pokes a dry-looking triangle of coffee cake with one finger, then sighs.

"I just... I guess I wanted to offer you some insights. Things you might not be aware of when it comes to Langan Corp."

Beth nods. "You mean Jim's cash-flow problem?"

Jerry looks up at her, eyes wide. "You know about that?"

"He essentially told me he's broke, or getting there. He's putting a reporter up my ass, forcing my machine down the world's throat so he can get the stock price up."

Jerry laughs, and for a moment Beth sees the man behind the scientist. The husband... likely the grandfather. A brilliant mind cast adrift because he didn't move fast enough, didn't push his people hard enough. Didn't sacrifice everything.

"Yes, well, don't believe everything you hear, or everything that man says. He's part shark, part snake. The point, and why I asked you to come here, is to warn you. I apologize if I'm being dramatic," he says, looking idly out the dirty café window. "Or perhaps I'm not being dramatic enough." He shrugs, sips his coffee, runs a hand through his disheveled white hair.

"Okay," Beth says. "I'm all ears."

Jerry nods. "I know you keep to yourself, that you're private, and that you're protective about your tech. Which I understand, believe me. That place is like an anthill; there are underground tunnels you don't even know exist. Technology you couldn't begin to imagine."

"It's not summer camp, Jerry. I'm not there to make friends."

The older scientist smirks, arches a bushy eyebrow. "That much is apparent."

Despite herself, Beth lowers her eyes, embarrassed.

"Look, I've been around a lot longer than you," he continues. "I have friends in that company. Old friends. Some of whom are still there, some of whom are not. Beth, what happened to me has happened to others." He stares at her with earnest, watery eyes. "Trust me when I say that no one is safe."

Beth frowns. "What do you mean, *safe?*"

Jerry leans forward, lowers his voice, as if—even in this remote location—Jim Langan is somehow listening to their every word.

Glad I'm not the only one who's paranoid, Beth thinks.

"Despite how it might seem, given Friday's ugly scene, my division was on the rise. Neuroprosthetics had just made a massive breakthrough. I mean... *massive*. I recently discovered a way to connect the brain to the body in ways that would not only give people a normal, happy life, but in many ways make them, well, something greater. Something humanity hasn't yet seen. Again, I realize I'm sounding dramatic, but the point is that I opened a door that may never close again. You'll have to forgive my coyness, but details are obviously classified."

Beth shakes her head, confused. "So why would Jim throw it all away? Why blow up something decades in development when you're on the brink of success?"

Jerry sits back, a taut smile on his face. "Jim's not blowing it up, Beth. Jim's taking it public."

"I...Sorry, I'm confused. Jim owns the science already. Why remove you from the equation? What's the upside?"

"That's why I'm here, talking to you." Jerry takes a deep breath, lets it out. As if steadying himself for what comes next. "I like you, Beth," he says. "I liked your husband. He was always kind to me, and I felt horrible when he died. And I can see how much it hurts you, how hard it's made things for you this past year. Losing staff, working long hours through unimaginable grief, pushing yourself... It's impressive, and heartbreaking."

Beth's hands curl into fists beneath the table as she begins to get an inkling of what this man might be trying to tell her, but she needs him to say it. "In the hallway, you said I'd be next. What did you mean?"

"I meant just that. You're next." His fingers scrabble toward her across the table—as if, in his excitement, he wants to clutch her hand and demand answers—but then retreat to hold a dull spoon, gripping it tight. "You're close, aren't you?" he says quietly. "Close to that final breakthrough, whatever it might be, that will allow him to take your discovery public."

"I can't really say—"

Jerry laughs, holds up his hands. "I get it, and to be honest, I don't want to know. All I know is that you're working on some groundbreaking technology, and I know—like the sun rising in the east—that once you reach the zenith of all your hard work, Jim won't need you anymore, and he'll do to you what he did to me. To many of us. Some of the things going on in that building, the science being twisted and bent to create the impossible... it would make your head spin. With the quantum computing power we have now, breakthroughs are coming faster than ever. Including yours, I assume."

Beth nods. "We're close."

"As I thought. Listen, I'm going back, Beth." He leans forward, eyes darting nervously. "Like I said, I've been around a long time. I have friends. And Jim doesn't know everything. There are ways to infiltrate that goddamn place he's clueless about."

"Going back? To what end, Jerry?"

"To get my life back!" he snarls, smacking the table with a closed fist, eyes blazing with sudden fury. "That man took my life from me, and I refuse to accept it. I'm going to get back what's mine, and if he wants to come after me with his lawyers, let him. I'll find another financier who will match him briefcase for briefcase. I won't let him cast me aside, Beth, and neither should you."

Beth shakes her head. "But why? Why get rid of the very people who created the tech in the first place?"

Jerry leans in once more, grinning like a man whose mind has been broken or, at the least, warped with hate. "Because he has very different ideas about how to utilize the toys people like you and I have created, have sold to him, albeit with the best of intentions. Beth, you believe you're creating something that will benefit mankind, as did I, but that's not always the most profitable path, as you can imagine. Once these inventions are completed, and it's no longer a matter of discovery, but of application, he will discard the creators and give the science over to his handpicked minions, people who have no qualms about using our hard work any way they see fit. Do you see?"

Beth's mind floods with variables she's never wanted to consider, has always found a way to ignore. Until now.

"I think so, yes."

"Good," Jerry says.

"Look, I have to go, I'm sorry, my daughter—"

Jerry waves a hand. "Of course. Thank you for coming."

Beth stands shakily, heads for the exit.

"Oh, and Beth?"

Beth turns, looks at the tired, angry old scientist and his cold coffee, wondering how much of him is genius and how much is madness.

"Watch your back, Doctor," Jerry says grimly, wearing the scowl of a condemned man. "And be careful who you trust."

"I will," Beth says, and pushes through the door.

The tinny bell rattles above her head.

"If you're as close as you think you are," Jerry yells after her, decorum and caution abandoned, "then his plans for you have already begun."

FOURTEEN

Beth is driving through a heavy rainfall. The sky beyond the windshield is an ominous slate gray. She glances out her side window and sees a dark, flowing mist; sulfurous clouds pour past, distorting the shapes of whatever lies beyond. She sighs as raindrops patter the car's roof, a steady rhythm that seems uncomfortably loud to her ears. Almost painfully so. She flips on the wipers, lets their metronomic song, like the beating of a mechanical heart—*squee-chud, squee-chud, squee-chud*—soothe her weary mind.

Behind her, someone is singing. Beth turns her head and sees Isabella in the back seat, strapped into a booster, holding Singing Sally tight to her body. Sally's eyes glow bright yellow as she croons a country song.

> *I hope to see you soon,*
> *In the country...*

Beth smiles at Isabella, who smiles back.

The car begins to shake. Beth turns around to face forward but sees nothing but more gray, as if they're encompassed in a storm cloud or surrounded by thick fog. The whole car is vibrating now, as if she's driving over rough, unpaved ground instead of a city street.

"What the hell...?"

She grips the wheel tight as the wind outside picks up, rocking the car with invisible hands. Within moments, it's *howling*, the wind screaming loudly enough to drown out even the sound of battering rain. The mist rolling past her window grows thicker. Blacker. Fighting a growing sense of panic, she twists her head to look through the passenger window but sees only more of the dark mist (*Smoke! It's smoke!*) pulsing by, thick and broiling.

"Mom?"

"Hold on, honey," Beth says, the car shaking uncontrollably now as she tries to hold on to the wheel, which fights against her grip like a living thing. She stomps the brake but the pedal drops effortlessly to the floor, doing nothing to slow the car, which moves steadily faster, faster...

"Beth? What's happening?"

Beth turns to see her teenage sister, Mary, miraculously sitting in the passenger seat.

Just fifteen years old. The oldest she'll ever be.

Mary's head is caved in on one side, her face obscured by a smear of wet blood. Her right arm is missing and there's a jagged tear at the shoulder where it was torn away. Her eyes are wide and white beneath the red veil of blood on her face. She's terrified.

"What's happening?" Mary says, louder now, almost a scream. Her chest rising and falling with large, panicked breaths.

"I don't know," Beth mutters. "I don't—"

Then Beth feels her stomach *lift*, as if the car has entered zero gravity. The engine is *roaring* now, combining with the sounds of wind and rain to create a cacophony so loud Beth can hear nothing else. She whimpers, clutches the wheel for dear life as the pulsing gray fog in front of the windshield clears away, as if blasted by a gust of wind.

And now she sees clearly.

She stares at a tilting blue sky and, far below, a carpet of dense green forest.

Isabella shrieks from the back seat.

"Hold on!" Beth screams, and the car tilts downward, the engine whining louder and louder. Black smoke billows past the windows as they begin to free-fall—plummeting down, down toward the trees—toward certain death.

"I'm sorry!" she yells to her sister, to her daughter...

The trees are coming so fast. "I'm so sorry!"

The first branches crash through the windshield. Glass implodes and the metal of the car shreds like paper as her body is ripped mercilessly apart...

∽⊕∾

Beth jerks awake, eyes wide.

She stares at brightly lit yellow walls. Past the foot of the bed, a white vanity topped by a heart-shaped mirror faces her. Her body is trembling, her breathing heavy and uneven as her heart searches for a rhythm. The air is cool but her skin is coated in a sheen of sweat. She swallows, forces herself to try and calm down, to get her bearings.

This isn't my bedroom.

"Mommy..."

A tired voice beside her. Beth turns her head and sees her daughter, half-asleep, rubbing at one eye with a perfect tiny fist.

I'm in Isabella's room. I fell asleep...

The book she'd been reading to her daughter is splayed open on her stomach. Her mouth is bone-dry but she manages to swallow, forces herself to relax. She sets the book aside, wipes sweat from her brow, pushes strings of matted hair from her eyes.

Just dreaming. Fell asleep reading to Isabella... then had that dream.

"I'm sorry, honey," she says. "I didn't mean to wake you. Go back to sleep, okay?"

One of Isabella's eyelids flutters partly open. A hint of dark brown iris looks up at her. "You had a bad dream?"

Beth nods. "Yeah, but it's okay now."

She kisses her daughter's forehead and slips from the bed. At the door, she turns off the overhead light. There's a faint *click* as the night-light plugged into the wall activates.

A whisper from the darkness.

"Mommy?"

Beth hesitates, one hand on the door handle. She gazes back into the depths of the room, lit weakly by the blue cast of the small night-light. She senses, more than sees, Isabella shift her body to face the doorway.

"Yeah?" Beth says.

"I have bad dreams, too."

Beth hesitates, not sure how to respond.

How do you tell your child that, sometimes, nightmares are real?

"We all do, honey. They're just parts of your imagination, right?"

For a moment there's only silence from the dark. Then Isabella's voice comes again, barely a whisper. "Sometimes I see Daddy in my dreams."

Beth feels a wave of unwanted emotion. She's tired. Exhausted. The nightmare has shaken her and she wants to do nothing but crawl under her own covers and fall into nothingness. But she nods patiently, choosing her words with careful thought. "Well, that's good, right? As long as you can imagine him, he's real. He's with you."

Isabella's hand comes into view, and Beth realizes she's shifted to the edge of the bed, toward the light. "Sometimes I dream that he's in my room," she says in a whisper, as if not wanting to be overheard. "Watching me sleep."

Beth shakes her head. She can't do this, not right now. She's losing patience with the conversation, with the raw, mind-scratching emotions frying her nerves. She refuses to snap at her daughter, to be anything but a stable, reliable force for her little girl, but she's *so tired*. "Okay, honey. I think it's nice you see your daddy in your sleep. But listen, Mom's going to bed now, okay?"

Isabella, voice rising, as if excited to finally reveal some long-held secret (and definitely more awake than she was moments ago), continues.

"But I'm not asleep. When I see him, I mean. I'm only pretending. And it's not in a dream."

Eyes adjusting to the dim light, Beth sees that Isabella is now sitting up, pointing to the foot of her bed.

"He stands right there."

Beth does her best to ignore the chill crawling up her spine.

No. No more.

Please, no more.

It's all Beth can do to shake her head, the exhaustion consuming her. "We'll... we'll talk about this another time, okay? Good night, Isabella."

There's a hesitation, a moment of consideration, perhaps, and then Beth sees her daughter lie back down, pull the covers to her chin. "Good night, Mom."

Beth begins to close the door, then pauses. "And hey, if you dream of your dad again? Put your mom in there, too, okay? It'd be nice to see him for a bit."

"Okay, Mom," Isabella says from the dark.

Beth hears her loud yawn and smiles. She closes the door, momentarily studies the construction-paper sign taped to the door at eye level—Isabella's name written across yellow paper in blue, red, and violet glitter. She touches it briefly with the tips of her fingers, then turns and walks unsteadily toward her own bedroom, mind and body desperate for sleep.

Praying it will be dreamless.

FIFTEEN

Beth takes the winding drive up the hill slowly, the hard rain making the pavement slick, the cutout of the road a vague gray ribbon she strains her eyes to follow.

She does her best not to think about the dream.

She crests the hill, sees the first security point—the small guard shack, dark as charcoal, the yellow-and-black-striped iron gate beside it, the fencing surrounding the lot—and thinks for the millionth time that it feels like she's entering a prison. The sullen, concrete structure beyond the expanse of flat pavement does little to dispel this sensation. For the first time—thinking of the reporter's comments about the reduced number of employees—Beth takes a moment to study the parking lot and is surprised to find that there *are* fewer cars than there were a couple of years ago. The realization makes her heart sink.

As she crests the rise to the guard gate, however, something breaks up the monotony of colorless shades and concerns about atrophy at her place of employment.

Near the building's entrance, she notices a tightly packed cluster of emergency vehicles. Police cars, a life-support unit, an ambulance—all the vehicles flash their emergency lights; smeared blues and reds decorate the stubborn drops of rain on her windshield.

She stops at the first checkpoint, shows her ID. "What's going on?"

"Nothing good," the heavyset guard says, not meeting her eye. He jabs a hidden button that raises the heavy gate. "Have a nice day."

Annoyed, but more curious, Beth drives onto the lot, settles into her parking spot near the front of the building. *Whatever happened*, she thinks, *happened just outside the building's entrance. A heart attack? Was there a break-in? Oh God…*

She feels a tinge of anxiety in her gut as she powers off the car, pulls the hood of her coat over her head, and plucks the umbrella from the back seat.

The lab.

She walks quickly toward the animated array of emergency vehicles. As she gets closer she can make out dozens of employees—many of whom she's never seen before—waiting to get through a small, newly formed gauntlet of black-clad guards. Instead of showing their IDs and continuing into the lobby, as they normally would, each employee is first being frisked, patted down, bags and purses opened and rummaged through by the burly, menacing, and very much *armed* security personnel.

Tariq stands near the back of the line, his umbrella one of many creating a canopy over the small, grumbling crowd. Aware of a stretch of yellow caution tape strung between the emergency vehicles, Beth doesn't bother trying to cut through but walks around the scene toward the growing queue of employees, each of them wearing a slightly different expression: Some are annoyed, but more than a few, she realizes, appear downright angry.

Many look scared.

She tugs at Tariq's elbow and he spins to face her. There's a momentary, unspoken debate about whether he should step out of line or try to sneak her in. The man behind Tariq—tall, with long shaggy hair and wearing thick glasses—solves it for them. "Go ahead, Dr. Darlow," the man says, smiling. "It's okay."

Beth studies the man, doesn't recognize him, but nods. "Thanks," she says, uncertain how she feels about having these mysterious employees know her by sight. She leans closer to Tariq, careful not to knock her umbrella with his, and lowers her voice as much as she's able over the patter of rain, the off-kilter rhythm of disconnected voices surrounding them. "Okay, what the hell's going on?"

Before he can reply, she adds hastily, "Is the lab okay?"

Tariq meets her eyes for a beat. "Lab's fine," he says, then shifts his gaze to a spot just over her shoulder. "Have a look."

Beth turns, realizing she now has a better view of the building's entrance through a gap in the vehicles. For a moment she's not sure what she's looking for... then it becomes clear what all the fuss is about. She gasps.

On the sidewalk just outside the lobby doors, splayed on the pavement like a broken doll, is a body. A white sheet covers a majority of whoever's underneath, but she's able to spot a pair of men's loafers extending from just beneath the sodden covering, the leather now soaked a dark brown. Jutting from the sheet near the man's midsection is a clawed hand, fingers turned skyward, exposed to the heavy rain.

Beth's eyes trail up the shrouded body to the head, sees a misshapen red splotch where the face would be. It's only then she notices the blood leaking out from beneath the sheet, mixing with the rainfall, running in rivulets toward the curb's edge.

"Oh my God."

Tariq nods. "Jerry Wilson."

Beth spins on him, eyes wide. "No! Jerry? I just saw him..."

Tariq raises an eyebrow, a question in his eyes. "Just saw him?"

"Last week," she replies quickly. "When they escorted him out."

Tariq nods, and they shuffle forward as the line moves. "He tried to break in this morning. Apparently, he left something behind he couldn't live without. Literally."

The tall man behind them leans forward. "I heard the guard on duty shot him three times as he ran from the lobby. Once in the back and then, when Jerry spun around—maybe to give himself up, who knows—he got another in the chest, a third in the head. Poor guy didn't have a chance. He was dead before he hit the ground. They don't mess around here."

Beth swallows tightly, finding it impossible to keep her eyes off the sprawled corpse, trying to recall snatches of their conversation.

Trust me when I say that no one is safe.

She shivers, pulls her coat tighter to her body. Watching the scene, she notes a cluster of police officers interviewing a Langan security guard, who, to her eyes, appears more annoyed than shaken. She debates whether he was one of the ones who escorted Jerry out that day, perhaps knowing it might come to this. Perhaps hoping it would.

"No amount of research is worth risking your life," the tall man says, and Beth finds herself itching to be away from him, away from the swollen, wet group of Langan employees, and down in her lab.

I'm not so sure I agree with that, Beth thinks.

Staring hard at the rain-soaked loafers, the upturned claw of a dead hand, Beth wonders—if it came down to it—what she'd be willing to sacrifice to save her own research, her own invention. To take back her life's work.

"You can say that again," Tariq replies to the man behind them, but his eyes linger on Beth, as if relaying a warning. As he if knows what she's thinking.

She meets his eyes for a moment, then forces her gaze forward, away from the bleeding body of the old scientist—the one who thought he had friends—and shuffles forward with the rest of the line.

TRANSCRIPT:

Pre-Travel Debrief of Dr. Beth Darlow
March 22, 2044 | 11:15 AM
Location: Forum Room—Langan Corporation
Attendees: Dr. Beth Darlow, Dr. Jonathan Greer, Dr. Abigail
    Lee, Dr. Terry Adams

[ALL QUESTIONS PRERECORDED: AUDIO FILE 232-B]

Q: Please state your name and today's date.
BD: Beth Darlow. March 22, 2044.

Q: Who is the president of the United States?
BD: James Whitmore.

Q: Describe your marital status.
BD: Widowed.

Q: In one word, describe your childhood.
BD: Happy.

Q: Name two members of your immediate family.
BD: My uncle, Brett Hawkins. My daughter, Isabella Darlow.

*Q: If you could change one moment in your life, what would
    it be?*
BD: I would stop my husband from leaving on the day he
    was killed.

[RECORDING ENDS 11:18 AM. FILE TRANSMITTED VIA
LANGAN OPTIC DRIVE TO SATELLITE MK-JOURNEY,
11:19 AM.]

SIXTEEN

The viewing platform is wide and spacious. The floor is covered by gray industrial carpet, giving the broad balcony a softer feel than the bleach-white concrete of the main laboratory on the ground floor. There are two elevated rows of padded folding chairs and three clear-tech screens, lowered from the ceiling, that hover just past the balcony's edge.

Jim settles into a seat at the end of the front row. Already seated in the row alongside him are Chiyo Nakada, followed by Jonathan and program director Abigail Lee. Seated behind them are physician Terry Adams and a trio of suits, each representing the interests of the three highest-ranking board members—with *members* being an operative word, since the seats are filled not by individuals but by corporations, goliaths of space travel, pharmaceuticals, and microtechnology. Their interests are not in Beth—or even, necessarily, in the machine itself—but in the technology buried within, the hint of a transformative way to process the human mind into digital bits and send it through time, to blast an organized consciousness into a swarm, a sea of transportable data, then rebuild it into something new, at a day and time of their choosing. Or, potentially, shoot it through space to a distant star, light-years away from the dormant flesh.

Perhaps a different flesh altogether.

The possibilities, Jim knows, are limitless.

Beneath the viewing platform, the machine is humming, generating an electric vibration in the air that keeps the suits fidgety and tickles the eardrums of the viewers. Lying in the heart of the machine is Beth, wearing dark leggings and a skintight black runner's top, an outfit designed to absorb any sweat from her torso, arms, and legs. Standing next to Beth is Tariq, who methodically secures her wrists and ankles with firm Velcro straps. He then moves to her head, where he places wireless electrodes to her forehead and temples, and behind her ears.

In front of the tiered balcony seats the clear-tech screens come alive, glowing a murky blue, as if showing images from an empty swimming pool, deep enough to shadow the sun. The viewers shift their bodies in nervous anticipation.

Jim Langan clears his throat, speaks clearly to the rest of the group. "The screens will show us specific images from Dr. Darlow's brain, accessed during travel. In a word, memories. That same data is also sent to the quantum computers monitored on the main floor below, where it is translated and stored. A split of the live feed will carry to us up here." Jim shrugs. "Put another way, we see what she sees."

"You mean we're seeing her stored memories," Chiyo says, her tablet already recording audio of their conversation. "To be clear, whatever she sees, albeit targeted, is something that already happened."

Jim thinks a moment, all eyes now focused on him, awaiting his response. He hesitates for only a second, thinking. "Yes...and no," he says. "Ms. Nakada, try to separate the dream state of a memory and the actual data of a stored event. This isn't a conjuration of the imagination; it's pure ones and zeros, if you take my meaning. Think of it as downloading a particularly large file to your tablet via light waves, yeah? Using the newest optic technology. Except—"

"Except my tablet is in the past," Chiyo says, nodding.

Jim smiles proudly, points a finger in her direction. "And the file...is *you*."

There's a heavy sigh from the second row, and Jim twists around to see one of the board member proxies shaking her head.

"You have a question?" Jim asks, and all three proxies look at him as one. The two men say nothing, but the woman looks toward the floor below.

"If this is so safe, Langan, why is he strapping her down? It's only her thoughts that are traveling."

Jim glances past the balcony's railing toward the machine, watches as Tariq secures a final, firm strap across Beth's forehead.

He turns back to face the proxies, smiles, and waves a hand in the air, as if swatting a fly. "Purely precautionary," he says, then glances below. "Look, you see what he's doing now? That disc he's placing just below the strap? That chip, no bigger than a fingernail, is a quantum processor. It uses photons to gather and encode the electromagnetic vibrations of her mind."

He points to the head of the laser, hovering just above Beth's prone body.

"When the energy from the laser splits, the processor chip acts as a transistor through which that energy is converted to virtual photons. Those photons reach *into* her brain, capturing the data file...or the memory, if you prefer. The chip is small, as you can see, but it has the computing power to run a space station, and that's not hyperbole. Regardless, to answer your question: It's essential she does not move during this process, even involuntarily. The laser must be *absolutely* precise."

"Or what?" the woman asks, her face a mixture of fear and astonishment, tinged sickly with greed.

Jim shakes his head. "Unknowable consequences. Which is why we are so careful."

Chiyo speaks up. "And that file of her mind? The one grabbed by photons? That's what travels."

"Correct," Jim says, smiling wide enough to show teeth. "Then, when that same negative energy pulse, now split three ways, hits the spheres, the wormhole opens and...well...away she goes."

Everyone nods, but Jim notices their lack of enthusiasm. Of comprehension.

It irks him.

Chiyo turns her back to Jim, focusing her attention on Jonathan. "Dr. Greer, tell me how you feel about Dr. Darlow traveling again so soon. My understanding is this will be her third trip over the last year. Isn't there typically a longer processing and recovery time between trips?"

"Who told you that?" Jim says gruffly, but Chiyo ignores him. Her eyes stay leveled on Jonathan, who stares forward, watching Beth's preparation.

Jim leans forward, points at Jonathan, not bothering to lower his voice. "Don't answer that," he says sharply, then swivels his attention back to Chiyo. "You're not authorized to question anyone on this platform except me, understand? Later, you will have time for a follow-up Q and A with Dr. Darlow. That's the deal. Or do we call this off right now?"

Chiyo sighs, sits back, lets her eyes drift back to the monitors. "Fine," she says, and is about to say something further when all three of the milky-blue screens go dark.

After a few seconds, the far-left monitor flickers to life, showing a bird's-eye view of Beth laid within the confines of the machine, straps across her limbs, waist, and head. Below, Tariq, having finished securing Beth, now settles into the chair at his station, just a few feet from the machine. When he speaks into a slim microphone extended from his monitor, his voice comes through speakers embedded within the screens. He addresses the group.

"Now that Dr. Darlow is in place, I'm going to begin the final stage of powering up the laser. The left screen is a live feed of Dr. Darlow here in the lab. Once we begin, the middle screen will show you a feed of her visit, a view of her perspective during travel. The quality may be poor, even swimmy at times, but this is normal. Even quantum processors have their limits. Lastly, the screen to your right will show a readout of travel time."

There's a rapid *clickclickclick* and the electricity vibrating in the room seems to double, then triple. Tariq's calm voice comes back as the screen to the right lights up, showing a digital readout.

1:30

"A countdown?" Chiyo asks.

"A timer," Jim corrects quietly. "As I'm sure Dr. Darlow told you, we're only able to sustain the wormhole for approximately ninety seconds."

Chiyo's eyebrows rise. "I didn't think she was being literal."

Jim scoffs, plucks at the lapels of his suit coat. "It's just a base-line. If we needed to, we could likely double that, but not without risk."

"What risk is that?"

"A potential risk," he says quickly, modifying his response. "If—*and only if*—the traveler were to be...say, *cut off* from their present consciousness, the traveling memory snipped like a piece of string...well, we're not sure if it would have a tem-porary, or even permanent, effect on the traveler herself. So we use ninety seconds as a way of proceeding with the most caution possible. When that timer hits zero, the machine pulls back the traveler's consciousness, then safely closes the wormhole."

Tariq's voice comes through the speakers once more.

The balcony lights dim.

The observation deck goes quiet. The seated guests go still.

Only Jonathan seems perturbed, crossing and recrossing his legs, a deep furrow of worry on his brow.

"Sending pulse in three...two..."

One.

It's dark.

"Keep your eyes closed," he says. A luxurious voice. A voice I know as if it were the beating of my own heart.

"They're closed, they're closed," I say. Irritated. Thrilled. Slightly turned on.

Movement. Beyond the dark veil of my closed eyelids, a throbbing light comes closer.

"Seriously, don't cheat."

I won't. I would never. "Sweet Jesus, man, whatever you're doing, do it already," I say, laughing. Then my voice softens. "You know how much I hate the dark..."

Did I say that? Then? I have no recollection of saying those words.

Why would I say something like that?

When his voice comes again, it's soft and close. Right next to my ear. The light beyond my sealed eyelids is dancing.

I can almost feel the heat of the candles, the sugary sweetness of the cake.

Oh Christ. Oh, fucking hell.

NO.

Not this. Please God in heaven, not *this*.

"Open your eyes."

I open my eyes and see my dead husband holding a birthday cake.

It's mine.

"Make a wish, baby," he says, smiling.

I want to scream.

"Oh no..." Jonathan says.

Heads turn from the video screens to look at him.

Jim leans over, murmurs from the corner of his mouth. "Shut the fuck up."

On the screen to the far right, the timer continues ticking down.

1:22

1:21

1:20...

The lights in the lab have been dimmed. The room is full of shadows.

We'd come in on a Sunday, wanting to catch up on things before a busy week, happy to let our work consume birthdays, holidays, even time with our daughter. A selfishness I now find hard to remember, or fathom.

I push myself up from my sitting position on the bed of the machine. For a fraction of a second I feel a pulse of heat and shame as I think about how many times Colson and I fucked on it. I estimate the number is somewhere between seven and ten.

I blow out the candles and he laughs.

I wonder if he's thinking the same thing I am.

I lean forward, over the small white cake, and kiss him.

It's the best kiss of my life. Whether that's a feeling I have now, or then, is unclear. I only know the warmth of my love for him sweeps through my body, a wave so powerful it sends shivers through me. I'd gasp if I could.

If I had any control at all.

"Hold on," he says, pulling back from our kiss. "I gotta get plates, and...uh...forks." He laughs self-consciously because we both know he's terrible at organizing a moment. For instance, giving a surprise birthday cake to your wife. And yet he can build machines most scientists only dream about, process mind-breaking calculations as if he were doing basic subtraction, harness the most elusive power of the universe.

In the past, I laugh along with him, but inside I'm being torn apart.

Because I know what this is.

What this *moment* is that I've been taken to.

March 27, 2043.

My birthday, one year ago.

The day my husband dies.

"Wait... I know about this," Chiyo whispers, then looks at Jim with concern. "Is this what I think it is?"

Jim takes a breath. His eyes shift to the timer.

1:01

1:00

0:59

0:58...

"Please remember that this is still, essentially, beta testing," he says calmly. "The whole reason these early tests are done is so we can properly examine new monitoring techniques, discover advanced targeting systems. The ultimate goal, of course, is to travel to a *predesignated* point. The applications of such a device—"

Below, one of the computers begins to *whoop* loudly. An alarm.

Jonathan stands and grips the balcony's railing. He yells down to Tariq. "What's happening?"

Tariq, obviously flummoxed, starts to speak into the mic. Then he stops, curses under his breath, and turns his head up toward Jonathan. "Her heart rate is spiking. But it's fine. It's... uh, normal. But what she's experiencing is raising her vitals."

Anxiously, Jonathan turns to Jim, sees the old man's annoyed scowl, and shifts his attention to Dr. Adams. "Terry? What do you think?"

The physician looks harried but keeps his composure, obviously balancing his response between what's happening and Jim's desire to temper any negative reactions in front of the reporter and attending board proxies. He clears his throat, gets up from his chair, and steps to the balcony. When he speaks down to Tariq, he's able to keep his voice authoritative, steady. "Tariq? Would you please put her vitals on one of the monitors?"

Below, Tariq punches in a sequence. The monitor showing Beth's prone body flickers to black, then turns into a series of multicolored boxes staggered with shifting numbers and pulsing lines, a staggered flow of data. The doctor takes a step back, studies the screen for a moment, then turns to Jim. "I don't see anything dangerous."

Jim crosses his arms. "Then everyone relax, and watch." He raises his voice. "And turn off that goddamn alarm!"

Below, Tariq types a command into his console. The alarm goes quiet.

The middle monitor, the one showing Beth's memory experience, displays a slightly warped image of her cutting a cake, setting a slice onto a small red paper plate that reads HAPPY BIRTHDAY in garish yellow letters.

Jonathan looks at the timer.

0:39

0:38

0:37...

He glances to Jim, then down to the laboratory floor, his features strained with worry.

"I'm going down there."

I hand a plate to Colson, who takes a quick bite of cake, then rolls his eyes and sets it down, looking sheepish. "You're not going to believe this. I forgot the champagne at home."

"Honey, who cares? Then we'll have it at the house, or tomorrow."

"No. No..." he says. "It's your birthday, and you deserve champagne on your birthday. Look, I'll be right back. There's a liquor store five minutes away."

I nod, but inside my mind I'm screaming: *STOP! DON'T GO! STAY HERE. STAY WITH ME.*

"Colson, you're being dumb. Don't worry about it. Besides, Isabella—"

"Isabella is with Marie Elena," he says with a proud, knowing smile, obviously pleased with his foresightedness. "And I informed her we'd be late."

"Look at you, planning ahead."

His smile widens and I want to reach out and touch his face, but I don't.

Reliving this experience, I feel the same urge strike me again with an almost unbearable power. Of course, I don't reach out.

Because I can't.

Instead, I nod stupidly, grinning like a schoolgirl as I hold a paper plate topped by a piece of birthday cake with vanilla frosting. I didn't know it then, of course, but I will never eat cake again. The very idea turns my stomach.

"You won't even know I'm gone," he says.

He leans in and kisses me quickly on the lips.

It's the last time we'll touch.

It's the last time I'll see him alive.

Jonathan stands beside Tariq, watching Beth's vitals as they appear on the assistant's monitors. After a few moments, he's surprised by the appearance of Dr. Adams, who apparently followed him down for a closer look. Jonathan catches his eye, gives him a grateful nod.

"Thirty seconds to go," Tariq says, typing furiously. "Her heart rate is seriously spiking. Look, I'm sorry, but I need to make sure all this data is getting routed properly. You guys do what you need to do. I just work here."

Jim, standing against the balcony railing, bellows down. "What's the problem?"

Jonathan turns, looks up. "We need to get her out, Jim."

Jim works his jaw, then looks to the physician. "Terry?"

The old doctor takes a moment to study the screen filled with Beth's vitals. Then he looks up at Jim. "She's obviously distraught. Not life-threatening, but if she escalates..."

Jim nods. "Fine, fine. Thirty more seconds. If her life's not in danger, leave her be. It's what she'd want."

Suddenly—and for the second time in as many minutes—an alarm *whoops* through the laboratory. One of the board representatives in the back row stands up, his face glued to the monitor, features strained with worry. "Langan, what's happening here? Is this woman in danger?"

Jim offers a weak smile. His eyes dart to the reporter, who's watching the monitor intently, her right hand moving rhythmically against the tablet, as if on its own, as she types notes into the virtual keypad.

"Everything is fine...She's..." He turns and glares down toward the machine, to the three men at the main console. "What's going on?"

Jonathan looks up, his face a mixture of anger and fear. "Her vitals are hitting dangerous levels. Neural activity spiking across the board. She's having a panic attack."

"Can we turn off that damn noise?" Jim says, yelling over the sound of the alarm. "I can't hear myself think."

Tariq punches keys, and the alarm goes quiet once more.

Jim takes a step back, looks at the timer.

0:22

0:21

0:20...

His eyes move to the middle screen, where he sees the warped tunnel-vision view of Beth's POV. On the monitor, the ghost of Colson Darlow is lifting a coat from a nearby table.

Dear God, he thinks.

I watch Colson put on his raincoat, the thin one with the hole in the right pocket.

"Honey, it's pouring outside," I say. My voice is impossibly calm.

Don't go... don't go... PLEASE DON'T GO.

"Relax, okay? This is important to me. You've earned it. I'll be back in a jiffy." He walks to the elevator, Beth following. He steps inside, turns, looks back at her.

He meets her eyes.

For a moment, he looks confused. Concerned.

My God, does he know?

My traveling self can't help but wonder if my husband sees the fluttering white shutter of a dual consciousness behind my irises. In the dim light, it would be almost impossible.

Almost.

Or is it simpler than that? Perhaps he notices something in my expression. Something that gives him pause.

Can he sense me screaming behind this placid mask?

Can he hear my beating fists pounding against this cage of the past I've been thrust into? Begging him to stop, to please, please, just...*stop*.

A tear slips from the corner of my eye and I know, in the past, that didn't happen.

Not then.

On this day I wasn't worried or sad or scared. I was thinking about getting home to Isabella. I was thinking about wanting him to stay because I didn't want to be alone in the dim laboratory, waiting for him to return.

But I didn't cry.

That's new.

"Happy birthday," he says, and the concern is wiped from his face as if it was never there. He smiles at me for the last time. The elevator doors slide closed.

And he's gone.

"Five seconds," Tariq says through the microphone. "Closing the memory drive."

All eyes are glued to the middle screen, the one that just showed Colson Darlow leaving the laboratory.

Ten minutes later, he'd be dead. His body crushed.

Everyone on the observation deck is standing now, watching the timer tick down:

0:03

0:02

0:01...

Tariq's steady voice comes through the speakers. "Memory packet retrieved. Closing the wormhole."

The living, humming power in the laboratory immediately cuts in half, then slowly declines, declines... as if it were a roaring jet engine slowly shutting down.

The air molecules slow, then settle. The room grows deathly quiet.

Beth's eyes shoot open.

Her limbs and head strain and buck against the bindings as she screams, screams as if her mind is being torn apart, her skin drenched in flame.

Jonathan runs to her, rips open the restraints at her ankles, her wrists. He pulls the electrodes, tears away the strap holding her head.

"Beth," he says.

With a gasp, she jerks upward into his arms. She screams once more—a throat-shredding shriek of pure heartbreak—and then she cries, sobs relentlessly into his shoulder as he sits with her on the cold steel table.

Above, in the balcony, the reporter watches, hand flying across the tablet, recording her impressions of this horrific moment.

Jim grips the balcony railing, knuckles white.

After a moment, he turns, looks at Chiyo, then the board members.

He grins.

"Ladies and gentlemen," he says. "I give you time travel."

SEVENTEEN

Beth slumps into the small couch in her office. Jonathan has turned the Most Uncomfortable Chair in the World around and sits perched on its edge, elbows on knees, hands folded as if in prayer.

"I'm so, so sorry, Beth. I can't even begin to imagine."

Beth stares into an infinite distance just over his shoulder, her face sallow, eyes red from hysterical tears. Thankfully she was the last thing Jim wanted any of the visitors, especially the reporter, to see. He hustled them down and into the elevator while Jonathan and Dr. Adams shuttled an inconsolable Beth to her office. It was Adams who gave her an injection of a mild tranquilizer, likely a small dose of diazepam. Now Tariq sits out in the lab running analyses, the doctor has left her in Jonathan's care, and Jim is likely pouring champagne in his office, talking about the success of her public breakdown.

She shakes her head, sniffles, rips another tissue out of the box sitting on the couch next to her. "I couldn't stop him," she says, her pleading, bloodshot eyes meeting Jonathan's. "No matter how hard I tried to form the words, no matter how badly I wanted to warn him..."

"That's how it works, right?" Jonathan says quietly, gently. "The traveler can only observe. And by doing so, can't affect the past."

"You throwing my rules back at me?"

He smiles, raises his hands in supplication. "Yes and no. Just reminding you there's nothing you could have done."

She nods, lets out a ragged breath. "I know, I know...but my God, Jonathan. I was *fully aware* of what was happening. Of what was *about* to happen. Jesus, I felt him touch my cheek. Do you have any...?" Beth puts her face in her hands with a moan. Fresh tears spill into her palms, travel down her wrists. She sniffles loudly, wipes her face. "Fuck, man, Jim must be fuming."

Jonathan laughs. "I don't know, part of me thinks he lives for the high drama. Makes the whole thing more...human, I guess."

Beth rolls her eyes. "Yeah, well, I put on quite the show."

"I think that even someone as coarse and moneycentric as Langan understands the trauma of what you experienced. Through no fault of your own, of course. I mean, the destination...it's random, right? Which I believe is another one of your rules."

Beth looks thoughtful, lets her feet slip to the floor. "Yeah, that's right," she says. When she looks up, her eyes are focused. "You know what really worries me? I've traveled three times now. Random points in my timeline. The first, about six months back, you remember?"

Jonathan sits back, thinking. He nods. "Yeah, it was a high school memory. Your prom, right?"

"That's right. I was living with my grandparents at the time, on my father's side. I was getting ready to walk onto the dance floor with Tyler Higgins." She lets out a breath, shrugs. "He was a swimmer. State champion. Then I turned around...and standing at the gymnasium doors was my Uncle Brett."

"He was there to pick you up, right? But he showed up early. I don't remember it being especially traumatic for you."

Beth pauses, reliving the moment in her head, then drops her eyes to the floor. "That's because I lied to you. It was my first trip after Colson's death, and I...hell, I don't know...wanted to make a good impression, I guess."

"Beth..."

She wipes her nose with a knot of tissue. "He was there to pick me up because my grandfather had just suffered a massive heart attack. My grandmother, she was with him at the hospital... They didn't think he had long to live, but he was stable. He'd... he'd told my uncle not to bother me. That it was my prom..."

Beth takes a deep breath, lets it out. She studies her hands, eyes wide and lost. "He was gone before I got there. The man who essentially raised me." When she looks up once more, there's a fire in her eyes. "Can you believe that shit? I missed saying goodbye because of a prom, with Tyler fucking Higgins, who turned out to be just another asshole. I mean, it still burns me up, you know? As if I gave two shits about some dance."

Jonathan nods. Reassessing. "And then the airplane," he says. "And now this."

For a moment, they sit in thoughtful silence, then Beth walks to her desk, opens a drawer, and pulls out a half-empty bottle of Jack Daniel's. "You feel like grabbing a couple of mugs from the kitchen?"

Jonathan leaves, then returns a few moments later carrying two coffee mugs. "I think at least one of these is clean," he says, setting them on her desk.

Beth pours them each a double.

She picks up her favorite mug, the one that says ALOHA! across the face of it, a faded rainbow riding beneath. A souvenir from a trip she took to Hawaii when she was a child.

Jonathan picks up the other, the surface clean white ceramic imprinted in black with the Langan Corporation logo. They click mugs and drink.

"Ay..." Jonathan gasps.

"Only the best for you," Beth says, smiling. She pours them each a little more, then cups her mug in her hands and goes back to the couch. "Three trips. Three tragedies. All of them somehow focused on the death of loved ones. I mean, what kind of sick shit is that?"

Jonathan takes a sip from his cup, winces, and sets it down. "You tell me. It's your baby."

"Statistically, it's impossible," Beth murmurs, working the problem, for what feels like the millionth time, in her tired mind. "The machine's selection of arrival points is completely random."

"So you keep saying."

She scoffs, knocks back the rest of her drink. "Yeah, I do, and science agrees with me. But I wonder if it's...I don't know..."

He leans forward. "What?"

"What if we're messing with things here that we don't understand? Colson used to say we were trying God's patience."

"Beth. Come on...What's that supposed to mean? That God has a nasty streak when it comes to scientists? You think you're building the Tower of Babel in there? A testament to human pride?"

Beth shrugs. "I'm suggesting the universe may not like us pushing it around. Flouting its rules. Maybe it's, you know... pushing back."

"Uh-huh, and now you're anthropomorphizing the universe."

"I know, it's ridiculous." Beth rolls the empty mug in her palms, thinking. "But I'm telling you. Something about all this... it's just not right."

"Okay, fine. So let's examine this more closely." He plucks the bottle from her desk, angles it toward her. With a thin smile she holds out her mug, accepts another pour while he talks it through. "Colson traveled, what? Seven times?"

Beth nods. "That's right."

"Well, unless I'm forgetting something, or he was...I don't know, hiding some truth, like you were with the prom, I don't recall a single negative response. If I recall correctly, all of his arrival points were pretty boring."

"Yeah, that's true," Beth answers, replaying his travel sessions in her mind. Suddenly, she laughs. "One of his trips was a high school play. Remember? He was Caesar? Being stabbed with all those foil-wrapped swords. I think that one was my favorite."

"That's right! And another one was just all you guys sitting at a table, eating breakfast."

Beth nods, smiling at the memory. "He'd made pancakes for my birthday. For ninety seconds we watched him pouring batter onto a skillet. I thought Jim was going to explode with frustration."

Jonathan laughs and sits back. "See? No horrible deaths. No tragedies. No cosmic vengeance of a wrathful God."

Beth sighs, sets her mug on the floor, rubs her tired eyes. "So, what? I'm cursed?"

Jonathan shrugs. "Or maybe you've just had more heartbreak in your life. I mean, look, we don't know how the points are chosen, right? So let's forget the hocus-pocus for a second and go back to thinking like scientists."

Beth raises her eyebrows but continues to listen.

"Couldn't it be something more simple?" he says.

"Like?"

"Like...maybe the machine is reading your strongest, most emotional memories. Targeting the brightest stars in your inner universe..."

"That's very poetic," Beth says, her eyes dropping to the floor once more. She stares at the faded rainbow of her mug between her feet and feels a cold sliver in her gut, as if she's forgotten about something awful and is just now remembering. "It's also incredibly depressing."

"Why depressing?"

Beth reaches down and grabs the mug off the floor, cradles it in her hands.

"Because it means I have a very sad universe."

EIGHTEEN

When Beth finally arrives home, it's nearly eight o'clock. The house is quiet.

She walks down the narrow hallway, the wall on her left covered in drawings and other random artwork created by Isabella; to her right, an empty living room. She notes the newest addition, the bright red butterfly they'd taped to the wall just a few nights ago. She pauses a moment to study it, her tired mind snagging on something about it that's not quite right, as if she hung it crooked or...

Her thought is disrupted by the sound of her daughter's laughter. She continues down the hall, toward a yellow crack of light squeezing out from beneath the bathroom door.

"Hellooo?" she calls out.

Marie Elena's voice floats toward her, intertwined with the chimes of Isabella's laugh. "We're in here..."

At the door, Beth knocks lightly, then pushes inward. She blinks at the bright light; moist, warm air coats her skin. She spots Isabella in the bathtub, slick with hot water and covered in a bumpy hill of bubbles. Marie Elena is on her knees next to the tub, holding a shampoo bottle. They both turn to look at Beth, smiling brightly.

"Mommy!" Isabella yells, tossing a handful of bubbles out of the tub in her excitement.

"Hi, sweetie!" she says, heart filling with joy at the sight of her little girl. "Marie Elena, I'm so sorry to be late. It was not a great day."

"Don't you worry, mama. I would never turn down a chance to give Isabella a bubble bath. Although my knees aren't as strong as they used to be," she says, not unkindly. "Why don't you finish for me here and I'll heat you up some dinner before I go."

Beth steps into the small pink bathroom and helps the nanny to her feet, doing her best to swallow the guilt of being late (again) and of missing her favorite time of day with her daughter. "You're so kind, thank you. It won't be a habit, I promise."

Marie Elena grips Beth's wrist, her hands warm with bathwater, and gives her arm a friendly shake. "And I keep telling you, don't worry, Beth. I'm happy to help. Sit with your daughter and I'll see you tomorrow. I'll put your plate in the oven." She turns back to Isabella, who's now methodically working the shampoo into her tousled head of dark hair. "Good night, my princess. See you in the morning, okay?"

"Bye, Marie Elena!" Isabella says gleefully, her eyes closed tight against the dreaded sting from a stray drop of shampoo. She blows a few sloppy, soapy kisses as Marie Elena leaves, and Beth settles to her knees next to the tub. She picks up the plastic cup used to rinse her daughter's hair, dips it into the warm water. "All done scrubbing?"

Isabella lowers her hands, nods.

As Beth rinses her hair clean, the stress of the day washes away with the sweet-smelling soap. Her mind clears of the cluttered, painful memories, the data-crunching thoughts she can never seem to let go of quiet—then vanish—as Isabella giggles, wiping suds from her forehead, which Beth can't help but lean down and kiss.

◌

Later that night, Beth lies in bed, limply holding her tablet, the same thriller novel she's been reading for weeks—seemingly at a page-per-night pace—lit up on the screen. Her eyes are heavy, body and mind exhausted. She wants nothing more than six or seven unbroken hours of sleep, a long morning run, and a day at the lab where she can stop putting herself through the emotional blender of traveling and reporters and corporate interference and just go back to focusing on the science.

Of course, tomorrow morning there will need to be a debrief, followed by another therapy session with Jonathan to make sure her eggs aren't scrambled. Part of her is almost beginning to wonder if it *would* be smarter to have someone else do the actual traveling. The idea of sitting back as a spectator, watching the virtual feed, analyzing the data with an impassive, emotionless scientist's mind, is borderline luxurious.

But early on in their trials, she and Colson agreed—at least until they knew more about the impacts of traveling, both personal and scientific—that it would only be one of them going through the wormhole. They'd made the decision for multiple reasons. One, admittedly a somewhat selfish one, being that they both felt it vital to actually *experience* what it was like to travel, to send your consciousness through a rip in space-time and occupy your own body, relive a moment of your past self. They both knew there was just as much data to be mined from the subjective experience as there was from the objective analysis.

The other reason—and much more significant motive for its only being one of them, and no one else, who traveled during the early stages of the machine—was a reason they didn't often speak of, or even like to think about, if they could help it.

The risks.

Or, put another way, a more *truthful* way: the danger.

They both felt it important that no outsiders be in the line of fire for anything that could conceivably (or inconceivably) go wrong when traveling. Neither of them wanted to be responsible for having a random traveler end up brain damaged, or worse.

Lost.

Their consciousness forever damned to a purgatorial state between two points in space-time. Their minds irretrievable. Their bodies nothing but empty shells.

They both knew it was, at least scientifically, possible. If something were to go wrong with the wormhole—whether caused by bad data or a freak energy failure—the catastrophic result could, theoretically, happen to whoever was strapped into the machine.

That's also why they never went past ninety seconds. The risk was too great.

In many ways, the risk was *already* too great.

How did Tariq once put it?

It's like playing Russian roulette with a flamethrower.

"Enough," Beth mumbles, her mind so groggy with worry and exhaustion she can barely form the word. She sets the tablet on her nightstand, clicks off the bedside lamp.

In the dark, tired but wired, she uses a trick she learned from Jonathan to free her mind of the million things it wants to think about, to turn over and over and analyze. She imagines an empty sheet of white paper. Unblemished. She focuses on the clear white landscape.

Focuses on *nothing*.

Slowly, her mind settles, drifts. The white page looms larger, larger, covering her mind like a blanket. She feels herself dissolving, her mind slipping through a quiet entrance, into the void of sleep...

When a man's voice comes from the hallway.

Shocked at the sound, Beth comes wide-awake, her mental sheet of paper shredded into a thousand pieces. She sits up, then freezes, waiting in the dark.

Listening.

Did I imagine it? Was I dreaming?

Then the voice comes again—the muffled voice of a man trying to speak quietly.

It's followed by the sound of light laughter.

Isabella's laughter.

He's in her room.

"Isabella!" Beth yells, leaping from the bed. Her feet hit the cold floor at a run and she lunges toward the bedroom door, rips it open, and bursts into the darkened hallway. She turns toward her daughter's bedroom, sprinting through ten feet of hallway, and slams through the door. The blue haze of the night-light offers dim outlines of the furniture, of her baby girl sitting up in bed.

Standing at the foot of the bed is the dark shadow of a man, slightly hunched, as if whispering secrets.

When Beth enters, his head turns.

The whites of his eyes glint in the dim blue light.

"Get away from her!" she screams, instinctively slaps her hand at the light switch.

The room bursts into existence as the overhead light comes to life, the yellow walls and white bedspread near blinding after the darkness.

The man is gone.

There is no man.

Isabella turns her head, looks at her mother through sleepy eyes.

"Honey," Beth says shakily, running to her daughter, wrapping her in a hug. "Are you okay?"

"Yes, Mommy," Isabella says quietly, leaning into Beth's chest, arms wrapped around her mother's waist in a loose embrace.

Beth pulls back, looks at the spot where she would have sworn she saw a person standing, leaning over her daughter's bed...

I saw him! I saw someone.

He looked at me.

She turns her attention back to Isabella. "I heard...I heard talking. You were laughing."

Isabella's face scrunches in thought for a second, then she spins and grabs Singing Sally from the pillow beside her. "I was talking to Sally, that's all. It was pretend." She hugs her mom tight. "I'm sorry."

"It's okay," Beth says, her racing heart finally slowing, but her mind still a jumble of fear and confusion. "It's okay..."

I'm going crazy.

A chill slithers up her spine, denying her the warm comfort of Isabella's embrace.

It's the machine, she thinks, knowing deep down in her heart that it's real.

That her worst fears have come true.

The machine is tearing my mind apart.

NINETEEN

When Beth wakes the next morning, she's exhausted from lack of sleep, her mind lost in a fog.

After the incident with Isabella, she'd finally surrendered to taking one of the pills Jonathan had given her, forcing her mind to slow down, her tightly strung muscles to relax. In doing so, however, she'd slept straight through her first alarm, waking too late for her desired run, and only just managing a quick shower before Marie Elena showed up to take care of her daughter for the day.

Now Beth drives to work in a dull haze, her body twitchy. Her mind is a battlefield between the emotional memories of her past fighting tooth and nail against the logical problem-solving of her present and future. She knows the clock is ticking on reaching that next level of discovery with the time travel. If the machine is to have viable potential, she *must* figure out how to control it. How to target the arrival point. But to do that, she needs to spend weeks—maybe months, maybe *years*—studying the data collected from the trips she and Colson have already logged. Sending herself through the machine again, at this point, will do nothing but add more variables she doesn't need.

And, of course, there's the danger component. The possibility that traveling is causing very real trauma—both physical and psychological—to her person.

Which is why it can only be she who travels. For now. She won't risk hurting someone with her invention, with her and Colson's incomplete science.

When Beth arrives at the office, she does her best to ignore the fading crimson Rorschach smudge on the sidewalk in front of the entrance, wondering if Langan plans on ever cleaning it or instead leaving it as a warning to other employees.

Fuck with me and this is what will be left of you.

Beth shakes away the feelings of disgust—of *fear*—and puts her mind back on task.

On the machine.

She walks through the lobby, past security and the sliding glass door, to the elevator that will take her to the lab. As she nears the end of the corridor, there's a soft *ding* and the copper-colored doors slide open, revealing a harried-looking Jonathan. For a moment they study each other. Beth wonders if she looks as terrible as he does and suspects she just might.

"You look like hell," she says, trying to smile it into a jest.

He nods, steps from the elevator, grips her elbow. He looks at her with feverish eyes, as if he's been crying. Or screaming. "We need to talk."

Beth eyes the open elevator for a moment, then sighs as the doors slide shut. "Okay, what's up?"

"Not here." He turns and looks down the hallway. "Come on."

The hairs on the back of her neck stand up when she realizes he's taking her to what was, a few scant days prior, the offices for Neural Prosthetics. Her mind serves up an image of Jerry lying dead on the pavement under a rain-soaked sheet, his blood running into the gutter, one clawed hand pointed toward the sky.

Before she can protest, however, he's pushing through the door and pulling her in behind him. She takes in the empty front lobby and feels a pang of fear, fighting off visions of her own lab emptied, the machine pulled apart and hauled off to God knows where, her files confiscated. She shivers involuntarily, and Jonathan gives her a questioning glance that she shakes off. Instead, she pulls her arm free from his grip, takes a step deeper into the office as the door shuts silently behind them.

A narrow hallway leads back to more offices and the large open floor space of the Neural Prosthetics main laboratory. She's seen it only once, shortly after she and Colson first started at Langan. Jerry insisted on giving them a tour, proudly showing off his group's newest mind-controlled limbs, hands, feet. It was impressive, but once the time machine started siphoning off the budgets of other departments, any amicability turned to black ice.

She certainly never got another tour.

Now the lobby is barren and silent, paper strewn and dusty. Beth thinks it smells like a tomb. "I don't think we're supposed to be—"

"Beth, just let me talk, okay?" Jonathan says, and she can't help wondering if the space is bugged. She recalls Langan's words to her just last week:

I hear everything. I see everything.

Beth studies Jonathan more closely.

He's not just worried.

He's frightened.

"Jonathan, what the hell is going on? Look, if this is you warning me not to travel again, believe me—"

"I've seen the article, Beth," he says, cutting her off.

Caught off guard, she pauses, eyes on his. "And?" she says, the word nearly catching in her throat.

"It's... it's not good."

Beth takes a step back, folds her arms over her chest. "What do you mean?"

"I mean that Ms. Nakada did the exact opposite of what she was supposed to do. Instead of building up the possibilities of what you've created, she..."

"She what?"

"In so many words? She calls it a waste of funds. She suggests all the money spent on your research could be used to create something more useful. She refers to the machine, and I'm quoting, as 'a brilliant invention, assuming the future depends on regression instead of progress.'"

Beth's arms tighten around her body. "She said that?"

Jonathan nods, an angry frown creasing his face. "Once the interview portion with you is over, she gets into an opinion piece. At one point, she accuses Langan Corp. of 'throwing money at mad science.' Anyway, you get the gist."

"That's...but—" Beth cuts off her confused stammer. Her face hardens. "What the fuck happened to her being a ringer?"

Jonathan shakes his head. "I don't know, but it gets worse." He watches her carefully, as if making sure she's not going to faint or scream—or punch him in the mouth. "Much worse."

Beth thinks a moment, then nods. "She goes after me. Personally."

"It didn't help that you...you know..."

"Lost my shit?"

"Yeah. I believe the line was, 'I'm not sure what's more unstable, the underlying science or the woman responsible for it.'" Jonathan glances at the closed door as if worried about eavesdroppers. "Beth, it's a kill piece. This woman isn't a ringer; she's an assassin."

Beth scoffs, shakes her head. "It doesn't matter. Jim's got them under a blanket of NDA bullshit. There's no way he'll let it go to print."

"I'm not so sure. I think even the great Jim Langan was blindsided by this. Those NDAs cover a lot of stuff, but opinion isn't one of them. My guess is she was planted by a competitor. Maybe someone creating something similar? I don't know."

"There's nothing like this out there," Beth mutters, knowing she sounds defensive but not caring. "Regardless, this is on Jim, right? Yeah, okay, I had a freak-out, but it sounds like she was gonna burn us no matter what."

Jonathan lets out a held breath. His face softens, and he offers a limp smile. It's a look Beth is well-versed in. Remorse tinged with superiority.

"Beth, I think you need to start thinking about options."

Beth stares at him for a moment, as if studying a strange new species of predator.

"What the hell are you talking about?" she says, then takes a step closer. "And what were you doing in my lab?"

Instead of answering, Jonathan just looks at her with that sympathetic, infuriating smile.

As if he knows something I don't . . . something besides the article.

"Jonathan?"

"Come on, Beth."

"Fuck you. Don't 'come on, Beth' me. What aren't you telling me?"

But he only shrugs, stuffs his hands into his pockets. "Don't you think Colson would have wanted you to move on from all this? Get away from all the bullshit, the headache. Start fresh, you know? Create a new life?"

Beth can hardly breathe as she stares into Jonathan's face. She's missing something, not understanding. Not seeing what should be obvious . . .

. . . when suddenly, it all comes together.

The article.

Jonathan's muddled distress.

Tariq.

"Fuck me," Beth whispers, the conclusion hitting her like a left hook. She bites her lip, eyes darting from one corner to the other, mind racing.

Oh God. Please...NO.

Colson, what have I done?

Her eyes snap back to Jonathan, and his face sags at the realization that she's figured it out. That she's *caught up*. She takes another quick step forward and hardly notices when he shuffles a half step back.

"He wouldn't," she says, eyes wide with fright. With fury. "He wouldn't *dare*."

Jonathan lowers his eyes, says nothing.

"Shit!" she yells, pushing past Jonathan and jerking open the door of the empty suite. She all but runs for the elevator, tapping the lone button again and again and again. "Come on...come on..."

The elevator arrives and she steps inside, heart racing, mind already flowcharting next steps, playing out points and counterpoints, defenses. Offenses.

Moments later, the doors open on the lab. *Her* lab.

She takes a step into the large, quiet room (*too quiet, it's too quiet*) and looks around, already knowing what she'll find, but needing to be *sure*.

Nothing.

No one.

"Bastard."

Beth steps back into the elevator and taps the button for the main floor, knowing every second counts.

Praying she isn't already too late.

TWENTY

For the second time in the same week, Beth finds herself barging into the CEO's office.

Martha doesn't even try to stop her this time, simply gives her a cool, absent look as she storms by. As if Beth's fiery appearance is wholly expected.

Maybe even necessary.

When Beth bursts through the door—fists clenched, disgusted—she's not surprised, not at all, to see Tariq and Jim Langan sitting comfortably in leather chairs. *Surprised they're not smoking cigars and drinking cognac like a goddamn men's club.*

Jim rolls his eyes, palms turned upward. "And here we go," he says, and Beth has the overwhelming urge to punch the old bastard in the teeth.

"Yeah, here we go," she says, and focuses her blazing eyes on Tariq, who squirms beneath her glare. "Hey, Tariq. Man, I knew you were ambitious, but I never expected something like this. I thought you were better than this, I really did."

Tariq starts to reply when Jim sharply lifts a hand, cutting him to silence. "Tariq is here because I asked him to be here, and whether you seem to realize it or not, I'm the boss," Jim says calmly. "I was planning on speaking to you privately, but since you've inserted yourself into this meeting, we may as well speak openly. Bottom line? You're suspended, Beth. You are obviously under a lot of strain, and I can't rely on you to continue the project until you've taken some time to, speaking frankly, get your shit together."

Beth shakes her head. "You're unbelievable. You condescending motherfucker."

Jim's face reddens and he opens his mouth to reply when Beth continues.

"If I'm stressed, Jim, it's because of you. You're the one who needs money. You're the one who's cut my staff down to nothing. You're the one forcing repeated travels so you can get your press. Oh, by the way, I heard your ringer wasn't such a ringer, after all. That's right, isn't it? And that's my fault, too, I suppose?"

Tariq stands, hands held up defensively. "Hold on, Beth. Just listen for a second. All Jim told me was he was worried about you and that he felt you needed time. He asked me if I was comfortable continuing the project in your absence. But it's temporary; it's just to lighten your load for a bit, that's all."

Jim stands as well, sighing heavily. "He made it sound like a question. Allow me to make it into a statement. In your absence, Tariq is going to head up the search for someone to travel in your stead. I can't keep risking you, especially given your responses to the last couple of trips." Jim smiles, trying to soften the blow. "This is *good*, Beth. Jesus Christ, can't you see I'm trying to help you? You need to take some time off, get some rest, regroup. Spend time with your daughter. Meanwhile, Tariq will bring in a specialist to handle the risky stuff. Someone who's trained to deal with the potential of . . . hell, I don't know what you'd call them . . . *side effects*. You know, someone specially trained to withstand the travel, who's got the *right stuff*."

Beth looks at Jim blankly.

"Yeager? Glenn? Shepard? Hell, it doesn't matter. Look, think of it as a time astronaut. That's got a nice ring to it, yeah?"

Beth gives a harsh laugh, shakes her head. "You mean you want someone who isn't going to have a meltdown in front of reporters, is that it?"

Jim's smile fades, but he nods. "Yes, Beth. Since you've put it so bluntly... that's it exactly. Also, I'm trying to protect that brain of yours, if we're being blunt. I need it, and I need you. Sane and stable, preferably."

Beth's eyes shift to Tariq, then back to Jim.

Colson's voice whispers in her head.

You're losing, Beth. Time to pivot, find another angle.

Beth takes a deep breath, forces her hands to unclench, her voice to find a more even, soothing timbre. "Okay, okay. I came in a little hot, and I apologize. Can we... Look, let's take a step back for a second, all right?"

Jim shrugs, and Tariq sits back down, albeit tentatively.

"I know how it looks, Jim. I really do," she says, moving closer to the two men, lowering her voice as she does so. "And to some degree, I get it. But you need to understand something."

This man only understands one thing: money.

Well, here comes the hook, buddy. Bite down hard.

"It's not me, all right? It's the machine."

Tariq's eyes narrow, as if he is trying to understand where Beth is going, but Jim sits down, eyes never leaving hers. "I don't follow," Jim says, frowning. Waiting.

"I realize that," she says, not unkindly. "So let me explain. And Tariq will tell you the same thing I'm telling you now. The machine is *targeting*, Jim. The arrival points? They're not random."

Jim leans forward, clasps his hands over his knees. For a moment, he studies his shoes, thinking. Finally, he looks up, his face unreadable. "Maybe you should sit down."

Tentatively, Beth approaches the makeshift seating area, like an amateur trainer entering a lion's cage, and sits on the small couch while Jim settles back into his own seat. Tariq, looking trapped, stays where he is, eyes moving from Beth to Jim, as if watching a chess match, the victor of which is still uncertain.

"New analysis has shown the machine is targeting memories that, consciously or not, show higher-than-normal psychological and emotional vibrations," Beth says, speaking neutrally, clearly. Scientifically. "Spikes in the neural waves of the brain. What is sometimes referred to as a flashbulb memory. But it's more than that...It's...I don't know. *Deeper* than that. The machine...it's picking arrival points that are..."

Beth takes a breath, lets out a weak laugh.

I literally have nothing left to lose.

"God, I know how this sounds...It's picking moments that are *painful.*"

Jim watches Beth closely, as if looking for a tell. A lie in her words. Finally, he nods thoughtfully, looks at Tariq. "Is she bull-shitting me?"

Tariq glances at Beth, then meets Jim's eye. "No, sir. It's the truth. We just haven't had time to pinpoint the rationale behind it. There's so much data to process, and it's just the two of us. We need more time, more experimentation, to shake out the hidden formula."

Beth leans forward. "Jim, we're *close.* I know we can figure out how the machine is selecting these arrival points. Now that we know it's focusing on certain types of memories, it's just a matter of time."

Jim thinks a moment, then nods. "Okay, say I buy this. Here's my question: Why didn't we see these results with Colson? Why now? Why you?"

Beth sits back into the couch, relief surging through her.

Gotcha.

"Frankly, Colson didn't have these types of memories. He

lived a somewhat blessed life. At least in comparison to me, I guess. High school plays and pancake breakfasts were, for whatever reason, flashbulb memories for him, but not traumatic ones. Not hurtful ones. But they were still powerful. Meaningful to him in some way. So, to your point earlier, getting a time astronaut, or whatever you call them, might not be the answer. We don't want *stable*. We want fucked up. We want people who have had traumatic events in their past. People who have experienced pain on a higher scale." Beth sits up, unable to contain her own thrill at the idea of finally solving the biggest riddle of her invention, even if it is half-baked bullshit. "The machine will feed on those memories like a vampire, Jim. And then we'll *have* it. We'll know how, and we'll know why."

Jim looks up, naked excitement in his eyes. "And then we can control it."

Beth nods, smiles. "Yes. The golden goose you've been searching for." Beth leans forward, fingers bunched into fists on her knees. "I will deliver these answers, Jim. But I need more time. I need less interference... and I need you to trust me."

As Jim absorbs this, Beth looks to Tariq, who gives her a near-imperceptible nod.

Damn it, man, I hope I was wrong about you.

She nods back.

"Okay," Jim says, standing abruptly, then striding quickly toward the bar. To Beth's shock, he pours himself a large glass of whiskey, takes a quick sip, then turns around. "Okay," he repeats, that smirk back on his lips. "Here's my proposal. You stay," he says, pointing to Beth. "But I cannot have this reporter's last impression of you, and of the machine, be that howling, crying bullshit we went through yesterday." He sets his drink down on the bar, the clank of the heavy glass causing Beth to wince.

"Okay..." she says, wondering where this is going.

"That bitch is here for two more days, then she's gone and there's only so much I can do with whatever she decides to write. Yes, I can keep her from divulging technical details, but I can't keep her from voicing a negative opinion. So...I'm sorry," he says, unable to meet her eyes, "but you need to go through again."

Tariq's mouth drops open, but Beth only nods, her mind surprisingly calm at the idea. A part of her almost...*eager.*

If I'm right about this, I can work with it.

I'll be ready for it.

"I understand," she says. "Besides, whatever it throws at me, it can't be worse than what I've already gone through." She shrugs. "I've already watched them all die."

Tariq looks at her, his expression pained in a way she's never seen.

Jim stares at her questioningly. "I don't follow. Watched who all die?"

Beth smiles sadly, shrugs. "Anyone I've ever cared about."

TWENTY-ONE

Despite the drama of confronting Jim—and the desperation of buying herself some much-needed time—Beth still needs to adhere to test protocol, which means doing a debrief of her last trip.

Now she stands at the podium, one toe tapping against the lip of the wooden base in a desire to get *done with it* and get back to work. The knowledge that she is now on the clock for results is not lost on her, and wasting time on yet another round of test questions is not the best use of whatever precious days, hours, or minutes she has left before Jim drops the axe.

Mercifully, the panel agrees that reshowing a video of the travel event is not necessary. Beth is pretty sure it was upon Jonathan's insistence, rather than any concerns from the others. Apparently he thought reliving the night of her husband's death—*again*—would do more harm than good, and Beth couldn't agree more.

Big points for you today, buddy.

And since one goal of the debrief pertains to analyzing how reliving trigger events (such as the death of your husband) affects a person post-travel—Beth wonders if, perhaps, they already have their data. Her screaming and wailing in the immediate aftermath is a pretty fucking solid test result.

Besides, only moments ago it was decided she was going through (yet again) in approximately twenty-four hours. *So, hey, good news, folks! There's more data on the way! Although I'm not sure what the technical conclusion would be for turning me into a drooling, brain-damaged idiot. But that's science for ya!*

Beth shakes off the rogue thoughts, forces herself to stay in the present. She keeps her eyes down, does her best to keep her body still during the playback of the variable questions. She tries not to think about what she told Jim less than an hour ago.

That she'd pinpointed the machine's tendencies.

That the arrival points aren't random.

Does the machine really focus on pain? How much of my desperate speech was bullshit, and how much was a truth I wouldn't allow myself to believe?

Or is it something else? Something we're not seeing . . .

Because buried deep down in her web of critical thinking and scientific analysis, Beth has another thought.

Another hypothesis.

One she hasn't shared with Jim or Jonathan or even Tariq. And certainly not the reporter, although she'd hinted at it.

It was Colson who first broached the idea that by opening the wormhole in space-time, they were adding a variable to the targeting process . . .

Please state your name and today's date.

Beth Darlow. March 22, 2044.

What if it wasn't the machine at all?

Who is the president of the United States?

James Whitmore.

What if something else—something unseen, something

impossible to comprehend—was making the decision?

Describe your marital status.

Widowed.

What if the arrival points weren't based on pain or love or emotion?
What if they were meant to punish the traveler?

In one word, describe your childhood.

Happy.

What if the arrival points were ways of telling them to stop?
To go no further.
Or else.

Name two members of your immediate family.

My uncle, Brett Hawkins. My daughter, Isabella Darlow.

Beth feels her stomach sour at the idea of a cosmic consciousness turning its great celestial eye in her direction. Catching the attention of an omniscient intelligence seems like a very bad idea. Call it God, call it a higher power, call it the will of the universe...by any name you choose, the characteristics of such an entity hold true:
It is indifferent to man's suffering.
It is vengeful when angered.

If you could change one moment in your life, what would it be?

Beth listens, distractedly, to the playback of her own voice answering the last of the variable questions.

I would stop my husband from leaving on the day he was killed.

But I didn't stop him, she thinks as the recording ends. *I didn't change a goddamn thing.*

TWENTY-TWO

Beth ignores Tariq as she crosses the lab to her office. She's too exhausted, too stressed, and too overwhelmingly *done* with the seemingly constant battle of corporate politics to spend another minute debating what Tariq did or didn't agree to behind closed doors.

Tomorrow morning she'll be going through the wormhole yet again. Three trips in a week's time. *Pretty sure that's a new record*, she thinks, wondering if her nerves will survive another go-round with her tragic past. How many times had Colson gone through? Seven? But that was with a full staff doing all the work before and after, not to mention there were weeks—not days—between trips. But even so, she remembers that he'd been strained. Exhausted.

Beth thinks back on those times, tries to recall his reaction to the repeated traveling; she remembers the tiredness he'd worn like a heavy coat for weeks at a time. Sure, it was emotionally draining, but for the first time Beth wonders if there might have been something else going on with her husband, something not related to the work...something she missed?

Focus on yourself, Beth, she thinks as she collapses into her chair, tiredly puts her face into the palms of her hands. *Prep yourself for the worst. What could be waiting for you at the other end of that wormhole?*

There's nothing else… There are no other tragedies. No sudden deaths. No car accidents or plane crashes or pianos falling from the sky to crush the head of some old lover.

"It'll be fine," she mutters into her hands. "I'll be fine."

Beth drops her hands, spins toward her desk, and boots up her screen. She types in her password, a most unscientific and easily hackable combination of her daughter's name and birth date—*ISABELLA080840*—and prepares to open Tariq's report on her most recent trip. She knows that Jim will be assuaged for only so long. In twenty-four hours, she needs to have a successful (and drama-free) travel session. Following that, she figures she has a week, two at the most, to crack the code of how the machine chooses the arrival point. It's been the grail she and Colson had been hunting for the last couple of years, and she's always known it would be a prerequisite to achieve new funding, and new life, for the project.

But she thought she'd have more time.

Months, if not years.

Now she has a couple of weeks at the most, with no Colson to help, no staff to crunch data, and an associate who is, at best, untrustworthy.

At worst, malicious.

Beth sighs heavily, tries to refocus her mind, block out the emotions, fears, and anxieties. She's already thinking she'll have to call Marie Elena soon, that she's likely looking at an all-nighter at the lab, not to mention working through another weekend.

The ultimate irony, Beth thinks. *To build a time machine, only to run out of time.*

She scans the shared drive for the newest report from Tariq, then transfers it to her personal drive so she can access it from home if needed.

As she closes the shared drive, revealing the window of her private drive, she notices a bright red folder in the middle of the hazy blue backdrop of her screen.

It's labeled simply, only one word in all caps:

BETH

Her brows furrow in confusion. She knows for a fact that the folder was not on her device yesterday. Or any day before that. *I would have noticed something with my name on it.*

No, she'd never seen it before, and there was no way for it to end up on her personal device unless...

Unless someone loaded it from home? On my tablet?

She slides the tip of her finger across the screen, the pointer moving to hover over the strange red folder. She wonders if perhaps Isabella left her something to open. It would explain the cryptic title of her name, but she highly doubts Isabella would know how to do such a thing. *Maybe Marie Elena helped her?*

Feeling a tingle of anxiety in her stomach at the sight of the red icon, Beth glances at the top corner of the screen to check the time, and frowns.

Isabella would have returned home mere minutes ago.

Still, it was possible...

Despite lingering inner protestations, Beth taps her finger on the red folder. A window pops open to cover a quarter of her screen. Inside the new window are two icons.

One is a video file, titled ME FIRST.

The other is a second folder, this one light blue, titled ME LAST.

"What the hell?" Beth murmurs, leaning back in her chair, studying the two icons apprehensively. Finally, knowing her damned curiosity leaves her no choice, she taps the video icon.

The video player opens, revealing an impossible image. Beth gasps.

"No…"

Beth's husband stares back at her. A frozen image of Colson sitting at his desk, hands folded neatly in front of him. He's wearing a wry smile, as if holding back a punch line or making a concerted effort to keep a secret. One he badly wants to tell.

Beth looks out the office door, notices Tariq hunched over his monitor by the machine, fully engaged in his work. She looks to her right, to the darkened glass wall separating her office from Colson's. For the first time since his death, the sight of his dark, empty office gives her an unwelcome chill. As if it isn't an office at all, but a tomb.

Her own right beside.

"Fuck it," she says, and taps the button to play the video.

The video comes alive, as does Colson's visage. Staring at his face, she realizes that what she initially thought was a playful smirk has quickly devolved into a strained grimace.

He looks exhausted, she thinks, recalling once more how tired he'd seemed during those last few months before his death.

On the screen, her husband runs a hand roughly through his salt-and-pepper hair, exactly the way he used to do when he was overly stressed, when the anxiety and pressure were building to a fever pitch. His body is hunched, as if any second his head will drop all the way down to the desk's surface as he slips into unconsciousness.

Hi, Beth, he says, and Beth feels that unwelcome chill spread from her head to her toes, causing a breakout of goose bumps along her arms, a sharp sting of suppressed tears to her eyes.

In the video, Colson does his best to smile, but it fails midway, turns defeatedly back into a worn, tired frown.

Look, this is going to seem weird, but you have to take my word for it. What I'm about to tell you... it's absolutely necessary.

Beth shakes her head. "What are you talking about?" she says quietly, an old habit of replying to her partner's voice, the rippling customs of living a life with someone, an untamable side effect of having had a thousand—tens of thousands—conversations with a person you love.

Honey, there's something wrong with the machine. With the coding. It could be dangerous, Beth. You don't know how dangerous, because it was always me who was traveling, but you need to know there are things... things I kept from you.

He shakes his head, and for the first time Beth wonders when—when *exactly*—he made this video.
And how the hell did it end up on my device?
Involuntarily, her eyes shift to the dark glass wall of his office, then snap back to the video as he continues.

As you can plainly see, there's a second folder along with this video. Inside is a program that will show you the problems I'm describing, albeit poorly. But look, at the very least, it'll prepare you to defend yourself against the dangers I'm referring to. I know it's hard, but you have to trust me. When I'm gone...

Here he pauses. Tears flood his eyes and he lowers his head, wipes them away jerkily, frustratingly. Beth wishes she could reach out to him, put her hand on his head. Somehow help him, soothe him.

He takes a breath and continues.

. . . when I'm gone, it will become more clear to you what I'm talking about. By now . . . by now you've likely experienced a little bit of what I'm describing.

In the video he moves closer to the camera, so that his face fills the entire playback window. She stares at his eyes, sees the life in them, and wonders if she's ever missed him as much as she does in this moment.

I know you've traveled yourself. You've seen what the machine does.

Beth sits back, puts a hand to her mouth; a fingertip crawl of fear scurries up the back of her neck. "What the hell is this?" she whispers, not daring to say aloud what she's feeling. That she isn't simply watching a recording of her husband . . .

But that she's talking to a ghost.

On the screen, Colson looks past the camera, as if someone unexpected had come into the laboratory while he was recording. Then his eyes settle back onto the lens.

Beth . . . honey, I love you. But I'm out of time here. Just please, you know me, you know I'd do anything to protect you, to protect our family.

Beth shakes her head. One hand clenches into a fist that she rubs into her thigh, as if hoping to wake from a bad dream. Tears run down her face and she can almost feel her mind splintering— the logical, scientific parts of her brain dissolving into pink clouds of hysteria. Disbelief.

Madness.

She glances once more toward the darkened office to her right, as if expecting to see him sitting there in the gloomy dark, watching her with wide eyes before standing up and walking toward the glass divider, knocking to be let in, to come back to the world of the living.

The video continues and she does her best to focus on what he's saying, to clear her mind of emotion and *understand* what he's trying so hard to tell her.

> *Beth, listen closely. Here's what I need you to do. Open that other file, the program I left you. It'll explain everything. It'll fix the machine and... and I swear to you, Beth, it'll keep you from harm.*

He stares directly into the camera—directly at *her*. His brown eyes are soft, compassionate. He reaches a finger toward the screen.

> *It'll keep you safe.*

"No, wait!" Beth says, loudly enough to draw Tariq's attention, and then the video freezes, a blur of flesh and shadow. Breathing fast, heart pounding hard in her chest, she slides a finger over the icon and brings up the information menu for the video.

She wants to know when it was created.

She reads the date posted within the information menu, then reads it again, shaking her head. Not believing, not understanding.

March 27, 2043

My birthday. The day he was killed.

That's not possible.

Beth sits back in her chair, sucks in deep breaths, tries to calm her nerves, slow her heart. She feels as if she's touched a live wire—raw electricity surges through her veins, frying her nerves, ripping apart her logic in staccato bursts of blue fire.

She eyes the blue icon another moment, debating whether to open the file.

It'll keep you safe.

She reaches a finger toward the screen...

"Hey, you good?"

Beth nearly screams at the sound of Tariq's voice. She jerks her finger back and stands so quickly she almost knocks her chair over. Her eyes shoot to a confused Tariq standing at her office door, then down to the screen, still showing the blurry image of Colson's face. Deftly, she reaches out and flicks a fingertip up and left, closing the red folder's window.

"Hey! Yeah, I'm fine. I'm just...uh, there's a lot to deal with right now, and, well, I guess I'm feeling the pressure."

Tariq nods. "Understandable. And look, I'm sorry about the Jim thing. But, Beth, you need to know I would never do anything to jeopardize your project, okay? This is something *you* built. You and Colson. Yeah, I got ideas, and maybe one day I'll do my own thing, but for now? This?" He turns his head, nods toward the large metal machine across the lab. "This is all you. And I'm only here for one thing, and that's to help you succeed. That's it. That's *all*. I'm a scientist, too, remember. I got my pride," he says with a chuckle, before turning serious once more. "And I'm no thief. I would never steal this from under you, understand? I'd never do that to you, and I would never do that to Colson. Well, you know, Colson's memory."

Beth nods some more, feeling like an idiot through and through, but knowing it's the only thing she can do right now to keep from bursting into tears. "I know."

"Good," he says. "And I know you, Beth. I know you're gonna work through the weekend now that Jim's got his foot up your ass—*our* ass—so I'm telling you now...I'm here, okay? I'm with you."

"Thank you," Beth says.

"You go, I go. That's the deal."

Now Beth does cry. Then she crosses the office in three strides and does the most unprofessional thing she's ever done in a laboratory. She hugs him.

"I'm sorry I've been a bitch," she mumbles, her body almost reveling at genuine human contact, almost *feeling* the strain and pressure of the last week gently lower from a noxious boil to a persistent but manageable simmer.

Tariq steps back and smiles. "Don't worry, I'm used to it."

Beth laughs, scrubs her wet nose with the cuff of her lab coat sleeve. "Thanks."

"You ready to work?"

Beth nods, takes a deep breath, lets it out. "Yeah," she says, eyeing the tangled, gorgeous mass of steel, plastic, and mind-bending power she created. "Let's figure out what's got this machine so goddamn cranky."

TWENTY-THREE

When Beth looks at the clock, she knows she'll never have enough time to sift through all the essential data and still arrive home before Marie Elena needs to leave for the night. Desperate, she calls Lucy, who happily agrees to a sleepover with Isabella and Timmy. Hanging up on a somewhat frazzled best friend, she then calls home to let her nanny know Lucy will be by to pick up Isabella, and to please put some overnight clothes in her backpack.

Then comes the hard part.

"Mommy!" Isabella squeals over the phone, her exuberant voice sending spiderweb cracks of sorrow and guilt through Beth's heart.

"Hi, baby," she says, trying to keep her tone upbeat. "I have good news..."

Although Isabella is momentarily confused and dismayed when Beth tells her she won't be home that evening—as all young children are at the idea of their parents not always being there when expected—she's equally jubilant that she'll get to spend the night with Aunt Lucy and Timmy. *Her first sleepover*, Beth realizes. *And I'm not even there to take her or pack her bag or kiss her goodbye.*

After hanging up with her daughter, Beth swallows her guilt the best she can and gets back to work.

When Tariq knocks on her door, what seems only an hour or two later, she's surprised to see how tired he looks.

"Hey."

"Hey," he says, then yawns as he leans his weight against the doorframe. "I think I'm pretty much toast, and we got a big morning, so I'm gonna head out and get some sleep."

Sleep?

Beth looks at the clock on her screen and is shocked to realize it's nearly ten o'clock. "Oh my God, Tariq, I'm so sorry, I totally lost track of time. Yeah, please take off. I'll see you tomorrow. Is the machine ready? I know it's a quick turnaround."

"It's ready. I spent most of the afternoon prepping the system for the data dump you're gonna give it, and double-checked the chargers; we're all green."

Beth nods, feeling a rush of gratitude for her associate. She hadn't even thought to make sure the laser's power sources were fit for another go-round. "Awesome, thanks so much. Please get out of here, I'm right behind you."

Tariq smiles, acknowledging the lie but letting it go. "Cool. And I left you some pizza in the kitchen. There's Cokes in the fridge."

When the hell did he get pizza? Beth thinks, curiously alarmed at how engrossed she'd been in her own data crunching. "Thanks. I'm starving, actually."

"Call me if needed," he says, yawns once more, then leaves with a sloppy wave.

"Good night," she says, feeling a stab of envy at seeing him grab his coat and gather his things. Then her stomach grumbles and she forces herself to pause her analysis, stand up for a stretch, then take advantage of the food and cold caffeine her body is screaming for.

Minutes later, Tariq is waving from the elevator as the doors close, and Beth raises her can of Coca-Cola in return as she walks from the kitchen, her other hand holding a paper plate topped with three slices of room-temperature cheese pizza.

Settling back at her desk, Beth is already feeling reenergized by the few bites of food and a greedy swallow of soda, the caffeine and sugar hitting her tired brain like a blast of pure energy. While she eats, she studies a brain scan showing her neural activity in the moments prior to her traveling the day before. Pulsing purples, reds, and yellows show moderate-to-high activity in specific areas of her brain, fueled by a wide variant of potential causes such as stress, emotional spikes triggered by thoughts (or memories), even physical movement.

The scan she's studying has removed overlays of blood flow and electrical impulses, and with the twitch of a finger she can zoom into the recording of any one of the brain's eighty-six billion unique cells, easily targeting the pinpoint location of any abnormal activity. In the past, such monitoring would have taken several different types of scans, or even a surgical procedure. But now—assuming one had the correct equipment—it was as easy as taking a photograph, something done by default each time someone used the machine. And while Tariq is the neuroscience expert, Beth knows enough to recognize the types of things she thinks the machine might be drawn to—so-called hot areas of the mind that, in the milliseconds before travel, attract the attention of the software. A custom program that was built to randomly (although now, perhaps, not so randomly as they'd thought) select the arrival point of a traveler.

Historically they'd focused on areas where explicit (or flashbulb) memories were generated and stored: the hippocampus, the neocortex, and the amygdala. Lately, based on much of Tariq's analysis of the last two travels, they've been looking harder at implicit memory, buried deep in the basal ganglia, the part of the brain usually reserved for motor activity, but also the home of such human traits as learning, habits, and emotions.

The current theory: The machine isn't targeting memories; it's targeting extreme emotion.

But why?

The trillion-dollar question, Beth thinks, popping the last bit of pizza crust into her mouth.

Leaving the video of her brain's impulses running over the ninety-second travel period, Beth watches with a sort of fascination as the subdued colors representing stimulation—whether emotional, cognitive, or physical—cause the mapped image of her brain to explode like fireworks.

This is what it looks like to commune with the dead, she thinks. *To helplessly watch the people we love die over and over again. A beautiful, awe-inspiring light show of pain.*

As Beth stares, transfixed, at the screen, one name—one face—enters her thoughts.

Colson.

For the first time in hours, Beth remembers the video message tucked inside the mysterious red folder. The bizarre file of her husband on the day of his death. His warnings from the grave.

I know you've traveled yourself. You've seen what the machine does . . .

I'd do anything to protect you, to protect our family.

Beth finishes her soda, brushes her hands off on the thighs of her pants, and closes the map of brain-scan imagery with a quick tap of her finger. Her home screen appears once more, littered with hundreds of variously labeled icons linked to the server.

Sitting in the middle of the blue screen, as if waiting for her, is the red folder.

BETH

She taps it open, stares at the second icon in the window.

ME LAST

She shakes her head, slides her finger to the right.

"Okay, Colson," she says, voice heavy with exhaustion. "I'm trusting you. Show me what you got."

Beth taps the application icon and the screen flashes once— a wink of white—as if opening a new program. She holds her breath, watching the screen, waiting...

A couple of seconds pass, there's a soft *click* from her device...

...and then her screen goes an ominous, empty black.

Beth's eyes shift left and right, waiting for *something* to happen—to appear—that will explain this message from beyond, whatever it is that Colson wanted so badly for her to know. She's about to start tapping keys, desperate to know what the application will do, will tell her...

...when the screen bursts to life.

Beth jerks back as if shocked, jarred by the blast of activity as the screen fills with hundreds, then thousands—*tens of thousands*—of lines of code, all of it flowing by so fast she can barely register what she's seeing, what it means.

Ten, twenty, thirty seconds go by and still the code dump doesn't stop. Her eyes scan as fast as they're able. She's able to pick out repeated algorithms, commands...

And begins to recognize where the code is being pulled from.

It's her software.

The programming that controls the machine.

Then, just as suddenly as it began, it stops.

Having reached the end of what seemed an infinite amount of code, all of it now filling every inch of her screen in green digits, the cursor flashes for a moment, as if waiting.

Deciding.

Then it moves *backward*. Reversing direction, back into the data.

Lines of code begin to disappear.

"Wait..."

The cursor moves faster, *faster*. Lines of code are vanishing in a flash, then *groups* of lines, then entire pages.

"No no no...stop...STOP!" Beth shoots out of her chair, her breath fast and heavy, heart racing.

Colson, what the hell are you doing?!

Her machine. Her software. Her *life's work*.

It's being deleted before her eyes.

Erased.

"No!" Beth screams, and immediately begins tapping the button to power off her device, to cut it off from the main network before it can reach the servers.

The screen, now nothing but flashes of light as software is removed in massive chunks, stays powered up. Whatever this application is, this...*virus*...it's keeping her from shutting down her system.

"Goddamn it!" Beth looks around the office, frantically thinking, trying to figure out a way to stop this before it's too late. Pulling power won't help, as each computer in the lab has days of battery backup in case of power failure. Even worse, for security reasons, the lab's network is *contained*; her network doesn't touch anything outside the lab. The servers can't even access the rest of Langan Corp., which means there are no backups outside of the lab's private network, which she just gave some data-eating virus full access to.

The only positive, she thinks sickly, is she doesn't need to worry about wiping out the entire company.

As if I give a shit.

She bites down on the side of one finger, thinking...
thinking... the screen pulling down and destroying data at an
incredible rate, gutting the servers...

Beth releases her finger.

The servers.

Beth runs from her office and sprints across the empty lab. She
yanks open the door to a small caged area that houses the drives
containing all their programming and data. Until now, Beth had
never worried that the lab's network was completely self-contained,
cut off from the rest of the world. She knew her laboratory was
one of the safest environments a human could construct. The
entire mountainside could burn like an inferno for weeks and anyone trapped inside the lab wouldn't even feel warm. It was completely isolated, inside and out, from moisture, fire, heat, even
earthquakes. If someone were to make it down the elevator with
a bomb, the server cage would shutter-seal the second it was deto-
nated, the vibrations alone turning the cage into an impenetrable
steel box with enough sustainable battery power to last a full year.
From all physical dangers, the lab was a fortress.

From network dangers, it could only be damaged from the
inside. By those with access.

Like Beth.

Idiot!

As she enters the server cage, part of her is more angry with
her husband than she'd ever been during their life together. She
pushes through her harsh feelings of hurt and betrayal, of the pal-
pable *shame* at being so stupid as to open a program within their
data walls because of a mysterious video, embarrassed at letting
her feelings, and her exhausted mind, corrupt her judgment.

Reaching the access device for the servers, she flips open a
monitor and an archaic mechanical keyboard. Not incredibly
well-versed in server management, she figures she can't possibly

make things worse and begins furiously typing commands to shut down the servers and reboot the system to the last backup point, something it (thankfully) creates every six hours.

More than enough time to undo her fuckery.

She hopes.

But if it ate into the software itself, the code will have to be replaced, line by line. You're talking weeks of work, maybe months. Time you don't have!

"Shut up," Beth mumbles, chastising her inner thoughts as she finishes entering the commands and taps the ENTER key.

Immediately, the screen goes dark. The soft hum of the running drives goes silent.

Beth waits a moment, watching, praying. "Come on, come on..."

Soon, *clicking* and *whirring* sounds begin emanating from the console as the hardware starts the process of booting itself back to life.

"Yes!"

Beth runs from the cage back to her office. Her computer, still powered, shows nothing but a dark screen. She taps the power button, and this time the device obediently shuts down.

She falls roughly into her chair and huffs out a held breath, feeling as if she's just run through a burning building, which, metaphorically, isn't too far from the truth. She leans forward, eyes closed in a silent prayer to the gods of science, then opens them.

"Please..." she says, then reaches out and taps the stagnant power button on her device. The screen flickers, then lights up, showing her normal array of icons.

A message appears in the lower corner, informing her the system has been reloaded from a saved backup. The time stamp on the backup is 8:08:32. Just over two hours ago.

Before she sent a corrupting virus spiraling into her network.

She studies the screen closely, searching for the red folder, but it's gone. She feels both exultation and relief, followed by a pang of misery.

Gone.

The video, also, is gone.

A message from her husband she'll never see again.

One more part of him—of *them*—deleted forever.

TWENTY-FOUR

Asleep in her bed, Beth is stirred awake by movement in the dark.

The sound of her door creaking open, then footsteps.

The pressure of someone sitting at the end of her mattress...

She opens her eyes, fixing on the bright red digits of the clock on her nightstand. The time flashes: 12:00—12:00—12:00—12:00—12:00...

Power must be out, she thinks, her mind groggy.

Sensing a presence, she lifts her head and looks toward the foot of the bed.

Isabella sits there silently, in the shadows, her small, thin body a black scythe cut into the surrounding dark.

"Honey?" Beth says. "What's going on?"

The shadowed head turns, but Beth isn't sure which way her daughter is facing. When she speaks, it's quiet and distant, as if coming not from the little girl on the bed, but from another room altogether. "Are you there, Mommy?"

Beth sits up, disturbed. "What? Yes, honey, I'm right here."

Isabella's head jerks upward. "I can't see you!" she says loudly, sounding on the verge of tears. "I miss you so much."

Beth rubs at her eyes, desperate to clear the fog from her slow, sleepy brain. "Isabella, don't be silly. I'm sitting right here. Did you have a nightmare?"

Isabella is quiet for a moment. When she speaks, it's little more than a whisper.

It freezes Beth's blood.

"I forgot the champagne," she says.

"Isabella, please..."

"It's your birthday, and you deserve champagne on your birthday."

Then the shadowy form moves—crawls up the bed toward Beth until the face catches a splash of moonlight, and in the blue-tinted glow she can see her daughter's strained face, her wide, expressionless eyes.

Looking into those eyes, Beth gasps. Even in the dim light she notices Isabella's irises fluttering between brown and white, as if her eyes contained the repeated, rapid shuttering of an old film camera.

As if she were traveling.

Beth begins to whimper. "No, baby," she begs. "Don't go. Please don't go."

Isabella leans in closer, her eyes flickering faster, faster...

"I'll be right back," she whispers.

She climbs off the bed—too fast—and Beth tries to reach for her but she's gone, running away, her laughter coming from outside, from above, from beneath the bed...

"Isabella!"

Bright lights fill the bedroom window, growing brighter, blasting the room with a blinding yellow light. A horn blares and there's a wall-shaking *CRASH* as the window implodes and glass fills the air like a cloud of shattered death.

☙

"Beth!"

Beth jerks awake, nearly tumbling off the small couch she's

curled up on. She looks up and sees Tariq standing over her, one hand resting not so gently on her shoulder.

She's in her office. But she has no idea of the time... or if it's day or night.

"Tariq?" she says groggily, then forces herself to sit up, ignoring the jabs of pain from her lower back and legs, cramped from the awkward sleeping conditions. "What time is it?"

He removes his hand, takes a step back. "A few minutes past seven. I came in early to get things ready for your travel today. Found you here." He gives her a steady look. "Beth, you were yelling in your sleep."

She nods. "Nightmare," she says, the images of the dream already flitting from her memory. "Jesus, I feel terrible."

"Here." He turns to grab a steaming mug he set down on her desk. "God's elixir."

Beth takes the coffee in both hands and has a deliriously wonderful sip. "Thank you."

"Can't believe you worked all night," he says, shaking his head.

With a jolt of alarm, Beth recalls the previous evening. The virus. Rebooting the system, going through the software to make sure nothing had been lost or damaged. She takes another sip of coffee, wincing at the heat but relishing the much-needed caffeine.

"Look, we had an issue last night. A corrupt file or something. I rebooted the servers—"

"You what?"

"...and I think everything is fine. But please, let's run diagnostics on the entire system before we stick my head in that machine today."

Tariq looks aghast but nods. "Yeah, okay. But we only have a couple of hours."

Beth sighs. "I know. Let's do what we can. I checked most of the code last night, ran some virus filters, checked for obvious anomalies, found nothing. But I'd feel better if you could run a complete set."

"Yeah, no problem. I'm on it. You want to run home? Get a shower?"

"No time. I'll be fine."

Tariq heads for the door, then turns. "Any idea where the corrupt file came from?"

Guiltily, Beth shakes her head. "One second I was analyzing data, the next all hell broke loose. We'll figure out our leaks later, okay?"

Tariq doesn't look convinced, but he nods once more and heads out to the lab, leaving Beth to get her head straight for the morning's travel. She's beyond exhausted. Her body hurts; her head feels thick and heavy; her eyes sting from lack of sleep and dehydration. To make things worse, her nerves are shot, and the very idea of going through the wormhole again twists her stomach into knots and sends a surge of acid reflux to burn her throat. But she also knows there's no choice.

She recalls her words to Langan in his office the day prior but takes little solace from them. *I've already watched them all die.*

She can only pray it's the truth. That wherever she goes, it's someplace good.

She doubts her mind will survive anything else.

TWENTY-FIVE

Beth settles back onto the bed of the machine as Tariq secures the Velcro straps and places the sensors around her head. The balcony isn't as full as last time, the board members' proxies apparently having seen enough. But Jim sits stoically before the monitors. Sitting alongside him is Chiyo Nakada, who offered Beth a surprisingly warm smile upon entering the lab. Despite herself, Beth smiled back, even offered a small wave. For whatever reason, she couldn't bring herself to be upset with the reporter's hit piece. Maybe it was how much it tweaked Jim that made it, in her mind, almost worth it.

The three directors are in attendance, of course, Abigail Lee seated in the balcony with Langan and the reporter, apparently content to watch the program she was (supposedly) overseeing implode on a monitor.

Terry Adams and Jonathan, however, are both on the main floor, seated in empty workstations only a few feet from the machine pit, as if on high alert in case she has a recurrence of the trauma and drama brought on from her previous travel. She notices Adams is gripping a black leather satchel in his lap and has no doubt it contains several hypodermic needles, each filled to the brim with 100 cc's of calm-the-fuck-down.

Tariq spent the entirety of his morning finishing every diagnostic he could possibly fit in before anyone arrived but thankfully found nothing wrong with the programming. The software, he assured her, was sound.

Still, the incident with Colson's video and the ensuing virus had left an irksome worm in Beth's mind, as if whatever damage she'd inadvertently done was deeper than they'd had time to find during their hasty review. Part of her thinks the virus is still there, hidden somewhere within the weblike framework of the code, biding its time. Having a massive laser shoot a burst of energy at the traveler's head is already terrifying enough; to think that the system controlling it might somehow go rogue adds an entire other layer of concern and fear.

It'll be fine, she thinks as Tariq finishes his preparations.

Jonathan comes over to where Beth lies, now strapped down and immobile. He leans close so as not to be overheard, his eyes heavy with concern. "You don't have to do this, you know. If you honestly think Jim is going to pull the plug, you're not thinking clearly. He's too close. You're too close."

Beth, unable to move her head, simply shifts her eyes over to his. "Jonathan," she says, her voice barely a whisper. "I need to tell you something."

Jonathan nods. "Okay."

"I'm scared."

A tear runs from the corner of Beth's eye, and she blinks quickly before more can spill.

Jonathan frowns, looks behind him, then quickly wipes the tear away with the back of one finger, not wanting it seen on the monitors when the feed goes live. "If there's something you're not telling us, Beth ... if there's a danger here, we need to abort. Fuck the article."

"It's fine, it's okay," she says. "I just wanted to say it out loud. I wanted you to know so you can ... I don't know ... " Beth takes a deep, shuddering breath, lets it out. "Keep an eye on me, okay?"

After a beat, Jonathan nods. "Of course."

Jim's voice comes from up high, like a confused god calling down from Olympus. "Everything all right?"

Beth holds Jonathan's eyes another moment, then her eyes move away, and up, toward the overhanging laser. "Let's go," she says, loudly enough that Tariq begins typing in commands.

As the machine begins powering up, Jonathan steps back, then takes a seat next to Adams at one of the empty consoles, looking down at the screen. Tariq previously activated the monitor stations for both him and Dr. Adams, and as Jonathan watches, the screen in front of him lights up with data. He has a front-row seat to Beth's vitals along with a window showing a live feed of her arrival point. He looks at Tariq and gives a thumbs-up, nodding his thanks.

In the balcony above, the clear-tech screens also spring to life. The countdown on the far left shows the time, currently stuck at **1:30**. As is was before, the middle monitor is a wash of blue, the third a repeat of Beth's vitals.

Chiyo leans over to Jim, keeps her voice low. "You didn't need to do this, you know. It's not going to change anything, and to be frank, it comes off as reckless. Desperate. She's your best asset."

Jim smiles, waves a hand toward the reporter. "Dr. Darlow knows what she's doing. And in a few seconds you'll see history being made. Again."

Chiyo frowns but says nothing further, eyes moving to the screen as electricity fills the air, the building *huuummmm* of the laser as it powers up tickling her eardrums and making the hairs rise on her arms.

Tariq's steady voice comes through the speakers.

"Sending pulse in three...two...one."

The triangle prongs of the laser ignite, pitchforking into three streams, one toward the receiver in Beth's forehead, the other two shooting into the curved receivers on either side of her.

The timer begins counting down as the viewing monitor swirls, stirring brilliant swatches of blue before distorting into a blur of colors, then separating into light and shadow.

Deep into the arrival point, Beth opens her eyes.

The monitor floods with light, showing them Beth's POV. There's a fish-eyed, distorted view of a white surface, possibly a ceiling. A hard, focused spotlight is pointed directly into her eyes. On the blurry edges of Beth's vision, there are people. Faces looking down at her.

Jim, watching closely, has only a moment to notice that one of the faces is wearing a surgical mask.

Suddenly, and without warning, the monitor goes dark.

The feed has been cut.

Jim sits up, eyes darting between the three screens. Beth's vitals are consistent, unwavering. Whatever's she's experiencing, it's having little effect on her present biological state. The center screen is still dark, murky, as if Beth's vision of the past has been covered with a heavy blanket.

Or a blindfold.

The far left screen shows the countdown.

1:15

1:14

1:13...

Abruptly, Jim stands, steps quickly to the edge of the balcony, grips the railing with white-knuckled hands. "We've lost visuals."

Tariq, typing fast, doesn't turn around. "Little busy right now, Jim."

Jonathan turns, looks upward, and meets Jim's eyes.

"Do you have picture?" Jim asks, but Jonathan only shakes his head.

Suddenly, the screen showing Beth's vitals also goes dark.

"Lost vitals..." Tariq says calmly.

Jonathan stands, begins pacing behind Tariq. "What's going on? Is she in danger?"

Tariq shrugs. "I'm working on it, but I've got nothing." He turns his head toward Jonathan, his normally placid expression now lined with concern. "Should I bring her out?"

Jim, overhearing, yells down. "Don't you dare! And get me visuals!"

1:02

1:01

1:00

0:59...

"Working on it..."

For the next thirty seconds, no one speaks. Jonathan keeps his eyes on Beth, but her body lies still. Peaceful. Adams steps past him, muttering an apology, and gets close enough to press his fingers to her wrist. He nods, announces that her pulse is steady and strong.

With only ten seconds remaining, Chiyo looks at Jim. "How do we even know she's traveling? Without the visual of what she's experiencing, how do we know she's not just lying there having a nap?"

Jim rubs his chin. "The wormhole is open and she's connected to...*something*. The visuals, these monitors, are only here for show-and-tell, Ms. Nakada. The rest is pure data. Besides, there's a chance we can retrieve the video of her arrival after the fact. She's gone somewhere," he says, ruminating. "And when she comes back, we'll get answers, I promise you that."

Chiyo shakes her head, unconvinced, as the timer counts down the final seconds.

0:03
0:02
0:01 ...

Tariq's voice once more comes through the balcony speakers. "Memory drive closed. I'm closing the wormhole."

The sound of vibrating electricity inside the lab declines, then goes quiet.

All eyes are on Beth.

Jonathan goes to her first, begins unstrapping the restraints. He puts a hand on her cheek. "Beth?"

Beth's eyes open slowly, dreamily, as if she's indeed done nothing more than woken from a nap. She looks at Jonathan, confusion in her eyes. "Where am I?"

Jim, Chiyo, and Abigail Lee come down from the viewing platform. Jim rushes forward, pushes Jonathan aside, and stands over Beth's prone body. "Where did you go? What happened?"

"Jesus, Jim, give her a minute," Jonathan says.

"Fuck off," Jim growls, then looks back down at Beth. "Where?"

Beth, now free of the straps, only shakes her head, her eyes hazy and lost.

"I don't know ... I ..."

"Beth, come on. Focus."

Free from the head strap, Beth turns her head. Her eyes meet Jim's and, suddenly, they clear, her expression becoming one of interest rather than concern, as if she is trying to solve a riddle.

"I have no idea," she says.

"You were there," Jim says under his breath. "That's impossible. The data ... We know you traveled somewhere. Just tell us what you remember."

Beth sits up slowly, gently removing the sensors from her forehead and temples. Her eyes find Jonathan's for a moment, then she turns to gaze at Jim, so cool and steady that he takes a half step back.

"I'm sorry," she says. "I don't remember a thing."

TWENTY-SIX

Bullshit!"

Beth's never seen Jim so angry. Sure, she's pushed his buttons on occasion, and they've had their spats over the years (albeit with increasing frequency as of late), but he's not one to lose his composure, to *show* his emotions in such a raw fashion.

But he's showing them now.

Chiyo Nakada was escorted out of the lab by Abigail Lee and Terry Adams while the rest of them huddled around the machine like kids in a gas station parking lot, each of them with their own frustration, their own brand of disappointment.

No matter how hard she tries, Beth can't remember anything about the trip. She remembers that usual *lifting* feeling as her consciousness was being mapped and sent through the wormhole. She remembers the sensation of being *somewhere* . . . and she remembers feeling pain.

Lots of pain.

"I'm sorry, Jim. I don't know what happened," Beth says tiredly. "Tariq is in control of things when I'm, you know, being blasted through a rift in space-time, so I have no clue why the feed went dark."

"Don't get cute with me!" Jim roars, taking an aggressive step toward Beth, one fat finger pointed at her forehead, face reddening. "You did this on purpose! This is some sort of... sabotage or some shit."

Beth shakes her head, incredulous. "Sabotage? Of what? My career? That woman who *you* let into *my* lab is about to smear my reputation and denounce my life's work. You think I'm doing this on purpose, Jim? Really? I got news for you; we're not all as petty as you are."

Jonathan steps forward, angling his body between Beth—still sitting on the machine's bed—and Jim, who's pacing like a pissed-off gorilla. "Whoa, okay. Time out, you guys. As trite as it sounds, we're all on the same team here. So why don't we cool down and try to figure out what exactly happened?"

Tariq raises a hand from his console, and all heads turn toward him. "I'm already running diagnostics to see if the machine did anything weird during Beth's travel. I'm also doing a deep scan for any bits of fragmented information that might have been lost during the data transit. It's possible we can rebuild a visual of Beth's trip, but it'll take some time. Regardless, once we have that information, along with the diagnostic report, we'll look it over and find out what happened, and hopefully reconstruct the travel session."

Beth stands and walks over to Tariq's console, glances down at the screen. "Can you bring up the map of my brain activity during the trip?" Tariq clicks a few keys, and a complex multicolored graph begins flowing across the screen. Beth points to one of the lines that shoots straight down to the bottom and stays there. "I don't know... it just doesn't make any sense. For my neural feed to shut down like that?" She shakes her head. "It couldn't be something caused by the machine. It's not a program glitch."

"Then what would cause it?" Jonathan asks.

Jim stops his pacing and turns toward Beth, eager to hear the answer.

Beth shrugs. "That's a direct feed from my brain. So, if it went dark, it's because of something that happened to *me*, not the software. My brain, for lack of a better way to put it, simply... turned off."

"Well, that's just great," Jim says. "You had a little blackout and now we're fucked to high heaven. This is *exactly* the reason I told you to bring in someone else to travel. Someone who isn't as, you know, *delicate* as you are."

Beth takes a menacing step in Jim's direction. "Fuck you, Jim. Why don't we send you through next time? Maybe you can feel what it's like to have a working dick again."

"And that's it!" Jonathan yells, raising his arms. "I'm calling it. Right now. Jim, this is an incredibly stressful situation, and Beth needs time to get us the answers you want. So let's all take a breath and return to our corners. First thing tomorrow, we'll run the debrief and start figuring this out."

Jim stares daggers at Beth, but when he speaks, his voice is level. "Today," he says. "We debrief today. This afternoon."

Beth snorts. "Fine with me. I'll tell Abigail to have the recording sent back. The answers will still be at least twenty-four hours behind any alteration in the present timeline."

Jim turns on his heel and storms toward the elevator. "Three PM sharp!" he yells over his shoulder.

Jonathan gives Beth a last, indiscernible look, and follows Jim. Once the doors close, Beth collapses into one of the empty console chairs, plants her face in her hands.

Tariq stands, seemingly unsure for a moment, then walks over and sits next to her, placing a tentative hand on her shoulder. "You okay, boss?"

Beth sniffs, raises her head. "I'm just tired, man. I'm wrung out."

Tariq nods. "I hear you." He pauses a moment, then sits back casually, folds his arms. "Think we're fired?"

Beth looks at him and, for the first time, wishes they had become better friends, rather than associates. She wonders why they've never had dinner or drinks. And she feels emptied out by that fact, by her own negligence toward caring about those she relies on.

She offers a weary smile.

"Yeah. I think we are."

☙

The elevator stops at the third floor, and Beth lets out a frustrated sigh.

"Because of course..." she mutters as the doors slide open.

"Beth."

Abigail Lee steps into the elevators, almost shyly, as if feeling bad for invading Beth's space, despite the elevator's being for all employees of their wing. "I assume we're both heading to the same place?"

Beth smiles lamely. "Another glorious debrief."

Abigail nods as the doors close.

This close, Beth gets a whiff of her flowery perfume, can make out the carefully applied makeup that sheds a few years from her features. Beth leans against the wall, anxious to be through the debrief, eager to be alone again with her work.

As the elevator begins to rise, however, Abigail reaches out toward the panel and flips a small red switch. The elevator halts.

Beth leans forward. "What are you doing?"

Abigail doesn't turn but keeps her gaze facing forward. Her jaw is working, as if she were chewing on a problem, or on words that may or may not want to come out. Finally, she turns to peer at Beth, wearing a pensive, guarded expression.

"Look, I know we aren't best friends, and that's appropriate because I'm, technically at least, your supervisor. But I..."

Abigail blows out a breath, gives her head a little shake, as if jarring the thoughts free.

"But I want you to know that I have your back, Beth. I want you to know that when I say something, I'm speaking the truth. I wouldn't... I'd never purposely lie or mislead you."

Beth crosses her arms, feeling uncomfortable with the enclosed space, the almost claustrophobic conversation, but manages to nod. "Okay," she says quietly. "Thanks."

Abigail looks back at the elevator panel, as if debating what floor they should go to... then continues. "I don't think you could say the same for everyone in this company," she says. "Most people here have two mouths, Beth. Two faces. But... while I won't say you can always trust me... I will say that you can always count on me. If needed. You can talk to me about anything."

"I appreciate that," Beth says, then chuckles, going for levity to break the awkwardness of the encounter. "I'll be sure to let you know all my darkest secrets."

Abigail scoffs lightly. "There are no secrets here, Beth."

Beth is about to reply, to ask a hundred questions—one of which being what spurred the normally demure program director to have this conversation in the first place—when Abigail reaches out and flicks the switch once more. The elevator jolts to life, and only seconds later there's a *ding.* The doors slide open to reveal the second-floor hallway.

"See you in a minute," Abigail says, then steps quickly from the elevator, leaving Beth to wonder what the hell—what the hell *exactly*—is going on with the employees at Langan Corporation.

First Jerry, now Abigail.

Warnings everywhere, she thinks, trying to subdue the rising anxiety creeping into her chest. *And all of them directed at me.*

"Well, booyah for me," she mumbles, stepping out of the elevator and away from the lingering scent of the program director's flowery perfume, a fetid reminder that their strange conversation ever took place.

TWENTY-SEVEN

Beth stands at the podium.

For the first time during a debrief, she has an audience other than the panel. Seated in the chairs behind her are Jim, Chiyo Nakada, and Tariq. The hope is that, during the Q and A session, they will be able to extract some pieces of information to explain where Beth went and what exactly happened there.

If anything, she thinks, distracted by the presence of the reporter, curious as to why Jim is still letting her hang around—as if she didn't have enough to worry about without being scrutinized by an outsider.

Beth and Tariq spent what remained of the morning and early afternoon trying to decipher what had caused her blackout and why she couldn't remember her time at the arrival point, but came up with nothing.

I remember pain. I remember screaming.

"If we could begin," Abigail says. "We weren't able, in the short window of time we've had, to assemble any video of Dr. Darlow's trip this morning. However, with Mr. Igwebuike's help, we were able to create some still images, which I'll put on the screen now."

The tech screen to Beth's right lights up with a bright white image. There are smeared shapes—what appear to be people—

standing very close to her. Notably, one of the faces is partially covered with a surgical mask. Beth reaches for the memory—*any* memory—desperately hoping to fill in the gaps, to remember what past point in her life she traveled to.

"We've discussed this image quite a bit," the program director continues, "and given the masked face, we believe it to be a hospital. Or possibly an operating room."

Jonathan interrupts, lowering his head to his microphone. "Director, I think we should get playback matching out of the way before we discuss more hypotheticals."

Dr. Lee nods. "Is that okay with you, Beth?"

"Yes, it's fine."

"Very well," Lee says, her nasally voice steady and patient, almost bored. "Please note we are beginning the redundant question session, matching to date of travel, which was this morning, March 24, 2044. Recorded the same day, 3:06 PM."

As usual, the room fills with a soft blanket of static from the hidden speakers, followed by a man's deep voice reciting the six variable questions.

Please state your name and today's date.

Beth lets out a breath, answers.
"Beth Darlow. March 24, 2044."

Who is the president of the United States?

"James Whitmore."

Describe your marital status.

"Widowed."

In one word, describe your childhood.

Beth thinks a moment, momentarily forgetting the answer she typically offers. Flashes of her parents, the plane crashing, her uncle holding her hand at the funeral...
"Happy," she says.

Name two members of your immediate family.

This time Beth doesn't pause.
"My uncle, Brett Hawkins. My cousin, Milly Hawkins."

If you could change one moment in your life, what would it be?

"I would stop my husband from leaving on the day he was killed."
There's a momentary pause as the recording concludes. The speakers *click*, then goes silent. Dr. Lee speaks into her microphone. "Recording ended. Please begin playback of pre-travel session, dated March 23, 2044, Dr. Beth Darlow."
Without warning, Beth feels sick. A heavy wave of nausea passes through her. She's suddenly lightheaded and is forced to close her eyes, gripping the sides of the podium hard enough to feel the ache in her fingers. She focuses her breathing.
Let's just get through this.
Once more, the speakers click on, and the computerized voice fills the room. Everyone remains quiet, waiting patiently as the recording of the prior day's questions and answers is played back. Beth takes a deep breath, only half listening to her own recorded answers, desperate to get out of there and back to her lab.

Please state your name and today's date.

Beth Darlow. March 23, 2044.

Who is the president of the United States?

James Whitmore.

Describe your marital status.

Widowed.

In one word, describe your childhood.

Happy.

Name two members of your immediate family.

My uncle, Brett Hawkins. My daughter, Isabella Darlow.

Beth freezes. Her lowered head shoots upward, closed eyes open wide. She notes the look of surprise on Jonathan's expression. Watches as he leans over and whispers something to Dr. Adams beside him, who doesn't seem to understand...

Beth's whole body has gone numb. Trembling, she leans into the microphone, speaking loudly enough to be heard over the playback. "Can you play that back?"

...change one moment in your life, what would it be?

I would stop my husband from leaving...

Beth raises her voice, all but yelling now. "What did I say?" she says, hating the tremor in her voice. A rushing sound has filled her head, and she fights to stay focused. "What...please, please play that back?" She smacks one hand against the podium, hard enough that Dr. Lee jumps in her seat ten feet away. "What did I say?!"

Jonathan leans forward, looking shaken. "Just...just wait a moment."

Beth turns around, sees Jim staring at her with a sort of befuddlement. Nakada only stares forward, eyes wide and curious. Tariq's brow is furrowed in confusion and concern.

Beth spins back toward the panel, grips the stem of the microphone in one hand. Her whole body is shaking now. "Dr. Lee, I need you to play that back." Her eyes dart to Jonathan, who is now standing, leaning over the other two members of the panel, all of them talking in hurried whispers. "Jonathan," she says, pleading. "Please play it back."

Jonathan, his face ghostly pale, leans back over his own chair, grabs the end of his microphone. "Director, I'd like to suggest we...that we..."

He pauses, and his eyes lock onto Beth. "I think we need to reconvene."

Beth steps away from the podium and approaches the dais. She points at the ceiling, in the general direction of the hidden speakers. "Play it again!" she yells. "Jesus Christ, didn't you hear? Something's wrong. There's something wrong!"

Jonathan steps down off the dais, walks toward Beth with open arms, palms up. She glares at him as he approaches, feeling her muscles liquefy. Her head is spinning. "Jonathan, what's happening? I said I had a daughter? What the fuck is this?"

He grabs her, pulls her into an embrace. "It's okay, we need—"

The program director speaks loudly into her mic, overriding him. "Before we dismiss, please note for the record these recordings are anomalous."

Chiyo turns to Jim. "What happened? What does this mean?"

Jim shakes his head. "Nothing," he says. "It doesn't mean a thing."

Before she can reply, he stands and catches the program director's eye. He points to a corner of the room.

Abigail nods, types on her console, then leans into the microphone once more. "This debriefing is no longer being recorded. We will review the transcripts for technical anomalies out of session. Dr. Darlow, you are dismissed."

Beth pushes Jonathan away, glares at the program director. "What did I say, goddamn it?!" She approaches the table on the dais, slams her palms down on top of it. "You need to play it again. What the fuck did I say?!"

She feels Jonathan grab her from behind, and then the room is tilting and a voice shouts for Dr. Adams to *do something*, followed by the jagged sounds of someone screaming, crying.

As Beth falls backward, collapsing into a blessed abyss of unconsciousness, she realizes that the sounds of wailing despair, of unfiltered heartbreak, are coming from her.

TWENTY-EIGHT

Darkness swallows me gently, wholly.

I welcome it, luxuriate in the soothing folds of unconsciousness.

Slowly, a hard light pervades, seeps in like poison. Sound corrupts my cocoon, my sanctuary of death, and like the rending of a veil, my vision splits between light and darkness, solace and horror.

"I have no heartbeat."

A woman's voice. Not alarmed. Not screaming or hysterical.

Calm. Stoic. Professional.

"Beth? I need you to push for me."

Another woman. Her name falls into place like a puzzle piece completing an image of nothing, of flat gray mist. It's Dr. Hanna, my OB.

A memory within a memory: lying on a soft bed, cool jelly on my extended belly, the image of the child growing inside me. The pure joy of bringing this incredible new life into the world.

I shake my head. Tubes have been plunged into my arms. There are twice as many people in the room as there were ten minutes ago. I can't keep track; I'm focused on my breathing.

The breathing, and the pain.

But this isn't surgery. Because I'm not sick. I'm not harmed in any way.

I'm giving birth.

I have no heartbeat.

I look up at Dr. Hanna, wide-eyed. I scream in her face like a madwoman. No words, no curses, just a shrill, barbaric scream of horror.

Her eyes stay steady, locked onto mine. "Beth, you need to push. You need to push *right now* so we can try to save your baby. Do you understand? Right. NOW."

I push.

And I scream, and I push, and I scream, and I push...

I push to save the life of my daughter. To save the life of a child I feel I already know, know deep down in my heart. A child who will be all of me. The best of me. And so I shriek like a demon until my throat is raw and the veins in my neck are swelled to bursting and my eyes bulge because I need these doctors to save her, to save my child's life.

"That's very good! You're doing great, Beth! Now, don't stop, don't stop..." Dr. Hanna yells and yells like an insane cheerleader, encouraging me to keep on, to push through this wall of unfathomable hurt.

There's a sliding rush and the muscles of my body go slack all at once, as if my strings have been cut and I'm free to collapse. I close my eyes and fall backward into the bed, sweat-drenched hair plastered to my forehead and cheeks. *She's out,* I think, and I want to laugh, want to cry. *She's out, and now they can save her.*

With the last of my strength, I raise my head, force my exhausted, stinging eyes to open. I see Dr. Hanna seated at my splayed feet, handling the newborn child between my thighs.

The nurses behind her are no longer bustling. They're standing still, watching.

One woman crosses herself.

Dr. Hanna is wrapping her in a blue blanket. I think for a moment that she's getting ready to hand her to me. I wonder, absently, why I don't hear the baby cry.

The doctor turns her back to me, still holding Isabella—because that's the name we settled on, after much debate, Colson and I.

Isabella.

Now she's gently placing the baby into a plastic box. A nurse comes to stand beside me.

With a numb detachment, I feel the placenta arrive. No one notices.

The nurse is stroking my head like a mother would do for a sick child. She's saying, *Shhh now...you're doing great...shhh... just relax...relax...*

After a few moments, Dr. Hanna turns around to face me. She lowers her mask and tells me, in a soft, lilting voice, that my child was stillborn. That she had most likely died at some point in the last half hour, and there was no chance of reviving her. Of saving her.

Of saving me.

I hear Colson's rough voice by the doorway, so loud in the sudden silence. He's asking to come back in. He wants to come back because at some point they'd thrown him out...I can't recall when...

A nurse opens the door and he rushes into the room, looking from face to face. He catches my eye, then turns toward the plastic box holding our child.

He begins to bellow in agony and a nurse is putting her arm around him as he doubles over at the waist and the part of me trapped inside this body begs for release, begs to forget, and when the darkness finally comes for me I don't just welcome it, I *leap* for it, throw myself into it without reserve, without caution, because I need to be away from here; I need to be anywhere but here.

Most of all, more than anything, I need to forget.

0:03...

But then...something shifts in the new darkness.

Something here wants me gone.

0:02...

I feel a venomous *hate* surround me. The cosmic heart of a treacherous universe pounds in my ears in a language I can't possibly fathom; its rage surges into my veins like a dark drug.

With an undeniable force I'm thrust away, out of the dark. Discarded.

0:01...

And I wake.

And, for a while, I'm allowed to forget.

And then, like a vision of hell, I'm forced to remember.

With the pain of being pushed into a lake of fire...

I remember everything.

TWENTY-NINE

Beth, rising slowly to consciousness, whispers the words as she opens her eyes, squinting at the bright white light of the room.

I remember everything.

After taking a moment to let her eyes adjust and her mind clear, she raises her head and is surprised, but not frightened, to find herself lying in what appears to be a hospital bed. She turns her head and sees Jonathan in the far corner of the sterile cream-colored room, sitting vigil in a molded plastic chair and tapping busily into a tablet.

"Hey," she says, loudly enough so he can hear her.

He looks up, eyes wide with surprise, then sets down the tablet. He stands and walks to her. "Hey yourself. How are you feeling?"

Beth looks around the room, taking in the smooth, plain walls, the line of beds, the medical equipment. "Where am I?"

Jonathan smiles. "Don't tell me you've never been to our state-of-the-art medical bay before."

"Wait? This is . . . I'm still at Langan?"

Jonathan nods. "Yeah, this is part of the South Wing. Don't imagine you'd get over here much. Essentially biolabs, medical treatment, and development. There's an entire floor of pharma below us. You wouldn't believe what those guys are cooking up down there."

Beth nods. "Good to know I'm not Jim's only plow horse." She pushes herself up to a sitting position, then shifts her body to let her legs dangle off the edge of the bed. The room sways for a moment, then steadies.

"Hey, take it easy." Jonathan puts a hand on her shoulder, looks into her eyes with clinical focus, as if for anomalies or aberrations. "You want me to get Terry? He checked you out pretty good when you were under, and there's nothing to worry about. But still, maybe I should—"

"No," she says quickly, stalling. "No, please. I just need a minute." Beth puts a hand to her forehead, takes a few deep breaths. Then she lifts her eyes to meet his. "What happened in there? Seriously, Jonathan...what the fuck happened?"

Jonathan shakes his head, brow furrowed. "The previous answers can't be explained. Maybe you were...hell, I don't know. I can't explain why you'd say what you said."

"But if it's not true...if I was wrong...why wouldn't you have said something *then*? No one questioned it. So why now?"

"Honestly?" he says, pressing fingers into his tired eyes. "I have no fucking clue."

Beth nods, and they sit silently for a moment, neither of them having the words for what just occurred, what Beth has been through.

When Jonathan lowers his hands, however, he appears newly determined. His tone is confident. "But look, I know what you're thinking, and I know it's a mind-fuck, okay? But, Beth, listen, I've known you for more than three years. I knew Colson. I've been to your house for dinner, right?"

Beth scoffs. "You brought that blonde..."

"Right, right," he says. "Point is, Beth. I *know* you. And maybe I don't fully understand what weird glitch just happened with those debrief questions, but I guarantee you, beyond a shadow of a doubt, that you have never had a child. So yeah, the general thinking is that the recording is messed up, or something caused it to change, or ... I don't know. But I'm standing here as proof that it's wrong. It was always just you and Colson."

Beth lowers her head, nods. "I know. That's what I was about to tell you."

"What?"

"The arrival point. The one my brain apparently blocked out. I know where I went. I remember..."

Jonathan turns and grabs a nearby chair, a twin to the one he was sitting in previously, and pulls it over. He sits and stares up at Beth, his expression one of eternal patience.

"Tell me."

Beth sighs wearily. She doesn't meet his eyes but instead stares down into her folded hands, doing her best to remain impassive. "It was about four years ago. Before we came to Langan." She lifts her eyes to his, wanting—needing—to see another human face. "I was pregnant. It was a girl. I had no problems leading up to the birth, but something went wrong and ... well, the baby..." She takes a breath, tilts her head and stares at the bright lights set into the ceiling, shakes her head.

Don't cry, Beth. Please, no more tears. No more.

"She was stillborn," she says. "My little girl died during birth."

Jonathan put a hand on her knee. "I'm so sorry." Then his eyes widen in alarm. "My God, don't tell me that's where you traveled."

Beth nods, smiles sadly. "And here I thought..."

"What?"

"That I had no more pain left to give."

☙

After a final inspection by Dr. Adams, Beth is allowed to leave the medical bay, after which she goes immediately down to the lab, where Tariq is waiting to give her the highlights of the debrief aftermath.

"Honestly? Jim was freaked-out. Everyone was. I mean, that was some crazy shit, Beth. After you went down, Terry and Jonathan called medical for a gurney, and they wheeled you out. I wanted to go with you but Jim ordered me back here, told me to find out what went wrong. And that reporter? Man, she was taking a *lot* of notes. It was a scene."

Beth paces while he sits at his console, back to the machine, watching her.

"Well, I'm fine. But we need to talk with Abigail and find out what might have happened with those recordings. That anomaly, it must be something we haven't run into yet. I mean . . . it has to be a technical error, obviously."

Tariq nods slowly, his expression unreadable as he studies her. "Obviously."

Beth stops pacing, turns to him. "What's that supposed to mean?"

But Tariq only shrugs. "All I'm saying is there's a reason we do those questions. It's to verify there has been no disruption in the timeline. So, now we're saying the data from the questions is wrong, but it has to be a mistake? A glitch? I mean . . . hell, I don't know."

Beth wants to slap him, but she only points, anger rising to her cheeks like fire. "Get this straight, Tariq. I don't have a daughter. The arrival point? Where I traveled? That was the day she was stillborn. The fucking *moment* I gave birth to a . . . to . . . "

She begins hyperventilating. When he stands and takes a step toward her, she breaks down crying, sobbing.

"I'm sorry," he says, half reaching for her before she jerks away, her body a live wire.

"Don't touch me. I can't—"

"Beth. Please, I'm an idiot," he says. "You're right, it's the recording data. Something went wrong. I'll find it, I'll figure it out. First thing in the morning. But hey, right now, I think we both need to get out of here."

With a jolt, she looks at her watch, realizes just how late it is, that he waited past eight o'clock for her to come down from the infirmary. She wants to feel guilt, to feel . . . something.

He tells her to go home, to get some sleep.

She doesn't argue.

ℂ⊕つ

By the time Beth arrives home, it's full dark.

She slowly climbs the porch steps toward her front door, the entire house sunken in deep shadow, the moon nothing more than a dull slice of silver cut into the fabric of the night sky.

She disables the alarm before turning on the porch light and closing the door, carelessly throws the heavy security bolt into place. She flips another switch and the lights for the hallway stretching out behind her come to life. She kicks off her shoes and walks deeper into the quiet house, past the darkened living room, and into the kitchen. She dumps her bag on the table, opens the refrigerator—currently occupied by a half-full bottle of Chardonnay, three bottles of light beer, the remains of a packaged roasted chicken she'd picked up for dinner the night before, a plastic bag of tortillas, and a door full of aging condiments.

She ignores the chicken, takes one of the beers.

She wanders back into the hallway, her eye lingering for a moment on the broad swath of empty wall just outside the kitchen.

I should hang something there, she thinks absently, and passes the closed door on her left, which leads to what was once an office but is now used primarily for storage. The desk within was used more regularly by Colson than herself, and since his death she's fallen out of the practice of using the room for anything other than a place to put clutter. Now it's partially filled with boxes—mainly Colson's clothes, books, and other personal items—and the dusty desk pushed against one wall, stacked high with dated paperwork, old textbooks, and a tablet that hasn't been powered up in a year.

Swigging from the beer, Beth goes into her bedroom, walking numbly through the dark, and drops onto her bed, ignoring the spurt of cold beer that jumps from the bottle onto her wrist.

"Lights on," she murmurs, and the two bedside lamps come alive.

Beth takes a moment to let her body relax, then rolls over, sets the beer on her nightstand, and plucks up her tablet. She taps open her contacts, taps again on the grinning visage of her friend Lucy. Moments later, the call connects and Lucy's face fills the screen.

"Hey, you," Lucy says, seemingly distracted.

"Hey yourself. I had a shit day. Calling for comfort and stuff."

Lucy leans into the camera. "Yeah, you look like hell."

Beth smiles. "Exactly what I wanted to hear."

"Look, I'd love to lick your wounds, but I've got a full-blown Timmy crisis here. Why don't you come hang out with us on Saturday?"

Beth's heart goes cold, but she tries not to let it show. "I don't know…"

Lucy gets closer, lowers her voice. "Look, I know you hate being around kids, but, you know, they're the future or whatever. Be logical about it."

Beth laughs. "Yeah, okay. But just tell me that, at some point, there will be wine and adult conversation. Honestly, I need a friend right now. Things are bad."

Lucy moves back from the camera, brow furrowed with concern. "Shit, Beth. I'm sorry. Are you okay? I can definitely call you back once I put the monster to bed."

"No, no. I'm going to pass out soon. Go take care of the kid. And yes, I'll hang out with you guys. Shockingly, I have no plans."

"All right, cool. Get some sleep, and we will one hundred percent have some boozy girl-chat time on Saturday when the little man is napping."

"Okay, I—"

There's a child's scream from the tablet, so loud and shrill Beth nearly drops it.

Lucy rolls her eyes. "Shit, sorry. I gotta run. Love you."

"Love you."

The screen goes dark, and Beth sets it aside, picks up the beer, and chugs the rest of the bottle in giant swallows. She belches contentedly, then rolls off the bed, suddenly eager to peel off her work clothes, brush her teeth, and collapse into unconsciousness.

THIRTY

Beth's sleep is shallow, anxious. Her exhausted mind races in every direction, a pinball that continues to accelerate with no outlet, banging faster and faster against corroded bumpers, cracked rubber walls, rusted springs. She moans in the dark, her body tossing as if at sea, the sheets jumbled into a sweat-soaked clump at her hip.

She has a nightmare that she's buried in sand, with only her face exposed to the heated air, the bone-white sky, mere inches from an angry white-frothed surf that grows closer with each successive wave. Within seconds she's spitting out warm seawater. Soon it's pouring over her nose, stinging her eyes, climbing her scalp.

Then she's beneath the waves, holding her breath. Wave after wave crashes over her, the surface of the sea rising slowly, rising farther and farther from her prison in the wet sand, now a sea bottom. She stares upward toward that blank slate of sky, watches the repeating surges of water as they pass above.

There are faces in the waves. A man. A girl.

There are sounds. Laughter. Crying. Screams.

When she can hold her breath no longer, she closes her eyes and opens her mouth.

The sea rushes in.

Beth comes awake, gagging, choking. Her eyes are wide with terror, her body covered in a sticky sheen of sweat. She tries to breathe, to cry out, but her throat won't open, won't take in the air she desperately needs. Her fingers curl into the wet sheet at her side, gripping it tight, as if it will hold her to reality, pin her to this existence.

Finally her throat opens and she gulps in air, forces her lungs to inhale, exhale. Her heart is hammering and the logical part of her mind knows she's having a severe anxiety attack, but the emotional part of her is still staring up through those rolling waves at that pale, lifeless sky, waiting for death.

After her breathing steadies and her heartbeat slows to a relatively normal rate, she wipes her forehead and swings her legs off the bed, relishes the cool solidity of the hardwood floor beneath the balls of her feet.

She presses her fists into her bare thighs and bows her head, debating whether to attempt sleep once more or just get up, make a pot of coffee, and start her day. She looks to the clock, sees it's just past four AM, and decides on the latter. She stands, eyes heavy with exhaustion, but feels better knowing she doesn't have to worry about fielding any more nightmares. Not tonight.

Her tank top, saturated and cooling in the night air, sticks uncomfortably to her belly and back. "Shower..." she mumbles, already eager for the feel of hot water.

Beth turns toward the bed, grimaces at the ball of damp sheets, and knows they need a wash. She's just beginning to debate whether to pull the sheets now or after her shower when her bedroom door swings slowly inward.

Beth freezes in the dark, stares at the black void of hallway just beyond the door, which has seemingly, impossibly, just opened on its own.

She stifles a scream when she hears a voice, thin and weak, come from the hall.

A little girl is singing.

I hope to see you soon,
In the country,
In the country...

Beth's blood turns to ice as a cold claw of horror shimmies up her spine and grips the back of her neck. She takes a step toward the door.

Just follow my sweet croon,
To the country,
To the country...

"Hello?" she says, feeling like an idiot, as if whoever is out there would reply. As if she'd *want* to hear a reply—some echoing, idiot voice, amused as it responds: *Hello? Yes, I'm here. Why don't you come closer so I can see you?*

Beth shakes her head, forces herself to push away the fear, the timidity. This is *her* house, and if someone is inside it, she will deal with them. She looks around her shadowed surroundings but sees nothing that might act as a weapon. Feeling exposed in nothing but a tank top and underwear, she snags a pair of sweatpants from the floor, pushes her legs through.

If I'm gonna be murdered, at least it won't be without pants.

Feeling better with her warm sweats, she takes another step toward the open door, watching through strained eyes for someone to step into the room or burst from the hall toward her, arms outstretched, a butcher knife glinting from one clenched fist.

"Oh, fuck this," she says loudly, enjoying the way her firm voice shatters the anticipation in the air. She takes two quick strides, steps through the door, and looks both ways down the narrow hallway. One direction leads to a rear set of French doors and a worn-out deck, the other toward the front of the house. She notes that both the rear door and the front door are closed; the hallway, dimly lit by slanting moonlight, is empty.

When the voice comes again, she jumps and curses. But she can pinpoint the sound now. Her brow furrows when she hears the singing once more, because she realizes that it's not a *human* voice she hears, but that of a weak, scratchy recording.

It's coming through the closed door just ahead of her on the right.

From her office.

> *I hope to see you soon,*
> *In the country,*
> *In the country.*
> *Just follow my sweet croon,*
> *To the country,*
> *To the country . . .*

Beth takes slow steps toward the sound, stopping momentarily to glance into the kitchen, which is also empty. She reaches out and turns on the light, squinting against the brightness as it brings the house to life.

Feeling more assured with the light at her back, she walks to the office door, then just past it, peeking into the moonlit living room to make sure there's no one there waiting for her. She decides against turning on more lights, not wanting to give whoever might be hiding in her office a better view of her than she would have of them.

More determined now, she steps quickly to the front door and snags a closed umbrella from a stand next to the small bench she uses to pull on her shoes in the morning. The front door, she notices, is locked and bolted.

No one came in this way. Not unless they're the most courteous burglar in the world and locked up behind themselves.

Moving stealthily back to the closed door of the office, the umbrella gripped tightly in one hand, metal point protruding from the top like a fat icepick, Beth wraps her free hand around the door's handle and, steeling herself with a quick intake of breath, thrusts the door inward. The door glides on its hinges and slams against the opposing wall with a *bang*. She walks quickly into the room, pushing the umbrella's tip before her like a soldier stabbing forward with a bayonet.

Beth takes in the office—her cluttered desk straight ahead, pushed against a closed window. To her left, nothing but the usual stacks of boxes, overflow storage filled with Colson's things—old college papers and textbooks, the ephemera of her youth, of her lost love, gathering dust.

Otherwise, the room is empty.

"Shit," she breathes, lowering the umbrella and leaning back against the doorframe.

Then the voice comes again.

> *I hope to see you soon,*
> *In the country,*
> *In the country . . .*

Beth notices two pulsing yellow dots of light atop a short stack of boxes. Tiny pinpricks in the gloom, watching her. The recorded voice singing merrily, a demonic yodel.

> *Just follow my sweet croon,*
> *To the country,*
> *To the country . . .*

Confused, she turns and flips the wall switch, illuminating the room with the overhead light. On top of one stack of boxes is a doll. It's wearing a blue dress. Blond hair spreads like foam around a peach-colored plastic head. It's eyes glow, pulsing a sickly lemon yellow.

Beth hooks the nonlethal end of the umbrella over the door handle and warily approaches the singing figurine.

I never owned a doll like this.

When the singing stops and the eyes dim to show wide white eyes painted with bright blue irises, Beth reaches out and, after a momentary hesitation, snatches up the doll.

As her fingers grip the coarse fabric of the dress, she hears footsteps approaching from behind her.

She spins, clutching the doll tightly, eyes darting to the umbrella as the footsteps in the hall come closer. She hears voices as well.

There are people in her house.

Then they're at the door, and Beth gasps as a young couple fill the doorframe. Both are smiling brightly. They look around the cramped office as if it's the Taj Mahal, eyes wide and cheerful.

It takes Beth's brain a moment to register that she's looking at herself.

Herself and her dead husband.

Beth's mind and body go numb, as if her consciousness is traveling through the wormhole yet again, except this time without the machine, to a day and time of her past, when she and Colson were first looking at this house and deciding that the room in which she stands, clasping a doll that shouldn't exist, would make a perfect nursery for their future child.

A feeling eclipses her, a sensation similar to what she felt in her dream, as a wave of pure, unharnessed energy crashes over her. She can almost feel the sway of her body as the wave pulsates through the room. The couple at the door flicker, then they are suddenly walking past Beth toward the stacks of boxes. She follows them with her eyes, turning as they walk by her and *into* the stacks.

Her breath catches as the boxes dissolve and are replaced by furniture—a baby's crib, a rocking chair. The walls turn from dusky beige to a rich, vibrant pink. Beth of the past is now leaning over a crib, Colson standing beside her.

"How's my little girl today?" Past Beth says, the words flat in the air, as if spoken through a funnel. "How's my Isabella?"

The sound of her own voice whispering to her dead child hits Beth like an electric shock.

"Isabella..." Beth mutters the word as if casting a spell. She looks away from the beaming couple and down at the doll in her hands, who stares back at her blankly with wide, glassy eyes.

She watches with a mix of horror and fascination as the strange apparition of Colson looks up from the crib—and turns his gaze directly on Beth.

Not Beth of the past, but Beth of the *now*.

They stand a few feet apart, staring at each other. Beth's mouth hangs slightly open, the ridiculous doll clutched in her hands. She looks into her husband's ghostly eyes, not understanding, not believing. Colson opens his mouth, as if to say something...

When another wave rolls through the room, Past Beth and Past Colson disappear, ripple away into nothing. The crib also disappears, replaced with a twin bed and a fluffy white comforter. Plush toys rest against the pillow. A little girl sits on the bed reading a tablet, humming quietly to herself.

Beth steps toward her, hands shaking, eyes burning with a rush of tears.

She kneels, stares into the face of this little girl.

Her daughter.

Not dead.

Not stillborn, but *alive*.

Grown up and beautiful.

"Isabella," she says again—louder now, more determined—and the brimming tears break free and flow down her face as her daughter, somehow hearing her voice, looks up and into her eyes. She's smiling. Beth wants to reach out and hug her, touch her face, her hair...

"Oh, honey," she says, the words choking her. "What have I done?"

Another wave surges through the room and Beth feels the doll drop from her hands.

She looks down in a panic, searching the floor...

But it's gone.

The floor is empty, dusty. Beth, on her knees, jerks her head up...only to find herself staring at a pile of packing boxes.

"No," she screams, palms pushing against the lifeless cardboard. "No!"

She spins toward the door, but there's nothing. Only the gloom of a dim, empty hallway. She stands shakily, stares in horror at her unused desk, the dreary walls.

"No no no...please...no..."

But the visions have retreated, the memories faded and lost. Returned to the ocean of time. Beth sinks to the floor, curls into a fetal position, claws at the sides of her head as she moans through tears.

For the second time that night her breath is stolen away as she is pushed down into a world in which she does not belong, forced beneath the surface of time and space, buried chin-deep in the infinite quicksand of despair to stare helplessly skyward—desperate, searching—into a swirling, cosmic sea.

In which she is drowning.

THIRTY-ONE

"Knock-knock."

Beth looks up from the screen of data. It's early, not quite nine AM, and her eyes, tired and burning from the restless night (and excessive crying), create a momentarily blurred vision of someone standing just outside her office door. Absently, she wonders if it might be time to visit an eye doctor. Then her eyes adjust, and the figure crystallizes into the slight, smiling form of Chiyo Nakada.

Beth waits for a surge of anger to cloud her mind like black smoke and is surprised when nothing comes. She doesn't even have the energy to feel betrayal. All she feels is . . . numb.

"Oh," she says. "You're still here."

Chiyo ignores the chilly reception. "Can I come in?"

Beth rubs at her eyes, pushes her chair back from the desk. "Sure, why not."

Chiyo steps lightly into the office and Beth catches a glimpse of Tariq looking back over his shoulder, a deep frown on his face. Beth gives him a small wave—*it's fine, it's fine*—and turns her attention to the reporter, who once again sits on the edge of the uncomfortable office chair without the slightest impression of discomfort, as if she were a preening goldfinch settling on a pointed fence post. A *malicious* preening goldfinch, that is.

"Well, look, before I'm excommunicated, I just wanted to pop in to say thank you for your time these last few days. You've been more hospitable than I anticipated, and what you've accomplished here is truly groundbreaking."

Beth laughs. "Ms. Nakada, I've been briefed on your article. There's no reason to sweet-talk me. To be honest, I don't give a shit what you think. But thanks for stopping by." Beth stands, as if calling the meeting to an end, but Chiyo doesn't move, or seem even remotely put out.

"I know you think my piece skews negative, Beth…May I call you Beth?"

Beth shrugs, wondering whether to keep standing like an idiot or sit back down. After a heavy sigh of resignation, she sits. "Sure."

"Beth, you should know that what Jim Langan saw will not be the final version of what goes to print. In a situation like this, there are reasons to create a piece where everything is attacked, so when the lawyers push back, there are concessions. It's like any negotiation; you never start at your best offer, right?"

Beth nods. "Okay, fine. But if it hurts my funding, it still fucks me. So, while I appreciate your posturing, none of this has been good for me. The forced traveling alone for your benefit has been, frankly, detrimental. Physically and emotionally. No one should have to go through that. The machine isn't a carnival ride."

Chiyo nods, purses her lips. "Yeah, I was bummed that Langan forced that on you. It certainly wasn't a request that came from me or my magazine. But now that we're talking about it, I do have one or two follow-up questions?"

Beth laughs. "Jesus, you really had me going there. I honestly thought you were a real person for a minute. Sure, sure, hit me. Maybe I can dig my hole a little deeper."

Chiyo, again, doesn't seem the least bit perturbed by Beth's attitude. Instead, she places her tablet on the edge of the desk. "Okay if I record?"

Beth laughs again, but it's lost any humor. Her expression hardens, and she begins rethinking the whole "not feeling betrayal" thing, because the reporter is quickly beginning to annoy her. "You have two minutes, then I call security."

Chiyo nods, taps her tablet screen. "Quickly, then, I wanted to ask a follow-up about the mechanics of traveling. I'm no physicist, obviously, but when you mentioned before about only being able to observe, it got me thinking of the Thomas Young experiment from the nineteenth century, and the ensuing double-slit tests using quantum objects in the early aughts. I've skimmed Bohr and Heisenberg, most notably the idea that energy acts differently depending on whether it's being measured or not. In other words, whether it's being observed."

Beth nods tiredly. "Of course. Particles versus waves. Hidden variables. I see where you're going, but I should remind you I'm a physicist, not a metaphysicist. I deal with facts, not fantasy. That said, quantum theory is about probabilities, not properties—what we call a measurement problem, meaning that one's unique perspective and predisposed beliefs will greatly affect results. Back to your point, what you're describing is the theory that adding an observer to a scenario will somehow change the surrounding particles, create a different energy that modifies that reality. It's not the first time this has come up. And despite the tests you mention, it's all theoretical and not really applicable to real-world trials. Somewhat conflictingly, the way the machine operates is fairly straightforward. The portal it creates...that path...never strays, never splits or realigns. It's a two-lane road, Ms. Nakada. There are no off-ramps, no detours into alternate realities. It's objectively impossible."

"Yes, of course, I understand. And I'm obviously not the expert here..."

Beth sighs. "But..."

"But...you have to admit, there's so much we still don't know about how the universe works. And, with all due respect, you've leaped into an entire world of the unknown, the untested. You say you're about facts—"

"And probabilities."

"Fine, but what you're doing here is, frankly, mad science. You admittedly don't even know how the machine targets arrival points, much less what you might be doing to impact our existing timeline. And even if you are only *watching*, you could, admittedly in theory, be altering existence in meaningful ways."

"Chiyo—"

"In fact, based on what happened yesterday during the debrief, I'm a little surprised you have the nerve to dismiss what I'm saying so offhandedly. According to the *you* of two days ago, you had a daughter. And now you don't. How can you explain that?"

Beth thinks of the doll singing in the dark. The room dissolving to show a crib, then a bed. A little girl. She fights to keep her expression placid, detached. Part of her knows the reporter could be right. But to think of that, of what she may have lost...

"Two minutes are up," she says coldly, standing once more.

The reporter, however, stays seated, her dark eyes suddenly blazing at Beth, as if in accusation. "Fine. But I have one last question. I've watched you travel twice now, and I read about your past travel. The airplane?"

Beth says nothing; her lips compress into a tight line.

"I think you know where you were sent yesterday, but you don't want to tell me. It was painful, wasn't it? Tragic in some way."

Beth taps her fingers on the desk. "Time's up," she mumbles, annoyed at how weak the words sound.

Chiyo stands, her eyes continuing to hold Beth's with a hard glare. "Think about this, Beth. What if these tragedies in your life, the ones you've been forced to replay in the present, what if they aren't your true past at all?"

Beth shakes her head. "What are you talking about?"

"I'm saying, what if the tragedies aren't something you simply experience when you travel? What if they were *caused* by your travel?"

Before Beth can reply, a beeping comes from her device, a red dot flashing on the corner of her screen. "Excuse me," Beth mumbles, and taps the red dot.

Jim Langan's face appears. "My office. Now."

Beth nods, closes the window, but is unable to look up at the reporter. She doesn't want to see those accusing eyes, doesn't want to think about the gravity of what she's suggesting.

Is it possible?

But Chiyo spares her any further discourse. She lifts the tablet from Beth's desk, taps it, then stuffs it into her bag. She smiles at Beth warmly, as if they've been discussing plans for a potluck holiday dinner instead of theorizing that Beth was somehow responsible for destroying everyone in her life she'd ever loved.

"I have to run anyway. Think about what I said, Beth. And, you know, good luck."

The reporter turns and walks briskly from the office. Beth notices Tariq offer to walk her out, likely to grill her on what she and Beth had been discussing.

Beth waits until she hears the elevator open, then close, before following.

THIRTY-TWO

Beth enters Jim's office already on edge, but when she sees Jonathan sitting on the couch, her eyes widen with surprise, and a pinch of fear.

Shit.

After her nightmare, her...visions, the night before, she was desperate to connect with someone. She was so afraid, so alone.

So she called him.

Late.

Or, more accurately, early...somewhere in the ballpark of four AM.

"Just shut up and listen..." she said when he first picked up, not *wanting* to trust him. Not wanting to think of him as a friend, to feel as if she was misplacing hope, but needing someone to talk her through this storm of emotions, this impossible, invisible dagger of pain. "I feel like time is running out..."

She started crying. Sobbing.

"Okay, yeah, yeah...I'm here."

"You're a son of a bitch," she said. "So don't...please don't say...Shit, I'm sorry...I just need to talk to someone, okay? I feel like I'm being torn apart."

"Beth, take a breath," he said. "I'm here, I'm listening."

She told him about the visions of Colson, of Isabella. She confided in him about seeing her daughter. "I know what she looks like," she said, nearly hysterical. "Do you understand? I've *seen* her. Jesus Christ, I almost *touched* her."

Jonathan was nothing but understanding. He soothed her, told her to take one of the pills he'd prescribed. Explained how a state of half sleep could play wicked tricks on the mind.

"I'm not suggesting you dreamed all this," he said, sounding to her ears incredibly alert and stable considering the hour. "But I am saying that the imagination is more vivid than normal when in a lucid dream state. What you experienced was likely some form of hypnagogic hallucination, brought on by stress, lack of sleep...alcohol." He said the last word like a question, but she didn't bother—or care—to refute him.

After spending twenty minutes on the phone with the company therapist, she felt better, had a better perspective on what she'd seen and experienced. She didn't dismiss it, but she was at least able to shove it all into a closet of her mind, a locked-up space where it wasn't running willy-nilly through her head, smashing windows of sanity and causing general chaos to her emotional state.

But now he's here, and the vibe is...not great.

He wouldn't have, she thinks, recalling all his past promises of confidentiality, of support, of friendship.

Would he?

Still, she does her best to appear energized and pleasant, not wanting to let on that deep inside she's exhausted, splintered; that her mind is screaming at hurricane strength, her thoughts as loose and fragile as those of someone gone mad, bouncing their straitjacketed shoulders off the padded walls of her consciousness.

Her smile feels like a snarl, but she sticks with it, pointedly ignoring Jonathan's probing eyes from the other side of the room. "Hey, Jim, what's up?"

Jim sits behind his large desk, hands folded on the surface, head bowed. "Sit down, Beth."

Beth looks around, settles into a chair in the small sitting area, partway between Jim and Jonathan. "Okay. Why am I sitting?" She nods to the latter. "And why is he here?"

Jim lifts his head. Beth thinks he looks more tired than she does, but age is a bitch and exhaustion hits the elderly a lot harder than the young. Or so she'd like to think, praying the circles under her own eyes aren't as noticeable thanks to the miracle of concealer. Jim's heavy eyes shift to Jonathan, then back to Beth.

"How are you, Beth?" he says, and offers his trademark snarky, knowing smile.

Beth nods, keeping her eyes locked on his, refusing to look Jonathan's way. "I'm fine, thanks. Why am I here? I have a lot of work to do, as you know."

Jim stands and walks around the desk, then leans against it, facing her. "There's no easy way to say this, and I respect you too much to beat around the damn thing, so here it is. I'm suspending you, as of this moment, until further notice."

Beth starts to stand, wanting to scream, to shout at the old bastard. Instead, she fights to keep her composure, remains seated, voice level. "I don't understand. That makes no sense."

"Jonathan tells me you've been seeing your dead husband in the streets. That you, uh, think you saw a child who doesn't exist. That you're seeing ghosts." Jim wiggles his fingers in the air to emphasize his point.

Beth can't help herself. She turns her head and glares at Jonathan on the couch, who at least has the decency to look ashamed. "Confidential, huh?"

"I'm here as a friend, Beth..."

"Fuck your friendship."

Jim snaps his fingers. "Hey, hey...don't talk to him; talk to me."

Beth brings her head around, unable to keep the flush of fury from heating her cheeks.

Snap those fingers at me again and I'll break them.

"Now," Jim continues, "we all know you've been working too hard. That's on me, and I take full responsibility. You warned me to keep the traveling to a minimum, and I pushed. Jonathan warned me as well. So I'm taking the blame, you understand? But that doesn't change the fact that you need a break, Beth. You need some time to rest, to get your head together. You know... get your shit straight."

"My head's together, Jim," she says.

"No...no, it's not," he says, with so much despair in his voice she almost buys the idea that he gives a shit. Almost.

"Let me ask you this," he continues. "Do you *really* think you have a daughter? A child? Just because of some...anomaly in the questions? You think you've, what...changed reality? Seriously, I want to know."

Beth opens her mouth to refute the idea, to call him every name in the book. Instead, she takes a breath, doing everything she can to keep a clear head, to keep her emotions in check. "The point of the recordings is to allow for discrepancies such as this one. The entire reason we do the questions is to make sure we haven't altered the present. So why—"

"No again, Beth," Jim says, interrupting. "That's not entirely correct."

Beth closes her mouth, confused into silence.

Jim points at Jonathan. "Tell her."

Jonathan leans forward, hands folded. "The questions were created by me, Beth. The concept behind them is not to see if reality has been altered, even though that's how you and Colson

saw it, and we were happy to oblige your perspective because...
yeah, who knows, right? Maybe there was something to that theory, so we allowed it."

Beth barks a laugh. "You *allowed* it? You're just a shrink,
buddy. This whole project? This whole fucking place"—Beth
points at the air around her—"is still here because of me and Colson. We're the scientists in the room. We're the creators. We're the
old man's racehorses. You don't *allow* jack shit."

Jonathan takes a deep breath, and Beth wonders if she's the
only one fighting to keep their emotions under control. Everyone
in this room feels like a ticking bomb.

"Be that as it may," he continues, "as it pertains to Jim, and
to the panel of myself, Dr. Lee, and Dr. Adams, the point of
the questions is different than what you've been led to believe.
They have almost nothing to do with, say, physics. Do you
understand?"

Beth thinks for a moment, then it clicks. She grins darkly,
eyes twitching from one man to the other. "It's a mental test," she
says. "You do them to see if the traveler, in this case, *me*, has gone
bonkers. If my brains got scrambled while traveling, turned into
mashed potatoes." She scoffs in disbelief. "You're wasting all that
tech to see if the machine causes brain damage."

"More like cognitive loss, but yes, that's essentially correct.
We want to make sure whoever goes through that wormhole
doesn't come back thinking they're Napoleon. Or, in this case..."

Beth's smile drifts away. "That they have a daughter."

Jonathan nods.

"My understanding has always been that the questions,
and the science behind them," Beth says, "are to ensure that
going through the machine would not alter reality. *That's* the
point of the questions. If you've attached some psychological
test to that, that's a you thing, but it's not anything quantifiable.

Mental health was never instituted as a variable, and the results carry no weight for any conclusions you might conjure up. In other words, if that was something you wanted tested, you should have done it yourself."

"I have, Beth. Every time we sit down and talk, you're being tested. You know this."

"God, you're such a pompous—"

Jim interrupts again. "Regardless of why we have the questions, there's obviously something wrong with you, Beth. You need to take some time away. So that's what I'm giving you. With pay, I might add."

"Oh, la-di-fucking-da, Jim—"

"But my patience is not boundless," he adds, voice rising. "When you come back, I want you focused and energized. Take a week, take two, I don't care. At this point Tariq can handle the lab and I have enough material now to work the investors."

Beth's mind begins racing for solutions, for fixes. "The article? It's negative. It's a kill piece. Look, Jim, I can do another trial," Beth says, rambling now, desperate. "I can...hell, I don't know, come up with something to convince that little bitch the machine has value. Indeterminate value!"

"The article will be what I want it to be," he says coyly. "Ms. Nakada thinks she holds the cards, but she's not even at the poker table. Trust me on this."

Beth is standing, she realizes, and isn't sure when that happened. She looks around the room for help, but no one appears. No friends. No allies. "Okay, fine. I'll take the time. But I need a few more days first. I just need to finish the follow-up—"

"No, Beth. The second you leave this office, you're suspended. Security is waiting for you in the lobby. They have your things."

Jonathan sits up, glares at Jim. "Security? Jim, what the hell? We never discussed that."

Jim opens his palms at his sides, smiling grandly, as if he's bequeathed a great message on his flock. "Lucky for me I don't need your approval. It's my call."

Beth, shaking now, takes a timid step toward Jim. "Jim. I need a few days."

Jim turns on her, smile wiped away. "I don't think so, Beth. As I've said, you're not thinking straight at the moment. I think, perhaps, you're giving this whole…altered-reality mumbo jumbo some actual credence." Jim stands straight, puts his hands into his pockets. "We wouldn't want you doing anything foolish."

Beth drops her head, crosses her arms tight against her body. Jonathan is also standing now, the three of them in a ridiculous standoff, a triangle of hate and confusion, with billions of dollars—with *lives*—between them to fight over.

"Beth?" Jonathan says quietly. His best soothing voice. "*Do you believe the timeline has been altered? Are you planning something we don't know about?*"

Beth looks at Jonathan, eyes pleading. "I need to try to save her—"

"Oh, stop it already!" Jim snaps, and Beth jerks despite herself. He's an old man, but he's still a man. A bigger, stronger, more violent version of herself. An animal in human skin.

He slinks toward her, points a gnarled finger at her face as he approaches. "If what you say is true, Beth, then let me ask you this. What's this fictional daughter's birthday, hmm? What's her favorite color? The name of her best friend? What school does she go to?"

Jonathan steps closer. "All right, Jim, she gets the point—"

"What's her favorite fucking ice cream?"

"Jim," Jonathan says, stepping forward to put a hand on the older man's shoulder. "That's enough," he says quietly.

Jim steps back, away, shaking his head in disgust. "Yeah, it's enough, all right. Listen to me, Beth. You want to save your career? Keep your mouth shut and walk out that door. Get your shit and go home. For now, all of this stays between the people in this room, you have my word on that. But if you keep pushing me, if you keep *trying my patience*, I'll involve the board, the media... You'd never work again, don't you understand that? Not here, not anywhere. You'll be finished."

Jim turns away, walks back to his desk. His shoulders slump when he crumples into his leather chair. "Besides, even if you're right, Beth, even if those recordings are correct and you've somehow altered our current reality, in a day or so those old answers will catch up to our current timeline and be altered forever, washed away from reality. Any evidence of what's happened here will dissolve like melting snow."

He gazes at her with wet, sagging eyes, and she hates seeing the small glimpse of compassion—of *pity*—on his face.

"Either way," he says with finality. "This is over."

THIRTY-THREE

Beth arrives at the park slightly hungover.

After returning home in what she could only think of as a mixed-up state of shame, frustration, and white-hot fury, she immediately opened a bottle of cheap Cabernet and proceeded to dutifully drink it dry. Fortunately (or unfortunately as it turned out, given her pounding head), she had a second bottle tidied away in her kitchen cabinet, which met a similar fate.

Regardless, she promised her best friend she'd meet her, and she wasn't going to bail out because of a sourly churning stomach and a jackhammer headache. Her dark sunglasses were cutting out most of the harsh sunlight, and she could push through an hour of watching kids running in circles if it meant a little social time with someone she cared about, a rare treat in recent months.

She spots Lucy on a bench near the playground and pushes through the latched gate into the "Children and Parents Only" section of the park. The shrill, joyful screams of the playing kids scorch the exposed-nerve edges of her hangover, but she forces a grin as she waves to Lucy and walks toward the bench.

"Hey, there's the birthday girl," Lucy says, standing to give her a tight hug and a peck on the cheek.

"Hey yourself," Beth replies, eager to sit down and settle the brimming nausea that hasn't left her since she woke up an hour ago. "And please, I have a whole day before I'm, you know, *older*. Let me relish it."

Lucy gives her a quizzical stare. "Wait. Are you hungover?"

Beth gives a weak laugh and crumples onto the bench, almost sighing with relief. "God, you know me too well."

Lucy sits down, plucks two bottles of water from her bag, and hands one to Beth. "It's not hard, honey. You smell like spilled wine and you're pale as a ghost."

Beth accepts the water gratefully, opens it up, and takes a long swallow. "Ugh, I'm sorry. But hey, I'm here, right?"

"True," Lucy says, nudging her with an elbow. "And you never like coming to the park with us. If I didn't know better, I'd think you hate children."

Beth feels a fresh wave of sickness at her friend's words, swallows a bubble of acidic bile, and belches lightly. "No way. Kids and me? We're all good. You know, despite my having failed so miraculously at bearing my own."

Lucy turns to face her. "Jesus, that's a bit dark."

Beth shrugs. "Sorry."

Lucy gives her a meaningful look, then drops her voice. "No, I'm sorry, I didn't mean...Look, what happened to you was awful, Beth. Don't get me wrong. But it's been years, hon. It just caught me off guard, you know? Kind of came out of left field. I mean...are you okay?"

"Sorry, sorry..." Beth says, shaking her head, not wanting to burden her friend with her misery, but also tired of being alone with it. "It's just been a shitty week, and yesterday..."

"Yesterday what?"

Beth sighs, takes another sip of the cool water, already feeling better than she did only moments ago. "Just work shit. Sorry, stuff," she corrects, eyeing a nearby couple of young girls trying to unknot a jump rope. "I basically got suspended."

Lucy's eyes open wide. "Holy..." She drops her voice once more, this time to a whisper. "Holy shit, Beth. Are you gonna get fired? And if you do, will I finally get to know the big secret?"

"That's all you care about, isn't it?" Beth says, feigning hurt. "Knowing what I've been working on all these years."

Lucy laughs, leans into her friend's shoulder. "Well, no. But also, yes. I mean, let's call it a silver lining."

Beth smiles, watches children push themselves down a twisting plastic slide, then land on tiny, sturdy feet in a soft pile of wood chips. An unexpected pang hits her heart and she embraces it, almost relishing the pain in her chest, as if it's something to cling to. To remember.

"Honestly, I don't care anymore," Beth says, turning to her friend. "You wanna know?"

Lucy says nothing, her lips tight, eyes wide. She nods.

"Time travel, bitch," Beth says with a sad laugh. "Me and Colson figured out time travel. Or, you know, a version of it."

For a second, Beth is confused at the look of disappointment on Lucy's face.

"What?"

Lucy drops her eyes. "Nothing. I actually thought you were going to tell me this time."

Beth can't help it, she laughs again, loud and clean, the freedom of it dulling some of the pain. "Lucy, honey...I'm not kidding."

This time she gets the look she expected. Lucy goggles at her. "No way."

Beth nods. "Yes way. Been working on it for years. Got a big lab, a giant machine, the whole nine frickin' yards. Obviously, there are limitations, and it's not what you think, or what you've read in books or seen in movies. But still, it's pretty damn cool."

"Wow. I mean...wow, Beth. I figured you were...hell, I don't know, making biological weapons or something."

"Yeah, well." Beth looks away, back at the children. "It's all gonna come out soon, anyway."

"What do you mean? What's happening?"

Beth shrugs. "*Business Weekly* is posting an article about the whole thing. Our CEO's last gasp to raise more investment capital."

Lucy looks forlorn. "Aw, man. And here I thought you were finally opening up to me, you know? Giving me some exclusive information."

"Hey, you got the scoop, didn't you? First one in the world to know we've created..."

As Beth trails off, her eyes narrow, locking in on something at the far end of the playground. Lucy notices and follows her gaze, scanning the park in growing panic. "What? What's wrong? Shit, is it Timmy?"

Beth shakes her head slowly, as if dazed. "No...I think I know that woman."

"Oh," Lucy says, already standing up and walking toward her son, who is climbing a rope bridge, diligently making his way from a plastic pirate ship to a two-story structure with a green umbrella rooftop.

Beth gets up as well. She walks slowly toward the older woman she noticed moments ago. *I know her. How do I know her?*

As Beth gets closer, the woman turns, revealing a wizened but smiling face. She has a little girl hugged to her hip and speaks to her energetically, the child's arms wrapped tightly around the woman's waist.

"Excuse me..." Beth says, her mind racing to match that face to a name, to a place...

The woman's eyes shift to Beth, and her smile falters. The little girl tucks her face into the woman's jacket, and Beth can only see her long black hair, her skinny arms, a skin rash on her elbow from a recent fall.

Then, like a light bulb popping to bright life, the name comes:

Marie Elena.

"Excuse me," Beth repeats, louder now. She walks quickly toward the older woman, whose happy expression has all but melted away, her eyes full of wary concern at this approaching stranger.

"Beth?"

Beth spins around. Lucy stands behind her wearing a confused expression. She's holding her son, Timmy, in her arms. He's also looking at Beth, his face placid, neutral, as if the woman he's looking at isn't real. Isn't consequential.

"It's okay," she says, trying not to sound as crazy as she feels. "It's just . . . I know her."

Lucy tilts her head, looking past Beth. "Who?"

Beth doesn't answer but turns around once more. The older woman is staring back with pure contempt now, the small child released from her embrace so she can position her body between Beth and the girl, as if protecting her.

"I—I'm sorry," Beth stutters. "I don't mean to alarm you, but . . . do you recognize me?"

The woman shakes her head. "No, miss, I'm sorry."

Beth tries to smile, feels it twitching at the corners. "I'm Beth Darlow. Your name is Marie Elena, right?"

The older woman doesn't nod, doesn't move.

Beth looks down at the girl tucked away behind the woman. "Hi there, can I see you? Are you hiding?"

"Beth, what are you doing?" Lucy's voice says from just behind her, but Beth ignores her. She takes a step closer to the woman and the girl.

The woman takes half a step back, eyes now shifting, as if looking for help.

"I just want to see..." Beth says, trying to sound casual. *For fuck's sake, I'm just an inquisitive adult wanting to see how pretty someone's child is.* "Can I say hello? I just want to say hello to her."

"Beth..." the voice repeats from behind her. But it's far away now. Distant. Insignificant.

Beth reaches out a hand and the old woman, in a sudden, aggressive movement, slaps it away. Beth pulls it back, shocked.

"Ow! What's...? Look, can I just say hello...? I just—"

"Get away!" Marie Elena barks, eyes narrowed, her stature somehow growing—a mama bear protecting her cub. "We don't know you."

"But...your name *is* Marie Elena, right?"

At this the woman says nothing. Behind her, the little girl, no more than five years old, pokes her face around, wanting to see.

She has an olive complexion. Dark eyes.

Beth doesn't recognize her.

Marie Elena reaches down with one hand, presses the child's face back behind her.

"I don't know you," Marie Elena says. "And if you take another step, young lady, you'll regret it."

Beth stops, straightens. Suddenly, she notices that a quiet has fallen in the park. She looks around, sees parents watching. Staring.

I've been here before, she thinks. *This happened before.*

"Beth!" A hiss from behind her, and this time the voice is not distant, but close and aggravated. A warning.

Beth notices a few of the parents have moved closer, deep frowns on their faces, eyes alight with righteous anger. *An interloper,* Beth thinks. *I'm an interloper in this world. An outsider. And now...*

I've been spotted.

"Sorry!" Beth tries to laugh but worries it comes off as hysteria. She speaks loud enough that Marie Elena—and the enclosing parents—can all hear her plainly. "I mistook you for someone else. My apologies."

Beth turns around, sees Lucy staring at her as if she's gone mad.

And maybe I have, baby. Maybe I have.

"Really, I'm sorry," Beth says quietly, for Lucy's ears only. "I'm having a tough time...I don't feel well, and I think I need to go home."

Lucy nods, and for the first time in all the years of their friendship, Beth notices Lucy looking at her in a way she's never seen. As if she's not looking at Beth at all.

As if she's looking at a stranger.

THIRTY-FOUR

As Beth walks up the quiet street toward home, having left a worried Lucy at the park (clutching her son in a not-so-subtle protective embrace), she debates next steps. Her schedule, apparently, is suddenly wide open. She has the weekend, the week ahead... and, who knows, maybe the rest of her life to plan things out.

Will she return to Langan Corp.? She honestly doesn't know. She's been betrayed by Jonathan and is furious with Jim. Worse yet, she's losing the will to fight. To fight *back*. And that feeling, somehow, is the most depressing part of everything she's going through. It's always been part of her DNA to push back against dominating men, to fight for her rightful place in the hierarchy of the world's greatest minds, its greatest scientists. It doesn't help, of course, that her work is confidential, hidden from society, from her peers.

But that's all about to change.

Isn't it?

She's not so sure anymore.

Jim's coy statement that she needn't worry about the article has circled the drain of her thoughts for the last twenty-four hours, swirling around and around and refusing to vanish, to be sucked down into the netherworld of discarded memories. Given some time to reflect on her meeting—after the initial shock of the encounter, and Jonathan's betrayal, had dimmed—part of her

wonders if the article will ever see the light of day. She's beginning to think it might not and isn't sure how to feel about that.
Relieved? Or disappointed?

Regardless, she's been handed a window for introspection, a
time for the gathering of wits, for the resetting of a troubled mind.

But time isn't what she needs. Or wants.

What she wants is to travel. To find out if she can somehow
fix what's been broken. What *she* broke. Despite Jonathan's protestations about the briefings being a psychological test versus a
scientific one, she knows—better than most—that the possibility of creating a variance in one version of reality is incredibly
valid.

Chiyo Nakada's concerns were more on the mark than the
reporter realized, and Beth's casual deflections were mostly an
act, a calming reassurance that the machine isn't dangerous.
But the reality is that she knows better. In fact, she and Colson discussed it hundreds of times, assured themselves over
and over that the unknowable risk was well worth the tangible
reward.

Now, of course, Beth admits that their conclusions were
illogical, tainted by desires for fame and fortune. A mistake. An
ego-driven misconception of the potential damage that could be
done. Lives destroyed. Lives taken.

Vanished, as if they never existed at all.

As she arrives at the front gate, she grits her teeth. She must
figure out a way—no matter the cost—of getting back into the
lab. Of traveling one more time before it's too late.

She needs a miracle.

"Good morning," a voice says from her front porch.

Startled, Beth looks up to see a man sitting on her front steps.
She hardly recognizes him in casual clothes—jeans and a T-shirt,
sneakers, a baseball cap.

"Good morning. What are you doing here?" She doesn't say it unkindly, but with unguarded confusion. Part of her is even joyful at seeing a friendly face.

Tariq stands up, dusts off the seat of his jeans, and steps aside so she can get to the front door, but her eyes never leave him.

"You wanna come in?" she asks.

He nods, boyishly shoves his hands into his pockets. "Yeah, I think I better."

Beth steps up onto the porch, unlocks the door, pushes it open. "You want to give me a hint? I'm assuming this isn't a social call. Not that I'd mind," she adds quickly. "Trust me, after the last few days I could use a friend."

Tariq nods again, smiles. "I'm glad to hear you say that. Because I *am* your friend, Beth. But..." He looks away, toward the sidewalk, as if gathering courage. "I also haven't been completely honest with you. I'm here to correct that."

"O-kay," she says slowly. "Well, let me put on some coffee and we'll talk." She takes a step inside, then stops. "I hope it's not more bad news. Not sure I can take that right now."

"Nah, not so much," he says, then lets out a nervous breath. "It's just time, that's all."

"Time for what?" Beth asks, her heart picking up speed. She's never seen Tariq look so abashed, so uncertain.

He shrugs. "It's time for you to know the truth."

THIRTY-FIVE

Beth makes a pot of coffee while Tariq stands in the adjacent living room, toying with the remote for her wall screen.

"This is connected, right? I need access to my server."

"No, I'm a Luddite, that's why I built a time machine," she mumbles, greedily watching the hot water percolate, willing it to brew faster. "Yes, Tariq, it's connected," she says in a raised voice, not caring if she sounds irritated.

Because I am irritated. I'm also incredibly pissed off, hungover, embarrassed about creating a scene at the park, and terrified about my future. And apparently I'm missing a child. So excuse me if I sound annoyed, and why the hell are you here bothering me, anyway?

Beth closes her eyes, takes a deep breath, savors the smell of the fresh coffee. She holds the breath for a three-count, then slowly lets it out. *Relax, Beth. Just hear the guy out.*

Tariq hasn't told her anything further since his cryptic reveal on the porch, but that's fine with her. For now. She'll be a lot more ready to field some random bombshell after a large mug of caffeine-saturated black coffee.

"Okay, I'm connected," he says from the other room. "You almost done?"

"Yes. What do you want in yours?"

"I'm good, actually, but knock yourself out."

Beth nods to herself and pulls a mug from the cabinet as the machine spits the last of the brew into the carafe. Moments later, she walks into her living room, sipping happily. The heavy fog surrounding her brain is already lifting, and she feels her body slowly waking from its sluggish, alcohol-laden, sleep-deprived stupor.

"Okay, you have my attention," she says, sitting on the couch opposite the wall screen. The light from the window behind gives the screen a rectangular glare, so she lowers the diffusion shade, casting the room in a soft gray glow.

The screen shows a server desktop crammed with files and coded names, which Beth doesn't even try to engage with. Instead, she waits for Tariq to explain, willing to let him take the lead while her mind and body slowly return to life. He turns to face her, that chagrined expression on his face once more.

"Before I get into this, I want to say that I'm sorry I never told you before now. It's been eating away at me for months. Ever since Colson died, I've been living with this horrible, nagging guilt. And, in my own way, I've been trying to help, you know? But damn, Beth, you make it hard sometimes."

He laughs, but Beth only shakes her head. "I'm not following. What are we talking about?"

Tariq takes a deep breath in, lets it out. He drops his eyes to the floor like a shamed child. "I've been suppressing information from you. Like, analytics. Data. About the machine, the traveling."

Beth's eyes flare. "What?"

Tariq looks up, begins to speak more quickly. "But it wasn't my choice, okay? It wasn't my call."

"Okay, so whose call was it? Is this what you and Jim have been concocting behind my back?"

Tariq meets Beth's eyes and she's surprised to see something unexpected on his face. *Hurt.* "Damn, Beth, like I said, you sure make it hard sometimes. I'm trying to help you, and all you ever do is accuse me of shit. Treat me like a glorified assistant."

Now it's Beth's turn to look ashamed. She takes a beat to steady herself, then nods. "Okay, fine. I'll be all apologies once you tell me what's going on, and what Jim's been hiding from me."

Tariq shakes his head. "It's not Jim. I want nothing to do with that guy."

Beth's eyebrows rise. She begins thinking of possible culprits, people who would have enough sway over Tariq to make him... then she freezes.

It can't be.

As if hearing her inner thoughts, Tariq nods. "It's Colson, Beth. He's the one who told me to suppress the data. At least until we figured out why it was happening."

Beth holds up a hand. "Wait, back up. Colson told you to keep information from *me*? Do you really expect me to believe that? That he'd confide in you and not his wife?"

"He wanted to protect you, Beth," he says. "Everything he did was his way of trying to set things right. And then, when he died, I was gonna talk to you about it. Bring you in. But then Langan started cutting staff, and funding was drying up..." He shrugs. "I thought it was irrelevant. No need to stir a hornet's nest over the discrepancies. And I was worried, to be honest. Worried you'd think of it as a way of... I don't know, saving Colson. That you'd obsess over it. So I kept it to myself, waited for the inevitable dissolution of the lab. But then, over the last couple of weeks, with that reporter, and you traveling... and then the questions." Tariq chokes up as he speaks, wipes a tear from one cheek. "Damn it, I waited too long, and I'll never forgive myself. But he swore me to secrecy, Beth. Colson, he..."

Tariq stops, momentarily unable, or unwilling, to go further. Beth can't help feeling shocked. She's never seen the man cry, or, frankly, show much emotion at all.

What the hell is going on here?

She stares at Tariq a moment, trying to make some sense out of what he's telling her...but she comes up empty. Frustrated, she feels that familiar flare of impatience—of anger—but tamps it down. Buries it. Whatever's happening here won't be solved by anger or argument. She replays Tariq's words in her head, organizes her thoughts. After another long, thoughtful sip, she sets her mug down on the table.

"Okay, okay..." she says gently. "This is a lot to unpack, obviously. Let's start with the information. What were you and Colson holding back? What was he keeping from me?"

Tariq nods, seeming relieved at Beth's evenhanded response, and clears his throat. "All right, look. One of the things I'm responsible for is studying brain patterns, right? Before and after. That's my thing. But as the staff dwindled, I obviously took on other areas of analysis. It was soon after, during the period when Colson was traveling, that I first found the alteration."

Beth nods. "Explain."

"Okay. As you know, the basic wave function of a human mind is incredibly unique. I mean, at this point, we can use unique brain waves as fingerprints. They're one of a kind, and barring injury—or some other kind of destructive, outside stimulation—they never change. Not permanently. It's electric DNA. That's how specific the patterns are."

"Like you said, I know all this."

"Right, but what you don't know is that every time Colson traveled, his mind...his brain pattern...Beth, it *changed*. In essence—and this is going to make me sound like Grandma's fruitcake—it wasn't technically Colson who returned. Or, not his consciousness, anyway. It was someone else, someone *different*. Similar, yes. Exact? No. Like I said, even the slightest variation of a fingerprint—"

"And you become someone else," Beth says, her mind reeling to process this information.

"Exactly. But there's another possibility, one which you and Colson actually spoke about quite a bit. The idea that when you travel, you're not just observing; you're *re-creating* a moment of existence, which then sends out ripples of new data into reality. Like dropping a stone into a pond. And that ripple affects the entire lifespan of the traveler, and possibly others within range of the energy flow."

"I know what the inverse square law is..."

"Right, sorry. What I'm telling you is that it's possible the re-creation of those moments could account for the modifications to his brain pattern. Colson was still Colson after he traveled, but he was slightly different because he fucked with the program. He altered his reality. And yours, and mine, and...hell, potentially, anyone within Earth's atmosphere."

Beth stands up, begins pacing. "So, there is a butterfly effect. Even though we don't interact with the past? And you have proof of this? Something more than brain fingerprints?"

Tariq nods. "All the data is stored on my personal server," he says, lifting a hand toward the wall screen, the jumble of icons and folders.

"But the questions," Beth says, practically hearing the desperation in her own voice. "There's never been a discrepancy until this week."

Once more, Tariq looks chagrined.

Beth stops pacing and gapes at him. "You're shitting me."

"I'm sorry, but yes, it's happened before. Twice that I know of, that I can personally recall, even though others can't."

"Tariq? How could you not tell me this?"

"That's why I'm here. Now. To tell you what Colson was doing. All of this, everything you're going through? It's happened before. It happened to Colson, Beth. And I helped him fix it. But it's dangerous. You have no idea how dangerous it is. Colson...he became desperate. Obsessed with fixing the present—"

"What the hell do you mean?" she says, feeling an ice-cold terror creeping through her. "Fixing what?"

Tariq blows out a held breath, runs long fingers over his scalp. "Look, to your knowledge, Colson traveled seven times, right? That's what's been recorded."

Beth nods. "That's right."

"There were others, Beth. Two more times that I know of. That I assisted with. Two times he traveled totally off the record, trying to alter reality, to fix what he felt had been broken."

Beth scoffs. "Bullshit. I don't believe you. He would have told me, would have confided in me—"

"I can't speak for the dead," he says. "But I *can* tell you, with absolute certainty, why he kept at least one trip a secret from you."

Beth crosses her arms. "Okay, why?"

Tariq looks at her, eyes soft with apology. "Because you didn't exist, Beth," he says. "You'd been completely erased."

THIRTY-SIX

Early afternoon light gives the room a hazy, dreamlike appearance as Beth takes in the information, her mind reaching for denials, but something inside her, some small part of her consciousness, keeps them at bay, as if she is finally ready to accept the truth. The creeping terror she'd been feeling now slips into her mind like spilled ink and begins to scream.

"I don't believe you," she says quietly, more by instinct than conviction. "I can't—"

Tariq crosses the room, sits on the opposite end of the couch. "I get that. I do. I know it's…whatever. Impossible. But the truth is that you'd vanished. I mean, as if you'd never existed. No pictures. No office. Colson had never been married, had a completely different history. It was…man, it was insane, Beth."

Beth hesitates to ask, because she fears—she *knows*—what the answer will be.

"So how did he know? How did he know to…go back? To find me?"

"Because there were still, I don't know…*fragments* of you. Floating around Colson's head, I guess. Enough that it made him crazy. He wasn't sleeping, wasn't eating. He'd remember something about you, or dream about you…and it was like those ripples I talked about? It's like they were overlapping, two different timelines mixed together, and he was getting glimpses of both at the same time. Seeing, and experiencing, two separate realities."

"Yeah, I know what you mean," she says, rubbing idly at one temple. "And look, I understand your theories and am open to the idea, at least in principle... but to suggest traveling is like playing some version of neural hopscotch, that we're flipping between alternate realities, alternate dimensions, like a deck of cards? I'm sorry, but it's science fiction."

"Yeah, I thought the same thing," he says, settling back and crossing his ankles, hands resting on his stomach, as if able to finally relax now that he's unloaded the incredible weight of knowledge he's been carrying. "Colson, he could get pretty out there, right? Dude had some serious guru tendencies. Almost shamanic. Always talking about the spirit of the universe, some vast, intellectual energy pulling the strings..."

Beth nods and despite herself feels a smile on her lips. "That was him, all right."

"Yeah. But you and I? We're different. Unlike Colson, we don't rely on faith as much as we do science. Lucky for us, too. Because that's why I did what I did. I prefer hard proof." Tariq points to the wall screen. "This server is stored at CODEX. Technically, it's a Langan Corporation server. I say technically because they pay for it. They also have no idea it exists."

Beth stares at the screen. "CODEX? The moonbase? I thought that whole thing was still in testing. No one has access to that yet."

Tariq grins. "Well, let's just say I have old friends in high places. Call me an early adopter. Of course, I pay handsomely for it. Well, at least Jim does. Regardless, assuming the specs of the machine's energy don't change, or grow more powerful, those servers are outside the pulse of energy we create, beyond the range of whatever alterations the machine makes to our reality. As you know, the energy doesn't have the juice to travel that far. So, what's on my distant server..."

Beth's mouth opens, and she stares at the jumble of information on the screen in a new light. "Stays unchanged."

"Correct. Which is the only reason I know any of this is true. Or, more accurately, why I'm able to remember. Beth, I can recall proof of alternate pasts anytime I want." Tariq laughs, turns to look at the wall screen. "It's some crazy shit to get your head around, huh?"

Beth nods slowly, stunned. "But why? I mean, I'm obviously here. The present was apparently... healed, or whatever. So why did you—why did *Colson*—keep all this hidden from me?"

"That's a question for Colson. And like I said, I don't speak for the dead." He lifts a finger, one eyebrow raised. "*But*... I am going to show you something that may help."

Tariq takes a pen-size pointer from his shirt pocket and aims it at the icons on the screen. Beth watches as the cursor glides through the maze of icons as he navigates the pointer, then clicks open a folder marked CDARLOW031643. He clicks open a video file, and the screen fills with an image of Colson sitting at a darkened desk in his laboratory office. He looks haggard, unwell. Beth tries to recall the date she saw on the file. March 16, 2043. She can't think...

"Colson sent me these video logs the week before he died," Tariq explains. "Asked me to store them on CODEX. There's a short delay here... Satellites aren't the best routers. Okay..."

Beth sits back as Tariq plays the file, and Colson, hands folded on the desktop in front of him, speaks to her once more from beyond the grave.

THIRTY-SEVEN

Hi. Um, okay. This is Dr. Colson Darlow. Today is March 16, 2043. I'm at Langan Corporation. It's just past two AM.

    I've just concluded an unsanctioned travel. Assisting me was Tariq Igwebuike.

    If you include my travel sessions that are on record, this would have been my fifth trip... but it's the first unofficial trip.

On the screen, Colson wipes a hand across his face, scratches wearily at a day's growth on his cheek. Beth's heart swells at seeing her husband again, but breaks as well, knowing how distraught he is, how she didn't know, couldn't help him...

I think I've corrected the anomaly.

For the first time in the video, Colson smiles, albeit wistfully.

Beth was at the arrival point. It was such a relief, such a joy, to see her. She was... happy. Healthy. Whatever my last trip had altered... by traveling again, I was able to somehow reverse it, or... adjust it. Perhaps I just found a completely new timeline, a new reality, that suits me. Suits all of us. Because we're together again.

Since this travel was unofficial, there is no debrief, so I can only pray I haven't fucked something else up that I can't remember. Or wouldn't even know about.

When I returned, I called Beth at home, woke her up just to hear her voice. I told her I was working late, but I was worried about her and Isabella. It took everything I had to keep it together when she...when she told me our daughter was fine. She laughed because she'd fallen asleep in Isabella's bed again...

Like I said, I don't know the ramifications of what I've done.

But I have my family, and that's what matters. It's all I care about.

In the moments before I traveled, I focused—focused with everything I had—on Beth. On what I remembered of her. I think the machine looks for those mental spikes, those emotional flash points each of us have in our past. A day at the beach. An anniversary dinner. Making breakfast for the people you love on a beautiful summer morning. I think... with no evidence whatsoever, that it took me where I wanted to go. The machine saw the spike of awareness in my mind and drove toward it. Used it to select the coordinates of my arrival point.

Colson shrugs. For a few seconds, he doesn't speak. Finally, he shakes his head, continues.

I'm still trying to decide whether to tell Beth. If it gets out that there's a problem...a danger...it could blow the whole project out of the water. And, to be frank, Beth has a better heart than I do. She wouldn't risk it...

But I would. I will. I am. I pray we can find a way to

do this safely. I don't want to risk traveling again, but to put someone else at risk would be heartless. To tear someone's life apart... or erase their loved ones from existence. It'd be murder, plain and simple.

I don't know what to do. I don't know... but this is important. It's our life's work, and it could change... everything. If the questions come back wrong again, I'll have to correct it. Tariq can store the events, these logs, at CODEX, which we now think is far enough away from the experiment to escape the effects of what we do here.

That said, nothing is certain. Not the past, not the future.

Nothing.

THIRTY-EIGHT

The video ends and Beth sits back into the couch, trying to absorb this new information, the ramifications of it all. She looks at Tariq, her body numb with shock.

"He mentioned our daughter," she says slowly, cautiously, as if just saying the words could change the past, the reality of what she'd lost. "He said I fell asleep in her bed. But..." Beth stops, closes her eyes, thinking. "There's nothing, Tariq. I don't remember any of that."

Tariq nods. "That's why I'm here, Beth. Because you were right. You *did* have a daughter. Honestly, I wasn't sure, but I went back and watched this video again, and I knew you were right. That the questions were right. There *was* a discrepancy. The fact you can't remember is part of this new reality. A new you, I guess. But there's also that part of you that *does* remember. The visions you had, the dreams. Same as Colson...it's exactly what he was going through."

"I can't think like that, Tariq," she says, doing her best not to shout, to pull her hair, to howl in despair. "I can't sit here and believe I've lost a little girl."

"I know," he says calmly. "But look, there's one other thing I want you to see, and then we can talk, okay? We'll figure this out."

Beth slumps forward and puts her hands around the back of her head, as if trying to maintain some semblance of control. Of sanity. "What else could there be? Can you help me? Will you help me get her back? Jesus, Tariq, we need to figure this out. I mean, no offense, but we're wasting time."

"I know, I know," he says. "But this is important. It's something else. Something you don't know about the machine. About Colson."

Beth shakes her head in frustration. "What? Why can't you just tell me?"

"Because you'd never believe me," he says, then points at the screen. "Just watch."

Another video file opens, and once again Colson is sitting at his desk. He looks better in this video. Shaven and rested. But his eyes, Beth notices, are filled with worry.

She clamps a hand to her head, impatience and panic boiling within her, but forces herself to watch, to rationalize what she's hearing. To focus on anything that will help bring her daughter back.

THIRTY-NINE

This is Dr. Colson Darlow. It's March 21, 2043. I'm at Langan Corporation, and it's Saturday morning, just past ten AM. I've given Tariq instructions to upload this video, but that it be for Beth's eyes only, barring . . . well, barring my death. If that happens, I pray he'll know what to do. I'm sorry for placing that burden on him, but I have no choice.

With his help, I traveled about an hour ago. Beth and Isabella left this morning for a birthday party. Her friend Lucy's son . . .

Colson smiles sheepishly.

I begged off. Told Beth I wanted the morning to myself. It's been . . . difficult between us lately. We're both stressed. Tired. So tired . . .

Anyway . . . I was able to rope Tariq in for an hour this morning, to assist with another unofficial travel. It's easier on the weekends. Less security. Not that I want to make a habit of it.

Beth points to the screen. "I remember that day! My God . . . I was so angry with him . . ."

Tariq waves a hand at her. "Just watch, Beth."

This time, there was a problem. Tariq described it as a power glitch. The pulse stayed strong, thank God... but the computers rebooted ten seconds into my traveling.

That's never happened before...

I don't know how it happened, or why. But... the arrival point was... I was confused. I didn't remember... not at first. But then it all came to me in a flash. Like a doorway in my consciousness opened and...

Colson's eyes go blank, distant. Beth can't tell if he's lost in thought or if he's simply replaying the event in his mind.

I know that I was driving... I don't know what day it was, but I know it happened in the future because... there was an accident.

I think I was killed.

Beth's hand reaches out and clutches Tariq's forearm. "That's impossible!"

Tariq shushes her, gently pulls his arm away.

Colson continues.

It was terrifying... horrible, just horrible. My car was struck head-on... My God, it sounds crazy, but yes, I'm almost positive I didn't survive, that while traveling, I somehow, inexplicably, experienced my own death. It's theoretically impossible, of course... but I was definitely reliving something that hadn't happened yet. Something in the future.

If I knew when, knew the day... I don't know, maybe I could fix it? Change the future? This is all new territory. It's unexplainable. Frankly, impossible.

There's no scientific rationale for being able to travel forward. I suppose if one goes by the theory that our lives are...that time isn't real. Einstein's adage about time being an illusion...

I think about that. About the eternalists and the theory that all points in time are equally real. Then I think how what we're doing here—what the machine is doing—may have an unexpected side effect.

What if, by taking matter out of the equation, and by sending consciousness through space-time to destinations unknown, untargeted...what if we're throwing away the effects of perspective? Losing objectivity as it pertains to special relativity? Say there's no past, no present, no future... Say that time isn't linear. Okay, we've theorized that ad nauseam.

What I'm saying...what I'm theorizing here...is that we've removed the thumbtack in the universal corkboard. When we travel without our bodies, we're removing the fixed state of observation as it pertains to time. We've essentially freed our perspective, the set point that acts as the apex of the past and the future. The infamous razor's edge...

Colson shifts forward, looks directly into the camera.

What if we're traveling outside of time itself? Outside the rules of quantum gravity, of relativity, of physics? What if, for a minute and a half of Earth's time, we're gods?

Would that piss off the universe, or what?

Colson sighs, reclines. He turns his head, and Beth knows he's looking toward her empty office. Maybe he's thinking of her in this moment, or maybe—even likely, she thinks—he's not thinking of her at all.

Regardless, practically speaking, I don't know what I'm going to do. I'm scheduled to travel, officially, next week. Maybe I can correct the timeline and erase this accident...I don't know...I no longer understand the machine. The science doesn't make sense...

But there must be a way to do more than just observe.
For my sake, there has to be.
It's in God's hands now.

FORTY

The video ends. Tariq clicks a button on his pen. The screen goes dark.

He turns to Beth, who's in deep thought. "I hate to say it, but I think Colson was losing it a bit. Eternalism? That bit about time being an illusion? Einstein wrote that about a dead friend. It's not science; it's poetry."

"I'm aware, Tariq," Beth says distractedly.

"Point being, I wanted you to see this. The car crash? I mean...how did he know, right? If he really did travel into the future, that changes everything. It puts what we're doing on an entirely different level."

"Yeah, and that bit about perspective? About matter being the key to observation," Beth says, deep in thought.

"Right," Tariq says slowly. "I mean, it's a theory. Remove matter from the equation, give consciousness free reign to travel outside the rules of relativity." He shrugs. "Something to chew on, I guess..."

"No, I'm sorry, but it's impossible. We can't travel to the future because the future is always being created." Beth stands, begins pacing the room like a caged animal. "Every moment we interact with time creates a fluctuation. There's no target beyond the present. And yet, the machine sent him anyway."

Tariq shakes his head. "But it didn't work, Beth. He didn't

change the future. He still died in that crash. Just like your folks died in that plane. By traveling, the only thing that changes is *us*. Isabella didn't disappear from your world; you changed your world to become a place where you don't have a daughter. I know we can't change the future, but we can alter the present. I'm hoping I just proved that to you."

Beth rubs her eyes, groans. "Oh God. It's all so out of control. Tariq, I'm sorry. I need time to think about this, but right now I'm too damn upset, too damn hungover."

Tariq stands. "Hungover or not, if you want to fix this, I don't think you can wait."

"What do you mean?"

"Jim thinks he's got me around his little finger. He's all but offered me your job. *Multiple* times."

Beth scoffs. "I fucking knew it..."

"Regardless," he says, catching her eye, "there's one more thing I know that you don't. Which is that your suspension isn't a suspension. He needed you out of the lab next week."

Beth stops pacing; a chill climbs up her spine. "Tell me."

"He needed you gone so he could bring the new team up to speed. I'm sorry, Beth, but that's why I'm here. Now. Today. That's why I'm showing you all this stuff." He shrugs. "We're out of time."

Beth feels as if invisible fingers are at her throat, slowly choking the breath—the *life*—from her. She forces herself to breathe, to *think*.

"I'm being pushed out," she says, the horror of it almost unbearable.

Tariq nods. "I'm supposed to train the new team. Bring everyone up to speed with the tech, the software. In doing so, I keep my job. I get a nice raise. I'm on the new team."

"But I'm out," she says. "So why the false front of a suspension? Why not just fire me?"

"I've thought about that, and I think the crafty old bastard is keeping his options open, at least until the new team is in place. Wants to make sure they can do what you've been doing, keep things moving forward. Otherwise, I agree, he'd have just fired you. Torn up your contract. Stuck his lawyers on you like leeches."

Beth absorbs this. "Okay, then we have no choice. I need to get back in. I need to travel again. Today. I need to fix this. You'll help me, right?"

Tariq smiles, spreads his arms. "Why do you think I'm wasting my Saturday with you?"

"Thank you," she says, and continues pacing, brainstorming a strategy. "I'm suspended," she says. "There's no way they'll let me in."

"Yeah, I thought of that. I'm pretty sure the weekend guards don't know faces."

"It doesn't matter, Tariq. When they run my badge, it'll show I'm suspended. Those gun-toting assholes all but lifted me by the elbows as they escorted me out."

Tariq reaches into his pocket, pulls out an ID badge with a familiar name on it. "Like I said, I knew what was coming. Planned ahead." He holds out the badge and Beth grabs it, sees the VISITOR stamp where an employee's face would normally be. "Told her I'd turn it in for her. Whoops."

Beth wants to hug him. "That bitch owes me one, anyway," she says, unable to contain a smile as she stares at Chiyo Nakada's name typed across the bottom of the white cardstock sealed in laminate. She grips it tight in one hand, squeezes her fingers around it into a fist.

"You sure about this?" he asks, studying her. "Not trying to be dramatic, but it could be dangerous. And your career will be over if Langan finds out. I don't mean there...I mean *anywhere*. That dude has serious power, you know."

Beth nods, relishing the familiar rush of resolve. "Nothing matters but getting my daughter back."

Tariq studies her closely, then nods. "All right. In that case, I have just one request, and I'm in."

Beth waits, feet shifting with eager energy. "Anything."

"We do this. We *fix* this. That's it. No more traveling. No more machine. It's too dangerous, Beth. Colson didn't have the nerve to pull the plug, but I'm hoping you do."

Beth thinks for a moment. "Actually, that's not entirely true."

Tariq raises one eyebrow, waiting.

"When I did that all-nighter?" Beth continues. "Someone loaded up a prerecorded video from Colson, along with a virus, onto my lab computer. I had to reboot the servers to stop it."

Tariq frowns. "That wasn't me, I swear. I don't know anything about a virus. Besides, I could do that on my own."

Beth shrugs. "I know, I know, and it doesn't matter. When we're done, when things are put right? I'll help you wipe it out. All of it. I'll burn the damn thing to the ground."

Tariq gives her a suspicious look. "Really? Your life's work?"

"The machine's not my life," she says. "My daughter is."

"I believe you, mama bear," Tariq says with a grin. "Now, let's go find her."

FORTY-ONE

Tariq drives up the slim, twisting road toward Langan Corp. The sky is a coffin lid; heavy-laden with dark, swollen clouds, an undulating gray map of overlapping continents, dense and alive, consuming any stray speck of light, making the day feel dead, lost. Buried.

There's a light drizzle, and he has to use the wipers to clear the windshield as they climb the tall hill, giving the world a smeared, distorted view. As his sedan approaches the main guard gate, a small window slides open and a bearded man in a black uniform—heavy button-down shirt, baseball cap, sidearm—sticks out his head and waves them forward.

"Working the weekend?" the man says, baring a square of white teeth amid the thick facial hair, the approximation of a smile.

Beth, in the passenger seat, hands her visitor badge to Tariq, who holds up both badges toward the guard. He takes them in one hand, typing into his computer with the other.

"Ms. Nakada is a reporter for *Business Weekly*," Tariq says evenly. "It's her last day in town, so I'm giving her a quick tour. She's on your visitor log. We should only be an hour or so."

The guard nods, inspects a screen in front of him that Tariq can't see. "One second," he says.

After a nervous beat, Tariq, who's never been made to

wait at the main gate before, speaks up. "Sorry. What's the problem?"

The guard says nothing but turns away from the screen, then steps through the narrow door set into the side of the shed. He approaches the car's open window and leans down, his face now even with Tariq's and Beth's. His eyes glance at Tariq, then settle on Beth. She does her best not to squirm.

Fortunately, she had the forethought to wear dark sunglasses, realizing that while her black hair and complexion might allow her to pass as someone with an Asian name, her eyes—round and blue—would cause suspicion. "No problem," the guard says, before addressing Beth. "Do me a favor, Ms. Nakada? Hand this in when you leave today. Since you're leaving town, I mean. We don't like these things floating around, even if they're date-stamped."

Beth nods and smiles. "Sure thing."

The guard hands both badges back to Tariq, who in turn gives Beth hers while reclipping his own to the collar of his jacket. "Thanks, we won't be long."

The guard shrugs. "No worries. I'm here all day regardless. Have a good one." He turns around, reaches through the open window, and taps on something near his computer. The metal security pole rises to let them pass.

As the car drives toward the parking lot and the flat concrete structure beyond, the guard steps back into the shed, closes the sliding window to keep in the heat. Then he plucks the security phone off the wall and makes a call.

∽⊕∾

Inside the building, there's only one guard in the lobby. Hardly registering their presence, he does nothing more than wave at Beth and Tariq as they hold their badges aloft, walking through the body scanner and toward the sliding glass door leading to their wing and the elevator that will take them down to the lab.

"Jesus, security really sucks on the weekends," Beth mumbles as Tariq hits the button, calling for the elevator.

"Yeah..." he says, and Beth gives him a glance.

"What?"

"Nothing," he says, shaking his head.

The elevator doors open, and they step inside.

Moments later, as they enter the lab, the sensors catch their movement and dutifully turn on the overhead lights. Beth heads straight for the machine's console as Tariq pulls his white lab coat off an old-fashioned wooden coatrack near the kitchen entrance.

"You wanna go now?" he says, buttoning the front of his coat.

"No time like the present," Beth says, already typing in the commands to run the bootup sequence. "We'll need a few minutes while the laser powers up."

"Yeah..." Tariq says, nudging her aside and typing in his own entry codes. "Let me do what I do, boss."

Beth steps aside but keeps her eyes on him.

"Hey, I'm sorry I've been a shit to you these last few months," she says, watching him work. "I knew you and Colson were close, and...I don't know, maybe I resented that. Maybe I felt like I was outside the male bonding circle, or whatever. And, you know, trust isn't my strong point."

Tariq stops typing, turns to face her. "You've been under a lot of pressure, Beth. You had your right arm cut off and your heart ripped out at the same time. That's why I stayed here, and that's why I'm here now. Not for Colson, but for you. Okay?"

She nods. "Yeah, okay."

"Shit, if I was you and Jim was pulling all the shit he'd pulled, like with that reporter? And all those secret meetings with me? Honestly, I'd have fired my ass long ago."

"Well, I'd never do that."

"I know," Tariq says, and finishes typing. The rising energy for the laser hums gently, electrifying the air. "Let's get you suited up."

As the humming of the laser grows louder, Beth sits on the steel table, silently kicking herself for not thinking to change her clothes. A T-shirt and jeans wouldn't affect her ability to travel, but she'd have preferred more coverage on her arms where the straps would hold her down. *Too late now...*

Tariq applies the sensors to her head and neck, placing the processor chip, secured into a flexible band, over her forehead. "Okay..." he says, centering the chip. "Hey, do we need to record something from you? Something I can upload to CODEX? We don't have the briefing to tell us if we've, you know, screwed things even worse."

Beth laughs. "Very scientific. And yeah, I think that would be prudent. You have a tablet handy?"

Tariq nods, turns to his workstation, and plucks up a worn tablet. He points it at Beth, taps the screen. After a beat, he nods at her. "Whenever you're ready."

Beth thinks a moment, then looks directly at the small camera set into the tablet's backing. "My name is Dr. Beth Darlow. It's Saturday, March 26, 2044. Approximately three PM. I'm traveling today in an attempt to correct the timeline that took my daughter from me. Her name is Isabella Darlow. She has dark hair, brown eyes... She'd be four years old..."

Tariq looks over the tablet at Beth, waits.

She sighs. "There's no way of knowing if this will change anything. When Colson traveled, unofficially, he said he tried to focus on the things he wanted most, as if that could somehow set the coordinates for his arrival point. I'm wondering if we truly know what this machine really is." Beth pauses, gathers her thoughts. "Maybe it's not a time machine at all. Maybe it's a displacement machine, shifting the traveler from one reality to another. It's hard to know for sure. Are we modifying the current timeline? Or are we somehow bouncing between infinite universes? I don't know the answer, not yet...and if this works, I never will. Regardless, if I focus on my daughter, I'm hoping it will take me to her. One way or another."

Beth looks away from the camera, meets Tariq's stunned gaze. "That's it."

He nods, taps the screen. "It'll take a minute to send, but we can begin the sequence."

Beth smiles weakly, fighting the exhaustion and fear creeping into her bones. "Thanks, Tariq."

He taps at the tablet, entering the commands to send the file. "You really believe that? About shifting between universes? It's a leap."

"Honestly, I don't know. We'd have to work the numbers, but based on what you've told me, and what's happened, I think it's as viable a theory as anything."

"Yeah, I guess," he says, and sets the tablet down on the foot of the steel table. "You've just reinforced the idea that shutting this thing down is the right move. There's just too much we don't know." He looks at her steadily. "You ready?"

"I'm ready—"

A piercing, pulsing siren shatters the quiet of the lab. Beth and Tariq look up and around; the severity of the shrill, air-splitting noise causes them both to wince. Red emergency lights begin to flash, splashing a heartbeat of red across the walls of the sterile laboratory.

"Jesus, what is that?" Tariq says loudly, talking over the wailing sound. "A fire alarm?"

Beth's eyes go wide. "It's a security breach. We have to hurry!"

Tariq sees her panic. "Why? What is this?"

Beth grabs his sleeve, looks into his eyes. "It's *us*, Tariq. We're the security breach. Which means Jim knows we're here. He's shutting the place down. Our power source is independent, but security will be here any moment. Start the sequence. Start it now!"

Beth lies back on the steel bed as Tariq runs to his console. "All right, all right, stand by!" He begins hammering at the keys. "Thirty seconds!" he yells. "You're not strapped in, so whatever you do, *don't move!*"

The elevator dings. Three men clad in black burst into the lab. Their guns are drawn and pointed at Tariq.

Wearing a blue sweatsuit, as if his morning jog had been rudely interrupted, Jim Langan strolls out behind them. He points at the machine. "Stop them."

One of the guards strides quickly, aggressively, over to Tariq. Without hesitation, he presses the muzzle of a gun against his temple. "Shut it down!"

"Jesus, dude, relax! Jim, this is crazy..." Tariq yells, but his eyes shift from his screen to Beth, who now has her head turned to see what's going on. *If that laser goes off now and misses that processor...*

Their eyes meet for a moment as a second guard steps in close to Beth's side, gun aimed at her heart. "Sit up," he orders. Beth recognizes him instantly. *The guard from the gate.*

"I'd do what they say, you two," Jim says, sounding almost bored at the terror and chaos swirling around them. "Since you are here unlawfully, I've given the guards permission to use any force necessary. Including the option of shoot to kill. You are here under false identities and pretenses, and I must assume it's to steal my intellectual property."

"All right, I'm shutting it down," Tariq says, slowly raising one hand, then tapping some keys with his other. Instantly, the swelling sound of the laser's building energy begins to wind down. "It's canceled," he says. "Now, please, point that fucking gun away from my head."

The guard looks to Jim, who nods. The guard lowers the gun, takes a step back from Tariq, but keeps it aimed in his general direction.

Beth, knowing they've lost, sits up. She lets her legs dangle off the edge of the table, hands gripping its metal edge, her head hung in dejection. In failure.

Jim taps the shoulder of the guard standing next to him. "Turn off the alarm, will ya? I can't hear myself think."

The guard tilts his head to the small microphone clipped to his collar and mumbles instructions to an unseen recipient. Within seconds, the red lights stop flashing. The siren goes quiet. The sudden silence is a shock, as if they'd all been caught up in some game that abruptly came to an end.

"Put your guns away," Jim says, and the three guards sheathe their weapons in unison. He turns to address Beth, whose gaze remains cast downward at the concrete floor, as if she is unwilling, or unable, to accept the reality of her loss. "I think it's time we call a little staff meeting," he says.

Beth looks up, eyes wet. "Staff meeting?"

Jim nods. "I think this has gone on long enough," he says, and looks at her with the expression she hates more than anything else in the world.

Pity.

FORTY-TWO

Twenty minutes later, Beth is still sitting at the machine, now just waiting—and wanting—for it all to be over.

Tariq sits at his console, seemingly at ease with his fate, which he and Beth both know has gone from bad to worse. Beth assumed the worst thing that could happen to her or Tariq would be getting fired. Now she's hoping they aren't going to jail.

But despite her anxiety over how things have gone to hell, a part of her is still reaching for solutions—for ways to navigate this storm—to get one more shot at traveling and, theoretically, hopefully, finding her daughter.

Over these last twenty minutes, Jim (and the three very angry-looking security guards) has been joined by a mussed-looking Jonathan, as well as the program director, Abigail Lee, who looks as uncomfortable as Beth has ever seen her.

Men wielding guns can have that effect, she thinks, recalling the stomach-clenching feeling she had at having a loaded gun pointed at her chest.

Whatever happens next, she knows she'll owe Tariq a larger debt than she'll ever be able to repay; seeing the fear in his eyes when that gun was pressed to his head is an image she won't ever forget, or forgive herself for.

"Did you really think I wouldn't know?" Jim says, monologuing like a villain in a Bond movie while the rest of them sit around the laboratory, watching him pace, waiting to find out what the old man will do next.

When Jonathan arrived and saw Beth sitting on the bed of the machine, she thought—just for a moment—that he wanted to say something to her. He wore a pained, inquisitive expression that, had she not known better, suggested he was even worried for her. Wanted to *help* her. But she'd looked away from him, recalling his betrayal, how he took her private thoughts to Jim on a platter, letting him gorge on Beth's failures and shortcomings, her paranoia.

Now he simply sits quietly, looking antsy and haggard, while Jim lectures Beth about her naïveté, her stupidity. How it's all over for her now, as if she wasn't already fully aware.

"I told you before," he continues, "nothing happens in this building I don't know about. The second you were suspended I put our security force on alert, to let me know if the lab was accessed by anyone other than Tariq." He nods to Tariq, then glares at Beth accusingly. "Or if Dr. Beth Darlow—supplying the team with your photograph, of course—came within fifty yards of my complex. And like a rabbit hopping into a cage for a slice of carrot, here you are. As expected, I should say."

Beth rubs her head, picking at the electrodes that are still attached. "Jim, you need to listen to me. Please… *please*, for once, just listen. Not as my employer, but as a human being. Give me two minutes."

Langan stops pacing and folds his arms. He looks to Jonathan, who simply stares back, giving no indication one way or the other.

To Beth's surprise, it's Abigail who finally speaks up. "Jim, it can't hurt. We owe Beth that much."

Jim doesn't so much as glance at the program director. His eyes remaining locked on Beth. But, after a few moments, he nods. Once. Pursing his lips in mock disgust.

"Fine," he says. "But, in case you didn't already know, we are recording all of this." He points to the high corners of the lab, where Beth now notices—for the first time—a white plastic disc, no bigger than a baseball, set into the wall near the ceiling. "To that end," he continues, raising his voice, "allow me to state for the record that witnessing this conversation are three of Langan Corp.'s security personnel; program director Abigail Lee; corporate psychologist Jonathan Greer; myself, CEO Jim Langan; and lab technician Tariq Igwebuike. Speaking is Dr. Beth Darlow, who, while under suspension, entered the Langan Corporation grounds illegally, with the intention of committing a crime."

He looks to Beth, palms raised toward her. "All right, Beth, the stage is yours. Please, say whatever you'd like to say. And don't worry, the cameras have excellent audio capture capability." He lowers his voice to a conspiratorial whisper. "They always have."

"Fine," Beth begins. "Look, I just want to say that there was a discrepancy after my last travel. No one here denies that, right?"

She glances pleadingly at Abigail, Jonathan, and Jim. No one speaks.

"And...I've since discovered, just today in fact, that there have been *other* discrepancies in the past." Beth shoots Tariq an apologetic look, but he only nods. *Go on.*

Jonathan sits up in his chair. "I'm sorry, but that's not true."

"It is true," Beth says wearily. "And we have proof."

Abigail and Jonathan share a look, but Jim remains stoic, unmoving.

"Tariq has sent files that prove what I'm saying to CODEX, which is outside the influence of both the machine and any energy burst that would theoretically alter our timelines."

"More theory," Jim snarls.

"As I said," Beth continues, "there have been discrepancies before. After Colson traveled, and unknown to anyone in this room, our present reality was altered. Further, Colson secretly used the machine, at least twice that I know of—off the record and without authorization—in order to try to correct those discrepancies."

"It's true, Jim," Tariq says. "I have the travel logs as well as his video debriefs. All the files are stored at CODEX."

"Point being," Beth says, careful not to get her pleas entangled with the machine's disastrous side effects, "Colson *knew* these things happened. He knew that he had somehow *altered* reality. Just like I somehow knew, when I'd returned from my last trip, that my daughter was gone. Even though she never, technically, existed in this reality...I *know* she was here, Jim. I've been remembering her. *Seeing* her." Beth takes a breath. "Her name is Isabella. She has brown eyes and black hair. She's in preschool."

Jim shakes his head, and Beth, desperate, turns her attention to Jonathan.

"Jonathan, please believe me. I'm telling the truth. You heard the questions before I traveled. You know it's more than just some psych test. I *remember* her. I've *seen* her. Like a dream you have while wide awake, a vision of a fragment of displaced reality. I'm sorry, I don't know how else to describe it. But since Tariq showed me the stored videos Colson made, more information...more *memories* have come back." Beth laughs shakily, as if edging near hysteria. "It's like a goddamn flood! For instance, she has this dumb singing doll named Sally...and, one time, she made me a butterfly at preschool. It was blue."

"Enough..." says Jim, almost sadly. He turns to the guards. "Escort her off the grounds, please. And Mr. Igwebuike as well." He turns back to Beth and Tariq. "As of this moment you are both terminated from my employment. You will be removed from the grounds. If you attempt to return, you will be treated as trespassers. In the meantime, I will debate whether to pursue criminal charges, so I'd advise you both to think strongly about consulting personal attorneys."

"Jim, I'm telling you the truth!" Beth begs. "We'll show you the files. You can see for yourself."

Suddenly, Jim drops his arms, face flushed red with anger. "Christ in heaven, Beth, don't you think I know?"

Beth's mouth opens, closes.

She stares at him in shock.

Jim stands up straight, defiant; his well-worn smirk creeps over his face.

"And to think," he says. "I thought you were the smart one."

FORTY-THREE

The room goes very still. Very quiet.

Jonathan looks from Beth to Jim. "What are you talking about?"

Jim barks out a laugh. "My God, you people are dense. I feel like I'm repeating myself here. Over and over again. I've told you, all of you...I know everything that happens here. I built this place from the ground up." He opens his arms expansively. "This is my home. This is my domain."

Beth's mind is racing. *He knew. He knew and let me go on...*

"Jim, why the hell didn't you say something?" she asks. "This could have been avoided. We could've...I would have..."

"Would have what, Beth?" Jim says, his eyes feverish. "Stopped testing? Stopped your research? Killed the project? Do you really think I would have allowed that? As far as I'm concerned, Colson's so-called secret travels were just creating more data to mine. Honestly, it was gold."

Beth sees a crack in his logic and leaps at it. "Fine, then why stop me? You let him travel, and I'm only doing what he did. I'm trying to fix this reality. Like you said, it's just more data for you, so why now?"

"Because you have no idea what you've built!" he bellows, hands clenched into meaty fists. "This is *my* machine. My tech! Because we're *close* now, and I can't afford to have you fucking it all up. You? Your husband? Nothing more than guinea pigs."

Jim closes his eyes a moment, takes a breath, and tries on a crooked smile. "But to answer your question, since you asked so nicely, I'll tell you why—because the opportunities for this technology are far greater than your narrow-minded, altruistic perspective can fully realize. Digital consciousness sent through time? Sent to specific moments...specific *targets*. Think about it, Beth."

Beth does, and begins to see a picture that is not only haunting...

It's terrifying.

"You want to travel to other people."

Jim's smile widens.

"But...it's impossible," Beth says. "We can only travel to our own past."

"Says you," Jim says dismissively. "Which is why you, and others like you, are only necessary up to a point. I need fresh minds, fresh thinkers. This machine you've built is worth trillions, Beth. I don't need builders. I need winners."

Beth shakes her head, numb with disbelief. "You used us."

Jim nods, shrugs. "When the project ramped up a few years ago," he says, "it was still new, still in beta. So, yes, I allowed you little hamsters to hop on the wheel and run in circles. And yes, I watched Colson. Watched closely. I thought it was very interesting, to be honest, seeing him jump through hoops trying to bring you back. Hell, I was almost rooting for the guy. I even watched those videos he made. You know, the *secret* ones Tariq sent up to CODEX." He looks at Tariq. "Very clever, of course. But you used a Langan Corp. account, dipshit. Did you really think no one would notice?"

Tariq shrugs. "Didn't think you were spying."

"Wrong," Jim says. He grins, taps the corner of his eye. "I see *all*. I see everything."

Jim glances around the room, all smiles, his face a mask of pride and insanity. Then those red-rimmed eyes find Beth once more. He takes a step closer—close enough that she can smell his sweat through whatever cologne he splashed on before coming here. "But I have another answer to your question, Dr. Darlow," he says quietly, voice dripping with menace. "I'm stopping you because I don't *like* you. You're *uppity*. You're disrespectful. Even worse, I think you've held us back. Hell, if your husband hadn't been killed, I probably would have fired you the second the machine was ready. No more late-night fucks in the lab, I'm sorry to say. Although it did make great television."

Beth feels sick. "You're disgusting..."

Jim laughs. "Sure, sure... I'm the bad guy! That's quite a picture you paint. Let's see if I have this right. I pay you. I pay for the machine. I pay for the tech. I give you this beautiful lab so you can work on your creation, undisturbed. And what do you do? You break in. You hide things from me. You mock me."

Jim stuffs his hands into his jogging suit pockets, turns his back to her. He looks around the lab, as if seeing it for the first time. "Well... that's all over with now," he says quietly. "You're done, so... I guess time's up. I'll bring in some smart new guinea pigs, and we'll pick up where you left off. Easy-peasy."

"Jim, why wasn't I told any of this?" Jonathan says, his face flushed.

Jim waves a hand at him. "Because you're a fucking shrink, Jonathan. Mind your place."

Having heard enough, Beth stands, pulls two of the electrodes from her head, and steps toward Jim. One of the guards, the bearded one from the gatehouse, steps between them, a hand on the butt of his firearm. Beth halts her steps but keeps her eyes on Jim.

"Jim, listen to me. I don't care, okay? Fire me. Throw me

out. Arrest me, whatever. But let me use the machine one more time. Jim, she's *alive*. Somewhere, somehow…she's alive, and I need to bring her back. Let me save my daughter, I'm begging you…"

Langan wipes his mouth with the back of one wrinkled hand, then smooths the palm over his head of thin gray hair. "No," he says, so quietly it's as if he's talking to himself. "No, I don't think so."

He points at the guards. "Get them all out of here."

One of the guards grips Tariq by the forearm while another approaches Beth. She turns to Jonathan, desperate. "Jonathan, help me! She…she dressed as an angel this past Halloween. Please…you *knew* her, Jonathan. You had dinner with us. You…"

The guard grabs Beth roughly, begins pulling her toward the elevator.

"You called her Izzy once!" she yells. "And she hated it. Remember? So you kept calling her that, just to get a rise out of her…"

But it's Jim who answers. "Even if you had a daughter, Beth… and, if it helps, I actually do believe you did…she's gone now. Soon, the recordings will adapt to this timeline, and then in a few days, maybe weeks, you'll forget. You'll forget she ever existed. We all lose things, Beth. People we once loved…old memories that fall away like sand through our fingers…"

He looks at the machine, at Beth. "But, hey, life goes on."

Jonathan stares at the ground, as if in thought, an expression of confusion—then awareness—on his face. He stands as Beth and Tariq are dragged to the elevator, then he turns to Jim.

"You know, he says, almost casually, "I think I do recall an Izzy."

Jim gives him a perturbed look. "What are you talking about?"

Jonathan lunges toward the third guard, the one whose back is turned, his attention on the two scientists being hauled away. He snatches the gun from the guard's holster, then spins around, aims it directly at Langan's forehead.

Jim laughs. "You're joking."

Jonathan takes two steps away from Jim, and from the guard, who looks ready to murder, but the gun never wavers. "I won't let you destroy lives, Jim. I'm sorry, but this is something outside your control, and Beth deserves a chance to make it right." He takes a breath, lowers the gun, leveling it at Jim's heart. "Now, tell the guards to let them go, or I'll shoot you where you stand."

The two guards hauling Beth and Tariq across the lab come to a stop, then let their captives go in order to pull free their own sidearms, both of them pointed toward Jonathan.

Jim looks more confused than angry. His trademark smirk slides off his face. "I see, I see...Okay, Jonathan."

He looks to the guards almost happily, as if they were all in a play together, improvising a new scene. "Holster your weapons and step back, away from those two," he says, waving a hand at Beth and Tariq.

Then he turns, finds an empty console, and sits down, crossing his legs and putting his hands lightly atop one bony knee. "This is really getting interesting," he says. "To be honest, you've all got me curious as to how this is gonna end. I'm tickled pink about it."

Jonathan ignores him, turns to Beth. "This is your chance. Maybe when you come back, this will all be fixed. If not, well..." His words trail off, and he shrugs.

Beth stares at him, dumbfounded. "Thank you."

He nods but keeps the gun pointed at Jim. "Go on. And good luck."

Not waiting for a second invitation, Tariq walks past Beth toward his console, shaking his head as he begins typing commands. "This is nuts."

Beth hurries toward the machine. She quickly begins reapplying the sensors, pulls the band carrying the processor chip down over her head, centering it as best she's able. Tariq continues typing in commands.

As Beth lies down, the static hum of the powering laser fills the air.

Doing her best to lie perfectly still, Beth lets out a large, held breath. Distantly, she hears Jonathan talking to one of the guards, telling him to take a step back.

No more time, she thinks. *There's no more time.*

Tariq steps over to her and begins strapping in her arms, legs; he pulls the Velcro straps over her chest and head. She knows a red dot—guidance from the overhead laser—is reflecting off her forehead, and he centers the processor accordingly.

He looks down at her for a brief moment. "You ready?"

She can't nod, but she blinks her eyes. "Hurry," she whispers.

Then Tariq disappears, and she's staring into the eye of the laser, the energy behind its needlepoint face growing exponentially, creating enough power to blow the entire complex to dust if not channeled with meticulous care.

She closes her eyes, begins to focus.

Isabella . . . she thinks.

She tries to remember a moment in time that never existed. A memory that, in this reality, never even happened.

At first, she comes up blank. Fingers of panic begin to crawl through her stomach.

Then she recalls something Colson said in one of his video clips:

I think the machine looks for those mental spikes, those emotional flash points each of us have in our past. A day at the beach. An anniversary dinner. Making breakfast for the people you love on a beautiful summer morning.

"Thirty seconds!"

And then, on a breeze filled with the scent of jasmine, she remembers...

It's the first day of preschool.

Colson is following a few yards behind us, holding up his phone, shooting video. He records me and Isabella as we walk toward a white picket fence.

Beyond the fence is a blue schoolhouse. A cottage, really.

It has a bright yellow door.

We go through the fence and approach the door. Isabella, walking at my side, is holding my hand. A woman opens the door and steps outside. She's pretty. She has a warm smile. I trust her immediately, even though I've only met this particular teacher once before.

"You must be our newest friend," the woman says. She winks at me, then gives all her attention to my little girl.

I turn around to look at Colson. I let go of Isabella's hand and immediately miss her touch. That connection.

I find myself studying Colson. In this moment. His smile is big. Beyond happy. A joy that only comes with a certain amount of fear. I reach for the phone.

"Let's get you in here! Come on, Colson, hand it over."

"You got it?"

"I got it."

He takes two quick steps toward his daughter, who raises her arms to him.

"Daddy!"

I watch my husband and my daughter follow the teacher through the yellow door, hand in hand, and disappear.

I follow.

"Twenty seconds, Beth..." Tariq says. Then he's distracted by something. A loud crash. He begins to yell, panic in his voice. "Oh shit! Hey, man! Don't let him..."

Beth starts counting down in her head.

Nineteen

Eighteen

Seventeen...

There's a shout—it sounds like Jonathan—followed by sounds of a struggle.

Beth hears Jim's voice at full throat, a bullhorn in the open space. "Goddamn it! I said stand down! What are you doing?"

A gun fires. The sound is like a stick of dynamite exploding, the *BANG* echoing off the walls. Abigail screams, shrill and loud and horrified.

Beth wants to turn her head, to see what's happening.

Thirteen

Twelve

Eleven...

"Turn that fucking thing off!" A guard's voice. Enraged. He's very close.

"Just relax, it's not a big deal, man, just rel—"

The gun goes off again and again, and Tariq's words are cut through with a knife. Beth hears him groan, hears the unmistakable sound of a body hitting the floor. She smells the carbonized, bitter stink of smoke. The increasingly heavy whine of the laser reaching full power is roaring in her ears, vibrating her teeth.

"Tariq!" she yells, but she can't move her head, her arms, her legs.

She takes a breath, tries to focus on her thoughts, on her memory.

She continues counting down, knowing she has only seconds until hands are grabbing at her, pulling her away.

Eight

Seven

Six...

Jim's voice again. "Stop shooting! Jesus Christ, you've killed him! Abigail, stop screaming and shut down that damn machine."

Killed him? Killed who? Tariq? Jonathan?

The program director is sobbing, her words wet and broken.

"I can't...Jim, there's so much blood...The console was hit...I can't turn it off..."

Beth closes her eyes.

Like a whispered prayer, she says their names. "Tariq... Jonathan..."

Three

Two...

"Isabella."

One.

I'm in a bed.

I feel...weak. Tired. So tired. Too tired to open my eyes.

There's a soft humming noise that fills the room. It's comforting. I hear footsteps, distant. From the next room? A hallway?

Finally, as if spurred by the arrival of a rogue consciousness, I open my eyes.

It's dark.

My head turns slowly to the side, showing me a large window that frames a night sky.

Beneath the window is a comfortable-looking chair, plush and leather. Directly to my left is a small table with a lamp. The lamp is turned off. The idea of lifting my arm to reach it, fumble with the switch to turn it on, is laughable.

I sense, however, that I *want* to turn it on. That I want to get the attention of someone.

But my body is too weak. I doubt I could lift a finger.

Gratefully, I turn the other way. The pillow beneath my head is cool, soft.

To my right is an open door; the hallway beyond is brightly lit. The walls and floors are white. I hear voices, more footfalls.

Other than the light from the open door, the rest of the small room is in deep shadow. The version of me I'm inhabiting lifts her head and looks down at my body, as if taking stock. I'm covered in white sheets, a neatly tucked white blanket. I'm warm— comfortably so—and have no desire to free myself from my wrappings. The soft humming I hear is coming from a machine just behind the bed. There's a cord running from it, disappearing beneath the white blanket, toward my arm. I feel something plastic on the tip of one finger. A monitor.

I don't recognize this place. This feeling. This moment.

This never happened.

Regardless, I piece together the obvious.

I'm in a hospital. I'm very old.

And I'm dying.

As I stare blankly toward the hallway, a shadowed figure fills the door. A nurse, perhaps. Or a doctor. By the shape of her, definitely a woman.

She steps into the room, her face hidden in shadow.

Am I afraid of her? Of something else? I feel . . .

"Mom? You awake?"

The woman settles on the edge of my bed, her face now turned so the light from the doorway fills in her features. She has long dark hair and wide, beautiful brown eyes.

I recognize her immediately.

Isabella.

"Loosen the blanket, honey," I say. "I want to get my hand out."

The woman stands, and I see now that she's wearing a turtleneck and jeans. She begins gently untucking the blanket near my right arm, where the cable for the monitor has been run. I watch her closely as she does this for me, studying every inch of her with a sort of wonder.

At best guess, I'd say she looks to be around forty, given the worry wrinkles at the corners of her eyes, the smile lines at the ends of her lips. But...no, that's not right. She must be in her late forties—or even fifties—if I'm anywhere near as old as I feel.

I wonder what's wrong with me.

A form of cancer they couldn't root out? Maybe something else.

It doesn't matter. What matters is I'm here, at the end, with my daughter. She's alive and she exists and now she's taking my hand in both of hers and holding it. I relish the feeling it gives me, the warm surge of love and comfort, like drawing a deep breath after being underwater for far too long.

I don't understand how I'm here. In a future memory.

There's another tingling worry, a nagging red flag flapping in the back of my consciousness. It's telling me that it's been more than ninety seconds since I arrived.

But I'm still here.

And thankful to be. Grateful to see her again. To hold her hand one last time.

After smoothing the blanket down beneath my freed arm, Isabella sits again, still holding my hand. She smiles down at me. Her eyes are so beautiful, so kind, and I take a moment to study them. I search her face so that I can once more see my little girl, the one I loved so much that it breaks my heart just to think of her, to think of the pieces of the past I've lost.

She takes one of her hands from mine and gently strokes my forehead, pushes away a stray hair, slides it behind my ear. I close my eyes at her touch, the soft fingers of her caress, like the settling of a butterfly.

"Do you need anything?"

"I'd like a sip of water," I say.

She plucks a plastic cup from a bedside table. There's a bent straw stuck into the top, and she holds it to my lips so I can drink.

"Better?"

I nod. "Thank you, honey."

"How are you feeling?"

I smile, albeit wearily. "Tired. Not long now, I think."

Isabella frowns, grips my hand tightly. "Should I get a nurse?"

I shake my head, already feeling my heart slowing, a countdown from this life.

This memory.

"No, no...just you. Just me and you."

She nods, and I see the wetness on her cheeks. "I love you, Mom," she says.

Her love fills me. I feel it saturating my frail body like light.

I'm ready now.

And that feeling is so peaceful.

"I love you, too, Isabella." My voice is weak, barely a whisper. "I'll always love you."

She leans in and kisses my cheek.

The touch of her lips...I close my eyes...The darkness opens before me and I float into it. It embraces me gently as I detach from my body, pull away from bones and flesh, worries and laughter, heartache and joy. All those things that make us human. All those parts of *life*.

After a few moments, I dare to open my eyes—I decide I want to *see*—and find myself high above the hospital room. I look down upon my body—so still, so small. I don't recognize the elderly woman lying there, but I know the woman crying next to her. The one holding her hand.

My daughter.

I found my Isabella.

I blink, and the scene shifts. Like a globe sent spinning beneath my hand, a million moments pass by beneath me at impossible speed.

When I stop, I'm surprised—and saddened—to find myself looking down at my laboratory, although I don't know if *down* is the right word, the correct way to express what I see. To express *how* I see.

It's as if I'm seeing all perspectives of the room at once, merged in a vision my mind is only capable of thinking of as one perspective, and yet I'm simultaneously above and below, behind, and in front.

I'm everywhere.

I see everything.

My body lies very still on the steel bed of the machine. My eyes are closed, my limbs limp, unmoving. I don't know if I'm alive or dead. Near my office, a woman sits in a chair. She's sobbing. Two men are lying on the floor. One I recognize as a security guard, cradled in a fetal position, gripping his leg with hands covered in blood.

The other is Tariq.

He's face down on the concrete floor. Not moving. Not breathing. His pristine white lab coat has a dark spot near the spine. Beneath his body is a growing pool of dark blood.

Jim Langan stands nearby, unharmed, his face lowered into one palm, as if wondering how things have been taken so far.

Jonathan is on his knees, hands bound behind his back. His head is bowed, and I wonder if he's praying or just weighed down with defeat, sorrow. Guilt.

The two remaining guards are nowhere to be seen, but I've seen enough. Despite the near-indecipherable tug of my body, I pull away from it all. I want nothing more than to leave it all

behind. I rise away until the world blurs into a smear of black...
and continue to rise.

I climb higher and higher. There are lights all around me now,
moving past me slowly, then at a greater speed, and yet I don't feel
as if I'm moving at all. My spirit, my energy...this consciousness
now devoid of any physical entrapments...it's *free*, completely
untethered from my physical self. My humanity.

Instead of a body, I now feel myself becoming one with a
much greater energy. One that is eternal. That encompasses plan-
ets and galaxies. That holds billions of memories from millions of
years of life, of intelligence.

I realize that there's no turning back. No return.

Above me, in the distant nightscape, there's a light. I'm pulled
toward it, as if carried on the shoulders of a rolling stream, watching it grow larger, brighter.

In the next moment, I'm standing before it.

I step into the light as I would a doorway.

Or a portal.

The light expands outward in every direction. There is no up
or down in this place.

There's only everywhere.

I hear voices and a multitude of shadows float past me,
surround me, as if I'm enclosed within a white sphere, rolling
through a sea of dark angels, all of them calling out.

Hello? they say. *Who's there?*

I also call out. "Hello?"

An echo returns and I immediately realize that it's not an
echo at all. It's me. A countless number of me, passing through
this space. Searching...

I feel a pressure, as if I'm pushing through an invisible
membrane.

And from one instant to the next, I'm back inside my body.

The sun is overhead, pasted into a sky smeared with shades of blue, like a watercolor painting on an endless canvas. Below my bare feet is soft green grass. I'm wearing a lemon-colored dress I haven't worn in decades, since my first year of college.

In the distance, standing atop a sloping knoll amid an interminable meadow, is my husband.

FORTY-FOUR

He walks toward me slowly, grinning like a beautiful fool.

I run to him.

Colson catches me in his arms. He's laughing, and I laugh along with him. He's *real*. Solid. I can feel the texture of him, smell him. I kiss his mouth and taste him. It makes my head spin. It makes me breathless.

"Beth," he says, and there's so much inside that word, my name. Sorrow. Loss. Happiness. Lust. Wonder.

I kiss him again and hold him tight, and we stay like that for a while—minutes, hours, months, years—I have no idea how long. Time is in stasis. It's unquantifiable here. Elastic. Where we are is somehow outside its pull, its rules.

When I'm ready to let him go, I pull back and look at my surroundings more closely. Study the sun, the sky. It's vast but, at the same time, contained. As if we are in a hologram. A *rendering* of reality. Are we in outer space? Is this heaven? Or is it something else? Something undefinable. Something outside human knowledge, beyond science.

"I've missed you," I say.

Colson smiles down at me. "Let's take a walk."

He takes my hand. I grip his fingers tightly as we stroll through the meadow, heading seemingly nowhere, and everywhere, as if this world is continuously rotating like a gyro. Our own private moon.

"So," I say, trying to take it all in, my scientific brain doing its best to analyze a miracle, and failing. "What is all this? Am I dead? Is this the afterlife?" I laugh but have no idea why. Part of me thinks I should be frightened, but I'm not. I'm peaceful. Happy. "Are you here for me? To guide me to whatever lies beyond?"

"No, you're not dead, Beth," he says, squeezing my hand reassuringly. "And this isn't the afterlife. It's not purgatory, or heaven. It's just a place for us to have a chance to talk before you go back."

For the first time since I arrived here, I feel something other than euphoria. My stomach sinks at his words, at the idea of returning, being plugged back into Earth, into my physical body.

"Okay," I say slowly, unsure how else to respond, or what to think.

"I've been trying so hard to get back to you," he says. "To you and Isabella."

"I don't understand. You were always with us, until...until you ran out of time."

Colson shakes his head. "Time isn't what we think it is, Beth. Our science? Our data and algorithms and formulas? Totally wrong, hon. Not even *close* to the mark," he says, then laughs. "Our machine? Our life's work? It isn't a gateway, Beth. It's a randomizer. A cosmic slot machine. Every time we use it we're spinning the wheels, with no way of knowing what we'll get, where we'll be. We're ripping apart reality every time we fire up that laser, tearing through sheets of space-time that aren't meant to be torn through. We're not bending space, or connecting two quantum dots. It's not entanglement. It's *cheating*. It's throwing the bowling ball down any lane we choose and adjusting every scorecard in the building. But even more, we're tapping into an energy source that...well, it's more powerful than anything we can fathom. The negative energy the machine produces is enough to open the door a crack, yes, but it's another power altogether that throws it open wide, lets us pass into these other realms to reach what we think are random points in time." He chuckles again, but it's not joyful this time. It's disbelieving. "We were so arrogant, Beth. We think we're so intelligent, that we've figured out so much, but we're not even close. We're staring at a sheet of ice and reveling that we've discovered frozen water, but there's an entire galaxy hidden just beneath the surface, one that would blow our perceptions of reality to dust."

I stop walking and tug at Colson's hand to stop him as well. "How do you know any of this? And what are you, exactly? A ghost? A figment of my imagination?"

"No, nothing like that. I'm real, Beth. As real as you are. I'm just not in your world anymore or, I don't know . . . your version of it."

"So you're talking about dimensions."

He thinks about this. "Yes and no. Like I said, it's impossible to put it into a scientific construct you'd understand. That *any* human mind could even remotely comprehend."

For the second time since my arrival here (a place I've begun thinking of as the existential meadow), I feel something other than happiness. This time, however, the feeling is almost welcome.

I'm annoyed.

"Okay, well, this is all very interesting, Colson darling. And I'm delighted you've tapped into your inner guru, but you know that I've never enjoyed being spoken down to, so why don't we hold off on the hippy bullshit science and you just tell my poor, simple human brain what the hell is going on."

Colson laughs out loud, and I can't help but laugh along with him. The whole situation is so unbelievable, so bizarre, that it's impossible not to get caught up in a moment that's *real*.

That's *us*.

Who knows, maybe if Adam and Eve would've had a good old-fashioned argument once in a while, things might have gone a different way.

"Okay, okay," he says. "Brass tacks, got it." His smile fades a moment, and he studies the sky. I look up and see nothing. "Besides, believe it or not, we're running low on time."

"Ah, so time *is* passing here."

He looks as if he wants to correct me again, or philosophize about my definition of time in the eternal meadow of mother-fucking bliss, but he stops himself.

"Sort of" is what he comes out with, then continues. "Look, I won't try to explain what happened to me, but I can tell you that during one of my travels, something went wrong. I ended up somewhere I shouldn't have ended up, and I...fragmented, I guess you'd say. Parts of me went in different directions, rode different waves of space-time. I was multitudinous, but I was also overlapping with myself. With reality. See, when our conscious-ness goes through that wormhole, through that rift in the elegant design, we slip through layers of different realities. It's like cutting through a cake with a laser. It's discordant, chaotic. And because what we send through is nothing but pure energy, the rules, as it were, don't apply. We can spread out like a blanket, or tighten to the size of an electron. When I saw myself die, I was being shown one possible outcome. It wasn't real because it hadn't hap-pened. Just like the past isn't real. There is only the present, you see? There is just one moment, and that's all there is. You think of traveling as going backward or forward, but really all you're doing is altering the present. Changing that *moment*."

I nod, trying to absorb what he's telling me. I unconsciously take a step back, away from him, needing to clear my head, to *think*. In the distance, I hear what sounds like the rumble of thunder, and I notice that the meadow is getting darker. I glance up at the sun, which shines brightly as ever, and it's only in this moment I realize that it doesn't hurt my eyes to do so.

Just where the hell am I?

"Okay," I say, finally. "That's a bigger conversation. Let's just...put a pin in it, shall we?"

Colson nods. "Of course. You want to know how to get back. Get back to our daughter."

I grab Colson's hand, hold it tightly in my own. "Do you know how?"

He nods again. "As you probably figured out by now, if Tariq is the big softy I think he is, I ran into the same problem. I messed with time and lost everything I loved. That's why I tried to stop you, to warn you."

I think a moment, then it comes to me. "The virus."

"Yes, another overlap I was able to exploit. I've been able to insert myself at points in place and time with only a thought. I've watched you, watched Isabella."

"I thought I was crazy, that I was hallucinating..."

"No," he says. "You were seeing the overlaps. Waves upon waves. Seeing a construct of me that you could understand, that made sense. From here," he says, motioning all around us, "I can do things I could never do when I was, well..."

"Human," I say, knowing it's true.

That whatever he is now, he's not that. Not anymore.

He shrugs. "Humans are energy, Beth. And I still feel. I have dreams and wants. Desires. I feel sadness and joy. But there's so much of it coming in at once, from so many sources...so, yeah, I suppose that makes me something else."

"Tell me what to do," I say.

There's a loud *crack* from above, as if the sky is splitting in two, breaking apart like the hull of a sinking submarine.

"How do I find her?"

He studies me for a moment, and I see desperation there. "What if I told you that you could pick any point in time? Any memory, any moment...any reality?"

"I'd say I don't understand. How?"

"You saw my debrief videos, right?"

I nod.

"Remember what I said before? After I'd secretly traveled, one of the times you didn't know about? What I said about traveling outside the rules of quantum gravity, of relativity. Of physics? Of time itself?"

"You said we'd be gods," I say quietly.

"Our memories are the constitution of who we are," he says, eyes intent on mine. "They are the reflections of a billion lives on infinite planes...We only need to know how to open the door and we can travel to any of them, because they're all happening right *now*."

He nods to something behind me and I turn. There's a blur of white about ten feet away. Not a doorway, exactly...but an absence. As if someone had taken an eraser to the drawing of this world and rubbed out a section of color, revealing the blank page beneath.

"From here, the door is always open," he says. "From here, *we* choose our fate."

I turn and face him once more, surprised to see that he looks tired. Maybe even sad. Lost.

Above and beyond him, the sky is no longer blue but an angry purple combed with dark streaks of gray.

The meadow is dying.

"How can I do that? The machine..."

Colson smiles, and my heart hurts to see it. "The machine never chose the arrival points, Beth. *You* did. It's not an algorithm or a glitch in the code. It's human emotion. It's your desire to relive the most important, the most impactful parts of your life. Maybe it's joy, or maybe it's guilt. Maybe it's desire. Once the consciousness is freed, it can choose to be *anywhere*. That's the secret of the machine, of your work."

I run a hand through my hair, trying to take it all in. There's a *CRACK* of thunder overhead and I jump. "Fine, so tell me. What do I do?"

"You choose," he says with a shrug. "Do you understand what I'm saying?"

I nod. "Yes, I think I do."

"And know that I love you," he says. "That I'll always love you."

"I wish we had—"

He pulls me toward him and I kiss him one last time. When I pull away, I place a hand to his cheek and memorize his face, his mouth, his eyes.

"I love you," I say.

Then I turn away from my husband and run.

Into the white.

FORTY-FIVE

When Beth opens her eyes, she sees morning sun filtering through the sheer white curtains that cover the bedroom window. The window itself is cracked open an inch at the bottom. A jasmine-scented breeze flowers through the air.

She glances at the clock. Nearly eight AM.

I've overslept, she thinks, feeling a stir of panic. Then she remembers it's a Sunday, and it doesn't matter how late she sleeps.

And not just any Sunday.

She groans into the pillow, not wanting to think about it.

Hello, forty. I'd say it's nice to meet you, but to be honest, you can...

There's a loud clatter from deeper within the house, startling her. She jerks up into a sitting position, the sheet falling away from her, pooling in her lap. The air through the window feels cooler now, and she's surprised to notice she's slept in the nude. Shivering at the chill air, she looks around the bed for underwear, sweats, a T-shirt. Anything.

"The hell..." she mumbles, slipping out from under the sheets and heavy blanket and stepping quickly to her dresser, where she pulls out thick socks, underwear, flannel bottoms, a tank top. She gets dressed, then spots a black hoodie hanging from the handle of the closet door and snatches it greedily, pulling it on, takes comfort in the warmth of it.

Another loud sound from inside the house. The heavy *clank* of something hitting the floor. She approaches the door, opens it, and slips into the hallway.

As she walks toward the kitchen, she hears voices.

A man is talking.

A little girl giggles.

Beth steps into the kitchen, crosses her arms, leans against the doorframe. "You guys are up early."

Isabella sits at the kitchen table, an assortment of crayons splayed out in front of her, a half-formed drawing of a blue flower on a yellow sheet of construction paper. She looks up and smiles wildly. "Happy birthday, Mommy!" she yells, dropping off the chair and running to Beth, who bends down to scoop her into her arms, pull her tightly against her chest, breathe her in.

"Good morning, pumpkin," she says, kissing her little girl's head, ear, cheek. Isabella giggles and squirms, and Beth sets her down. She lifts her eyes to the man standing at the other end of the kitchen. "Let me guess, your famous birthday pancakes."

Colson turns from the stove, glances back at her mischievously. He's wearing a white T-shirt, jeans. No socks or shoes. Beth thinks he looks amazing.

He raises a spatula, points it toward her. "I wouldn't want to disappoint you." He does his best version of a comedic double take. "Wait a second, did you turn forty or thirty? I'm confused."

She laughs and eases toward him, wraps her arms around his waist, kisses the back of his neck as she surveys the mess he's created. A mixing bowl half-filled with lumpy batter. The portable grill on the stovetop crusting four misshapen golden-brown circles. Beth inhales the sweet scent of them, feels her mouth water. She lets him go and pulls a mug from a cupboard, fills it with hot coffee from the fresh pot he's prepared.

"Just the way you like them, too," he says. "Mushy inside, burnt outside."

"Please, they look amazing," she says, and walks over to the table to sit with her daughter. "And what are you working so hard at?"

Isabella keeps her eyes down, deeply focused. Beth notices the tip of her tongue poking out from the corner of her mouth, fights the overwhelming urge to pull her into her arms once again.

"A flower," Isabella says. "But it's a special flower."

Beth sips the coffee, relishes the rush of it. "Oh?"

"It's a birthday flower."

"Isabella, you want to hit pause on that so I can give you a plate?" Colson says. "Or did you want to skip pancakes this morning?"

Isabella looks up, an open-mouthed look of shock on her face. "No way!" she says, and dutifully pushes the crayons to the middle of the table, sets the flower drawing gently to one side.

Colson sets a plate in front of Beth, another in front of Isabella. He snaps his fingers. "I warmed up some syrup, and there's butter there in the dish. Bacon is, uh, pending."

As Colson heads back to the counter, Beth has another long sip of coffee, then leans in toward Isabella to help with the butter. "That waiter's kind of hot, don't you think?"

Isabella giggles, and Colson arrives with a small pitcher of syrup. "For my lovely ladies, I offer the finest maple syrup the grocery store had to offer."

"Why, thank you," Beth says, picking up the small ceramic pitcher, drizzling syrup over Isabella's pancakes.

"When!" she says, and Beth stops.

She pours a somewhat larger amount over her own pancakes before turning to look at Colson, who is standing at the kitchen sink, his hands resting on the countertop.

He stares out the window that leads to their small backyard. Through the window, Beth sees that it's a beautiful day. The sky is blue.

Their lone tree, a cherry blossom, is in full bloom. From where she sits, she can just make out the soft pink flowers coating the thin branches, a breeze plucking away a few petals to send them skirting through the air.

"Hey, mister," she says, ignoring the light flutter of unease in her chest. "Aren't you eating?"

But Colson doesn't move, or answer. He continues to stare out the window, as if transfixed by the floating petals of the cherry blossom.

As if lost in a daydream.

"I'm good," he says.

Beth sets down her fork. She glances to Isabella, who is neatly cutting a tiny bite from one pancake before daintily scooping it into her mouth.

She looks back to Colson. "Did you want to go in today? I know we have a lot going on. I don't mind, honestly. We can call Marie Elena, have her come over..."

Colson steps away from the window, walks over to the table. He pulls out a chair between Beth and Isabella and sits down. He puts his elbows on the table, leans in close to his wife, who watches him closely.

"No, I don't think so," he says. "It's a beautiful day. It's your birthday. I think we should all hang out. Go to the park, get some lunch. Pick up a nice bottle of wine for dinner."

Isabella's head jerks up as she overhears him. "Yes, the park!" she says giddily, a drip of syrup on her chin.

Colson turns to smile at his daughter. When he turns back to Beth, his eyes are lowered.

"That sounds nice," she says.

He nods, keeps his gaze on the table.

"Actually, I was thinking," he says slowly, carefully. "That you and I should talk about whether Langan is the right situation for us. For our work."

Beth sets down her fork, leans back. "Okay..." she says. "It's a little out of left field, but sure, we can discuss that, I guess. I mean, are you sure you don't want to go in today? Don't get me wrong, a day off with you guys sounds amazing. It's just not very like you...Colson?"

She reaches out, covers one of his hands with her own, squeezes it tight.

"As long as you're sure."

Colson looks up at her. A small smile plays at the corner of his lips.

"Yeah..." he says.

Beth stares into her husband's eyes, watches them silently flicker between white and brown, like the shutter of a camera taking a thousand snapshots.

Capturing a thousand memories.

"I'm sure."

Acknowledgments

As you can imagine, this was a tricky story to get right, but please know, dear reader, that every effort was made to keep the story logic on the straight and narrow, even with multiple timelines, blurred realities, a pinch of the supernatural, and time travel galore.

To that end, I want to thank my editors—Bradley Englert and Nick Burnham—and the team at Orbit Books for diligently putting my novel through the paces and helping me get it right. If there are failures or inconsistencies, it's on me (but beware—an irregularity could simply mean you've stumbled into an alternate reality).

The time machine I created for this book was inspired by the works and ideas of Michio Kaku and Kip Thorne. I was lucky enough to ask Dr. Kaku a question—during a live Zoom event—about the possibilities of sending pure data through a wormhole, and his affirmative response was a huge boon to the story (and a massive relief for its author).

The science (theoretical or otherwise) behind the digitizing of consciousness, the time machine, and the satellite-bounced questions and answers are all based, albeit with a layman's knowledge, in real physics. Just don't ask me to do the math.

As it pertains to some of that science, I was grateful for the help of NASA senior media writer, Rick Cross, for connecting me with his colleague, chief technologist at NASA's Marshall Space

Flight Center, and author, Les Johnson. Les was kind enough to read excerpts of the book and offer invaluable feedback and corrections on key parts of the story. Again, it's important to point out that any creative license taken, or mistakes made, are mine alone.

I want to thank my literary agent, Elizabeth Copps, for finding a home for this book (and all the others), and for doing her best to keep me sane and focused on the wins.

Lastly, I want to thank my family: my son, Dominic, and my wife, Stephanie. You guys make my world go round and I love you in every timeline there is.

Thanks for reading.

PF
Los Angeles
May 2024

meet the author

Stephanie Simard

PHILIP FRACASSI is the Bram Stoker Award–nominated author of the story collections *Behold the Void*, *Beneath a Pale Sky*, and *No One Is Safe!* His novels include *A Child Alone with Strangers*, *Gothic*, and *Boys in the Valley*. His stories have been published in numerous magazines and anthologies, including *The Best Horror of the Year*, *Nightmare Magazine*, *Southwest Review*, *Interzone*, and *Black Static*. Philip lives in Los Angeles.

Find out more about Philip Fracassi and other Orbit authors by registering for the free monthly newsletter at orbitbooks.net.